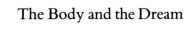

The Body and the Dream

The Body and the Dream

French Erotic Fiction 1464–1900

Translated and Introduced by
Jennifer Birkett

Quartet Books
London Melbourne New York

First published in Great Britain
Quartet Books Limited
A member of the Namara Group
27/29 Goodge Street, London W1P 1FD
Reprinted 1984

Translation and Introduction copyright © Jennifer Birkett 1983

British Library Cataloguing in Publication Data

The body and the dream.
  1. Erotic fiction, French
  843'.008'032   PQ1276

  ISBN 0–7043–2364–8

Phototypeset by MC Typeset, Rochester, Kent
Printed and bound in Great Britain
by Mackays of Chatham Ltd, Chatham, Kent

Contents

Acknowledgements

I should like to thank those libraries whose resources I have been able to use in the preparation of this book: the Bibliothèque Nationale, the Bodleian Library and the Taylor Institute, Oxford, the National Library of Scotland and the University Library, Dundee and, especially, the British Library and the University Library, Cambridge.

I should also like to thank those whose expertise and kind criticism was an invaluable help in the work of translation. I am especially indebted to Anne Smith, who has been a constant source of encouragement and enthusiasm, and to Stan Smith, who patiently read, corrected, revised, calmed and provoked until it was all finally written.

The Body and the Dream

The Body and the Dream:
Eros and History

Amor omnibus idem. We need to turn to the physical: it's the stuff of nature that imagination has embroidered. If you want an idea of love, go and look at the sparrows in your garden; look at your pigeons; look at the bull being led to your cow; look at the proud stallion led by two of his attendants to the mare, waiting quietly, flicking aside her tail to receive him; see how his eyes glitter; listen to him neigh; watch his leaps and bounds, his pricked-up ears, his mouth open and twitching, his swollen nostrils with their fiery breath, his erect, floating mane, the imperious movement as he leaps onto the object destined for him by nature; but don't be jealous, consider the advantages of the human species; in the field of love, they make up for all the strength, beauty, lightness and speed that nature has given to the animals.

Voltaire, *Dictionnaire philosophique*,
1764, art. 'Amour'.

That eros inhabits a domain outside history is an easy assumption. At its basis, as Voltaire's tableau makes graphically plain, is a physical and animal activity. The imagination's embroidery works over the physical: in eroticism, the body dreams its utopia, and since the body is a biological constant, the dream might well be expected to stay the same. The eighteenth century, indulging its rationalist inclination to invent universal categories, laws and patterns, filed away the life of passion in an archetypal model constructed by an old and impotent libertine, gazing back over his own career:

> He would lean on his spade and say to himself: Oh Lord, author
> of my being, what is man?
>   At the age of ten, as desire burgeons, the whole gamut of
> passions comes to assail him; at twenty, he enjoys them without
> moderation; at thirty, abandoned to utterly unbridled debauch-
> ery, he sets no limit to his desires; he avidly seeks out incest, and
> all the most lascivious satisfactions; at forty, a sophisticated,
> sensual libertine, devoid of all delicacy, having stayed a bachelor,
> he exploits every shameful device his hot blood inspires; at fifty,
> he turns for assistance to prostitutes; at sixty, he's impotent.
> Alack and alas, and that's where I've ended up. And what does he
> turn into then but a sage and philosopher, which is what I shall
> be. With these thoughts running through his head, Belleval
> would dig over the earth and water the flowers, comparing them
> to the destiny of man, and so he ended his career.[1]

However, the philosophy of an old and impotent libertine is only
half the truth. The constellations of sexuality are constantly re-
formed, and this is especially evident when the dream of eros takes
on literary form. The pleasure of an erotic text is a double one: not
just in the evocation of sexual experience, but in the form of that
evocation, the framing, the contexting, and the detail of the presentation. Mirabeau's libertine is complemented by Huysmans' des
Esseintes, who hangs the portrait of his ideal woman, Gustave
Moreau's Salome, between the rows of books in his study, and
constantly interrogates the representation to know what its sexuality means, and what styles have invented it.

The present collection of short stories and extracts taken from
some of the best-known if not always most easily obtainable classics
of five centuries of French erotic writing shows a small part of the
range of possible transformations of the carnal appetite in literature,
which have varied with historical moment and the individual's
place within it, cultural prejudice and literary convention. In the
earliest texts chosen, from Rabelais to Brantôme, much of the
pleasure is in the well-shaped anecdote, and the eroticism has the
joky slant of *gauloiserie*, the bawdy Gallic tradition that some
moderns would say is not genuinely erotic. 'Extreme licence
coupled with joking' argues Georges Bataille, author of some of the
most celebrated surrealist erotic fiction, 'goes hand in hand with the

refusal to take erotic truth seriously – by which I mean, tragically.'[2]
But *gauloiserie* too is a form of wish-fulfilment, 'with its wilful
neglect of all the natural and social complications of love, with its
indulgence towards the lies and egotism of sexual life, and its vision
of a never-ending lust . . . an attempt to substitute for reality the
dream of a happier life' but this time 'viewed from the animal side'.[3]
The laughter expresses a confidence in human ability to control and
order sexuality, in a combination that reappears in different forms
in the eighteenth century: an often crude sensuality woven into the
satire of Diderot and Voltaire, or, in Andréa de Nerciat's work, an
ethic of moderate self-indulgence which presents frivolous love as
the practical way of life. It finally vanishes with the Romantics, as
sexuality becomes more problematic: Balzac's racy tale of three
pilgrims is only a pastiche of an old tradition, and although the
melodramatic swift-moving accumulation of all possible perversions in the short space of Musset's *Gamiani* (1833) has its comic
edge, it is much more the macabre humour that looks forward to
the surrealist tradition.

The eighteenth century, with all its political and philosophical
upheavals, offers a wide variety of erotic styles, more or less loosely
connected by themes of exploitation, rivalry and competition.
Crébillon's games with the authority that violates and humiliates
are in a realm apart from Sade's evocation of the horror of inescap-
able domination. *Thérèse philosophe* (1748) indicts the exploitation
of the religious novice by the hypocritical priest, with a clever play
on the well-worn theme of the identity of religious and sexual
humiliation. Nerciat's *Félicia* and her aunt Sylvina engage in
carefully regulated rivalry for the pleasure of initiating the innocent
Monrose, who gains rather than loses from the dispute, going on to
star in a sequel of his own (*Monrose, ou le libertin par fatalité*, 1792) and
perpetuating the sequence of casual sexual initiations which is part
of this society's basic structure. It is a different story in Laclos'
world, where power is in itself erotic, and the rivalry of the Vicomte
de Valmont and the Marquise de Merteuil results in the casual ruin
of their victim and a severe shock to society's foundations.

At the end of the century, Restif de la Bretonne brings in a new
note, explicitly relating private sensuality to the social institutions
that channel or police it, writing of exploitation by prostitution in
the market-place or within the family, and discussing not merely
the sexuality of the aristocracy but that of the middle classes and the
lumpen populace. A disciple of Rousseau, Restif's style is con-

fessional, frank to the point of crudeness, and one that disregards all
limits of propriety in the articulation of a powerful and idiosyncratic
libido. At the same time, one of the less lovely children of the
Revolution, he longs for institutional structures or moral commands to shape his desire. Hence his interest in regulating and
categorising prostitutes and prostitution, and his conviction
(expressed in the opening Declaration) that his scabrous *Anti-Justine*
(1798) genuinely represented a contribution to the moral health of
the nation: ' . . . I composed this Work, savoury as it is, with none
but useful intentions. Incest, for example, is only included as an
equivalent to the corrupt tastes of the libertines and the dreadful
cruelties with which [de Sade] stimulates them.' This is, he claims, a
book written to save women from suffering and strengthen family
life. Self-righteous, melodramatic, grotesque, violent and realistic,
Restif is the new man of his time, the provincial come to Paris
demanding scope for his own personality and politics. And like the
Romantics, for whom he broke much valuable ground in terms of
freedom of style and content, his central preoccupation was to write
out his political and private fantasies into literary form: with Restif,
the text itself is the prime erotic experience.

   The nineteenth-century section gives samples of each of the
major literary schools from Romanticism to the end of the century.
The extract from Zola shows a side of his Naturalism often
forgotten, with a highly idealised, almost Lawrentian claim for the
beauty and legitimacy of 'natural', physical love, pressed in the
context of an attack on religious asceticism. It has, however, the
advantage of presenting an awesomely 'healthy' version of eros to
contrast with the dark and perverted forms otherwise proliferating
throughout the last years of the century, with the Symbolists and
the Decadents in particular exploiting the Sadean tradition of the
identity of love and death. Musset's Countess Gamiani sets the tone
early, 'a cold woman with no heart', whose lesbianism symbolises
the Romantic aspiration for the impossible Utopian fulfilment: 'I
know to my sorrow that I have parted company with nature. All I
dream of, all I can feel is the horrible and the extravagant. I'm in
pursuit of the impossible . . . Always desiring, never satisfied. My
imagination is killing me . . .' The pursuit eventually leads her to
poison herself and her partner in their last embrace, testing pleasure
to its extreme.

   In Huysmans' *À rebours* (1884), death is part of an eroticism
derived from impotence and neurosis, glossing an absence of real

desire with flashy displays of colour, light, violence and horror. This text is distinguished by its awareness of the context that frames it: the reconstruction of Moreau evokes an escapist landscape out of time and space but it acknowledges its real origins in its rejection of the mass life of the modern city. *Le Jardin des supplices* (1899), Octave Mirbeau's version of the identity of love and death, is also politically framed; its completion, indeed, was stimulated by the Dreyfus affair. But where Huysmans, motionless, contemplates an unmoving tableau of forces locked in confrontation, Mirbeau is engaged in a journey of critical discovery into the heart of the 'penal colony' of la Belle Époque in which the modern self is trapped. What happens in China reflects back on Capital and Empire, where subjects are controlled and incorporated by the institutionalisation of their complex instincts. As the Frontispiece explains:

> [Murder] is a vital instinct within us . . . it exists in all organised beings, and dominates them all, like the genetic instinct . . . most of the time the two are so well combined, merged so completely, that they form, in a way, one and the same instinct, and we can't tell which it is that presses us to give life, and which to take it away, which is murder and which is love.
>
> . . . We curb our need to murder, or diminish its physical violence, by giving it legal outlets: industry, colonial trade, war, hunting, anti-semitism . . . because it's dangerous to indulge in it without moderation, outside the law . . .

Other texts, such as Pierre Louÿs' *Aphrodite* (1896), try to forbid the real world entry to the world of the instincts. Inside the walled garden of the temple, incantatory rhythm and ritual create an atmosphere in which love and death, identified in the last ecstatic frenzy of the sacred prostitute, are all-important. Even here, however, eros is surreptitiously invaded by the market of trade and tribute in which love is for sale, and the buyer's power a major part of his pleasure. With an indolent phrase, Louÿs waves away the unsaleable, to lesbianism, starvation or slavery.

The modern mind makes heavy demands of erotic fantasy; sexuality is now the privileged area in which the 'authentic' self is constructed and explored. Various modern commentators have tried to colonise this function for their own philosophies. Denis de Rougemont argued that Western eroticism derives from the ideals and conflicts generated within our culture by Christianity.[4] Pierre Louÿs on the other hand, in his preface to *Aphrodite*, is interested only in sensuality that is materialist and pagan: 'Love, with all its consequences, was for the Greeks the most virtuous of all the sentiments and potentially the most glorious. They never attached to it the notions of shamelessness and immodesty that Jewish tradition brought into our culture by way of Christian doctrine.' His heroine, the courtesan Chrysis, has all the 'frankness, passion and pride of any human being following a vocation and holding a freely chosen place in society'. Sexual pleasure, however, still has for Louÿs a higher end than itself. For the *fin-de-siècle* aesthete, it is not death that is the climax of the chapter in the garden but art, the highest point of human perfection. Coarse sexuality is transmuted into the frieze encircling the temple wall, in which the artist includes himself, modelling the flower that symbolises the symbol, Aphrodite.

Georges Bataille, propagating his own idiosyncratic form of anarchism, lifts the discussion out of the limiting frames of religion and art, into more generalised psychological terms. At the same time, he articulates the political context that has given eros its present privileges. For him, erotic states are extreme states of being, divorced not only from a reproductive purpose but also from conventional contexts and standards. Their importance lies in the fact that they are not amenable to the regimenting, homogenising pressures exerted on individual subjects by modern, scientific, capitalist society; pressures described as 'the ideas which subordinate human activity to other ends than the *futile consumption* of their resources. The point is to destroy perceptions which are the basis of servile forms.'[5] And again: 'Sexuality at least is good for something. But eroticism . . . Here we have a sovereign form, *good for absolutely nothing.*'[6] Eroticism is autotelic, self-referential. It refuses to be confined. It is an invention and a transgression of limits that produces a sense of the volatility of the self. The transgression of limits is marked by blasphemy, where a belief in God exists, and where there is no belief, by the sadistic force of obscenity, violation and death. Sadism, explains Bataille in *L'Érotique* (1957), is not a deviation from human nature, but a 'sovereign and indestructible element' within it. Humans are creatures of excess and violence as well as reason, and human lives and language must confront and comprehend both in order to be complete.[7]

Following through this line of argument, the play of fiction in the erotic text can be viewed as consequence-free exploration and experiment in the realm of the symbolic. In both Crébillon's forfeit games and Sade's rituals, the sexual stimulus of humiliation is always doubly enclosed, by the game and the language which are its inventors. Unsuspected sides to personality are articulated by the forcing of limits within the rule of fantasy. Already in the Romantic period, Théophile Gautier's *Mademoiselle de Maupin* (1833) and Balzac's *La Fille aux yeux d'or* (1834) had explored through their bisexual heroines the ambiguity and mutability of sexual roles. Such texts provide the groundwork for the surrealists' creative play with all the traditional stock-in-trade of the erotic and, indeed, the pornographic tradition. Beyond the limits of the present study, the work of Apollinaire[8] contains some early intimations of a new approach fully realised in Bataille's own *Histoire de l'oeil* (1928), or, less well known but equally compelling, Robert Desnos' *La Liberté ou l'amour* (1927), in which the Corsaire Sanglot prowls Paris under the twin patronage of eros and capitalism (the Marquis de Sade and the giant pink Cadum baby on the hoardings), observing and participating in an imaginative and illuminating riot of love, violation, murder and death. In the boarding-school at Humming-Bird Garden, in a single orgasmic sentence, the violence of eroticism illuminates simultaneously the depths of the self and the social institutions that constitute it:

Humming-Bird Garden School for Boarders, for a long time, I know, you've been there in my imagination, a red-brick house surrounded by quiet lawns, with your dormitories where virgins, still asleep, turn and stretch with pleasure in their beds at the passing touch of midnight's gossamer threads, with the bedroom of the headmistress, a domineering woman with an arsenal of whips, rods and lashes, with your classroom where the white symbols in the depth of the blackboard correspond to the mysterious signs drawn by the stars on the sky, but while you stood motionless in a textbook landscape, the storm of all eternity was building up behind your slate roof ready to break in a flash of lightning at the exact instant when the marker's strap would rule its red furrow across the buttocks of a sixteen-year-old boarder and like a lightning flash carry painful enlightenment into the mysterious secret places of my erotic imagination. Is all this story only written to evoke your likeness: whiplash, lightning flash! . . .[9]

'Symbols' on the blackboard, 'signs' drawn in the sky, 'textbook landscape' and 'story': the emphasis is on fictionality, and even the marker's strap is a red line on the page. The writing is itself the lightning flash of transgression, illuminating briefly that which it transgresses.

The 'pornographic' edge to writing like this, and to a number of the other texts in this collection, raises a number of questions that have recently returned to the agenda for current debate.[10] The least answerable, though most often asked, is whether there is a distinction to be drawn between the erotic and the pornographic – a rationalist tactic that generally seeks to protect the enquirer's own sexuality under the former, 'acceptable' label, while consigning to the dangerous, transgressive category of 'pornography' the sexuality of the Other. Erotic writing as a whole belongs not to rationalist discourse but to what Julia Kristeva has called the 'carnivalesque' tradition, where the law and its subversion always co-exist. To this tradition she assimilates much of modern writing: 'Rabelais, Cervantes, Swift, Sade, Balzac, Lautréamont, Dostoievski, Joyce and Kafka. Its history is the history of the struggle against Christianity and its representation; this means an exploration of language (of sexuality and death), a consecration of ambivalence and of "vice".'[11] This is a more useful approach than those which attempt to dispose of 'pornography' on ostensibly literary grounds.

Beatrice Faust's *Women, Sex and Pornography* (1982), a curious mixture of the open and the censorious, rehearses some familiar arguments: pornography is interested only in content, not in form, lacks realism, over-simplifies, has no interest in the 'psychology' of people. Much of this overlaps with the arguments summarised and attacked by Susan Sontag in her essay on 'The Pornographic Imagination' (1967) and those deployed by Stephen Marcus in *The Other Victorians* (1966) – a work drawn on by Faust.[12] Pornography, further runs the creed, has a single 'intention', the sexual arousal of the reader, whereas genuine literature has a complex one; it lacks the beginning–middle–end structure characteristic of literature; it deals not in individual psychology and interpersonal relations but in depersonalised organs; it has no interest in language as such, being primarily concerned with non-verbal fantasies. As Sontag pointed out, the first error in such definitions is that they lump together good and bad pornographic writing; the second, that they show an unsophisticated understanding of what literature is and how language works. If we take, for example, the question of the use of language in well-written pornography, we find awareness of language as such, as well as a technical grasp of the trigger effect of words, images, rhythms as important for the pornographer as for the poet. Hence, perhaps, the success of a Musset or an Apollinaire in both modes.

Pierre Louÿs, who in *Aphrodite* lays such stress on the role of art in forming desire, created in its coarser modern complement, the *Trois Filles de leur mère* (1926) a heroine, Charlotte, whose sexuality is rooted in language and who constantly re-invents a paradoxically powerful masochistic subjectivity in a barrage of verbal self-abuse. Re-creating for the narrator, the latest of her lovers, the vileness of her past experiences, reciting for him, for example, the litany of animals whose sperm she claims she was forced to drink by an earlier 'lover . . . I mean customer' ('spunk from a horse or spunk from a goat, bull's spunk, dog's spunk, pig's spunk') she becomes, as the narrator says, 'more animated with every sentence'. As Charlotte tells it, that particular episode enters a strange space; whether or not it 'really' happened is uncertain, and (almost) irrelevant. For Charlotte, the story-telling is the exciting thing, the doubling of an event, more exciting than the real presence of the new lover, symbolically holding his hand over her mouth. What she wants is the erotic thrill of shocking a response from her audience, an orgasmic lightning flash to replace the mollifying paternal reassurances he insists on offering. Through the voice of the narrator (the modern consumer of sexuality, who wants the double pleasure of enjoying and censuring), Louÿs tests the limits of obscene language, constructing the dramatic force of his text by carefully timed movement from the explicit to the suggestive, and, indeed, from words to gesture. Shortly after telling her story:

> [Charlotte] went into the bathroom, stretched out naked on the tile floor, propping herself up on one elbow, her head thrown back, her mouth open, and masturbated frenziedly with one hand. She didn't seem to feel the cold from the floor.
>
> The more she masturbated, the more enthusiastically she reviled herself. I noted down once what she said then and I've just torn up the page; I hadn't the courage to read it through to the end. There are two things the young lady reading me couldn't

possibly imagine: the words I don't intend to tell her and my haste to have done with this chapter.

The last sentence – the narrator's paradoxical claim to silence – is a nice underlining of the point: this isn't reality, but the closed language-world of fiction. The parody appeal to the 'young lady', the 'gentle reader' of the novel tradition, confirms it.[13]

Musset's *Gamiani* is also word-play as well as play with sexuality, supposed to have sprung from a wager that the poet could in three days write a pornographic work 'without using the crude terms usually called naïve when they appear in the work of our worthy ancestors, such as Rabelais, Brantôme, Béroalde de Verville, Bonaventure des Perriers [sic] and a whole string of others whose Gallic wit would shine just as brightly if it were stripped of all the filthy words that defile the old language'.[14] When Fanny, the innocent recruit to the three-cornered relationship, describes her first experience of masturbation, the refusal of explicit obscenity is turned to psychological and erotic account. Lacking the vocabulary to understand or express what's happening to her body, Fanny becomes, as Alcide ironically comments, a poet, vividly conveying the visual and tactile responses that are within her range: charting the sensuous exchanges between herself, the objects in the room and the landscape outside, noting her own involuntary gestures and movements, finally focusing starkly on the physiological reaction that overwhelms her ('I leapt up in terror. I was soaked right through'). Her bewildering dizziness, the sense of swooning, are caught in the rhythm of her sentences and in the sudden capricious switches of perspective as she craves to roll on the ground, fly through the air. The obscenity of this passage is not in what Fanny says but in the almost silent presence of the experienced observers, Alcide and Gamiani herself, enjoying the power of knowing words which are the 'key to the puzzle'.

Teaching the right words is Suzanne's first concern in *L'École des filles* (1665). The beginner Fanny needs to know the technical terms, all their variations and their proper contexts in order not to be overwhelmed in the sexual power game. Suzanne's answer to the anxious enquiry 'why men sometimes like to use insults and dirty words when they're fucking us' is a witty, perceptive and affectionate deconstruction of what the other partner is up to:

First, when they have total possession of us, it amuses them to say the words that we find most embarrassing, so they feel they have an even more famous victory. Secondly, when their imaginations are steeped in delight and concentrated on the pleasure of coming their words don't flow freely and they talk in monosyllables, according to the promptness of their desire. So what they might one time call love's paradise, the centre of delight or the centre of love's desire, or that sweet little hole, they call quite simply a cunt, and that word cunt, besides being short and making us, so they think, embarrassed and ashamed (which they love to see) comprehends all the fondest imaginings of love. It's the same thing with the man's instrument, which they just call a prick, because otherwise they'd have to say: that nameless object, the virile member, the genital organ or some other such long silly explanation that love's frenzy leaves no time for. So instead of saying a long slow: 'Come, dear love, pray take the genital organ or muscle dependent from the lower part of my belly, and address it to the centre of love's delights!' it's much quicker to say in the heat of passion: 'Here, love, put my prick in your cunt!' or else: 'Let me fuck you, let me mount you!' Love excuses everything, and there are no dirty words when two lovers are fucking and mounting each other. In fact, words like that are terms of affection.

Fanny's reply pre-empts the reader's response: 'If it weren't so, cousin, you could convince anyone it were, just from hearing you, and you'd make anyone's mouth water for them, you speak of them so sweetly and skilfully.'

Suzanne quite properly warns her cousin against the dangers of using words out of context: ' . . . don't use them in society: they're naughty words, and girls blush when they're spoken'. In writing, however, as in sexuality, the inruption of difference heightens the transgressive violence of climax. Sade's *Justine*,[15] at the monastery of Saint Mary in the Woods, speaking in coyly precious terms of love's 'altar', the 'sanctuary', the 'porticos of the temple', the monk Séverino's 'gigantic faculties', provides a grotesque and terrifying counterpoint to the crude violence being practised on her body, of which she is also the direct and crude reporter, increasing the shock effect and underlining also that ludicrous element in her character, that determination to cling to the conventional, come what may, and make of it a virtue, that refusal to see what's really happening, that makes of her a deserving victim. Sophie, in *Aline et Valcour*,

presenting a monotone narrative from a single conventional perspective, produces a far less revealing text. Thérèse, in *Thérèse
philosophe*, capable of offering her own frank philosophical analysis
of her desire for sexual experience, its frustrations, diversions and
successes, engages in a knowing and ironic kind of self-exposure, a
voyeurism addressed to her own experience, that creates a novel
frisson.

It doesn't, of course, always work. Sentilly's Laura (*Le Rideau
levé*, 1786) is a simperer, plastering the clichés of sensibility and
enlightened philosophy over a text whose sole purpose is clearly to
provide explicit descriptions of the sexual act, but which would like
to pretend it's doing something more. As Sade said:

> If the writer had been explicit about wife-murder, which he just
> hints at, and incest, which he circles round all the time without
> admitting it, if he'd given us more scenes of lust . . . set in motion
> the cruel desires he merely hints at in his preface, the work, which
> is full of imagination, could have been delightful: but I can't stand
> tremblers, and I'd a hundred times rather they never put pen to
> paper than gave us half-baked ideas.[16]

Michel Foucault has pointed to the analogy between the detailed
analyses of the circumstances of sexual activity required by the
confessional and the form of Sade's own story-telling:

> 'Tell everything,' the directors would say time and time again:
> 'not only consummated acts, but sensual touchings, all impure
> gazes, all obscene remarks . . . all consenting thoughts.' Sade
> takes up the injunction in words that seem to have been retran-
> scribed from the treatises of spiritual direction: 'Your narrations
> must be decorated with the most numerous and searching details;
> the precise way and extent to which we may judge how the
> passion you describe relates to human manners and man's
> character is determined by your willingness to disguise no
> circumstance; and what is more, the least circumstance is apt to
> have an immense influence upon the procuring of that kind of
> sensory irritation we expect from your stories.'[17]

Sophie, confessing to Madame de Blamont, dwells on details of
circumstance, tone and gesture to an almost Richardsonian degree –
procuring in the reader, like Richardson, that strange response

which blends sympathy and 'sensory irritation'. For a novel like *Justine*, where the effects sought are more extreme, it is not simply detail itself that matters, but the way detail is selected and combined. There is no room here for sympathy; victims are portrayed in something approaching contemporary conventions of realism in the novel, but never granted the status of individuals rather than types. Justine's own responses and gestures always retain an edge of theatricality that prevents the reader from seeing her sufferings as real. The careful ritualism of episodes serves the same function, carrying the permanent reminder that this is not real life but theatre – structured fantasy.

This is perhaps also the place to deal with the unfounded charge that all pornographic writing lacks structure. Crébillon's *Tableaux des moeurs du temps*, like *Le Rideau levé*, *Félicia*, and *Thérèse philosophe*, variants on the *roman d'éducation*, and like the picaresque journeys of Justine and her sister Juliette, are certainly episodic – but so are most other eighteenth-century novels, and the ones cited here are not among the least rigorous. Works like *Gamiani*, or Mirbeau's *Le Jardin des supplices*, are written, for different reasons, to be read as a whole. For Mirbeau, the framing conversation in the gentlemen's club and the hero's preliminary adventures in Western politics are the context that gives meaning to the erotic adventure in the East. *Gamiani* is a short work packed with incident, accelerating to its murderous climax: both speed and intensity are calculated to generate an atmosphere of dizzy, outrageous fantasy. The importance of structure is particularly marked in the modernist and surrealist works that fall outside the present terms of reference: in Apollinaire's *Les Onze Mille Verges*, for instance, the cumulative effect of flagellations, violations, murders, scatological abuse, all the way up to the 'hero' Mony's death at the hands of the whole army by the ordeal of the rods, creates a new space in which obscenity can also be comedy, outrageous black humour – Rabelais confesses his collusion with Sade.

On purely aesthetic grounds, it is not possible to distinguish 'pornography' from other kinds of erotic fiction. 'Pornographic' is a label imposed for reasons purely external to a text: the text shocks and offends, and the degree of both shock and offence and, correspondingly, the definition of the pornographic, varies with societies and with individuals.[18] In this confusion, a political element comes into play in the extent of the control established authority thinks it necessary to exert over the sexual activity – real or imaginary – of its subjects. 'When States,' says Théophile Gautier, 'rested on fictions, they needed fictive virtues; they couldn't have survived without them.'[19] The attacks by magistrates and Right-wing critics on the 'obscenity' of Naturalist novels were prompted as much by their attacks on established institutions as by their sexual explicitness. Paul Bonnetain's *Charlot s'amuse* (1883), for example, arraigned and cleared, and then published again in 1885 in an edition that helpfully indexed and italicised the condemned passages, is in fact remarkably discreet in its language, if a little melodramatic in its moralising, as it traces the degradation and eventual suicide of a child from the slums. The real objection was that it arraigned the authority figures of the mother, religious teaching community and army who contributed to the child's corruption, and behind them a whole social system.

In the eighteenth century, charges of obscenity levelled against the *philosophes* often veiled a larger hostility directed against their desire to educate a wider public for a larger measure of individual responsibility. Pierre Bayle, for example, in the second edition of his *Dictionnaire historique et critique* (1702), the first great encyclopaedic work of vulgarisation published by the Enlightenment, has a number of footnotes and a lengthy appended *Éclaircissement sur les obscénités*, in which he recognises that what is at issue is the right to diffuse a different kind of information to a wider readership. Bayle argues for more openness and more knowledge; he also argues for more of a sense of enjoyment, finding space in his initial remarks to defend not only the right to know but also the right to invent, for sheer pleasure, fictions

> . . . where the author relates in a free, lively style a number of amorous adventures of pure invention as regards their subject, or at least the details and the elaboration; and brings into his tale a number of impure incidents which he tries to make as pleasing as he can to make of them enjoyable tales, more likely to inspire a desire for amorous intrigue than anything else.

Later in the same period the work of Diderot attacks as one of the foundations of despotic power the desire to regulate sexuality. The novel *Jacques le fataliste* holds the reader's interest in its complex innovatory notions on the relationship of individual and authority, freewill and responsibility by a seductive promise to tell the tale of Jacques' wicked love-life; and, in a clever twist, attacks the prurient but prudish reader's imputed shock at what he writes – the reader's uncritical collusion with the censor:

> If you gave the least thought to this prejudice of yours, you would realise it was based on wrong principles . . .
>
> I enjoy writing down your follies under borrowed names; your follies make me laugh; what I write makes you cross. To be frank, reader, I don't think I'm the worse of the two of us. I'd be delighted if I could protect myself from your foulness as easily as you can protect yourself from the boredom or the dangers of my work! Leave me alone, you wicked hypocrites. Fuck like donkeys out of harness, but let me say fuck; I'll let you do it, if you'll let me say it. You say kill, steal, betray with no hesitation, and the other word you only dare whisper! Is it because the less you let out into words of these so-called impurities, the more you have left to think about?[20]

And, of course, to confirm authoritarian fears, among the best-known authors of eighteenth-century erotic fiction were men actively engaged in the politics of the Revolution: Mirabeau, spear-heading the aristocratic revolt, Laclos, Orleanist and Jacobin, editing the Jacobin journal that strengthened the network of revolutionary Clubs, Sylvain Maréchal, journalist, chief editor of *Révolutions de Paris*, 1791–94, Jacobin, briefly Babouvist and imputed author of the *Manifeste des égaux*. Even Sade, between his liberation from the Bastille in 1789 and his re-imprisonment by Bonaparte in 1801, acted as secretary to his revolutionary section – and included in his *Philosophie du boudoir* (1795) the stirring pamphlet 'Français, encore un effort si vous voulez être républicains'.

If Michel Foucault's hypothesis in his *History of Sexuality* proves correct, the increased importance acquired by sexuality in modern times is in fact less to be ascribed to the writers of erotic fictions than to authority itself. From the confessional in the sixteenth century to the institutions of the nineteenth – family, teachers, psychiatrists – normative authorities have ensured the construction and diffusion of so-called 'perverted' forms of sexuality by the attention they have concentrated on them. Foucault sees in these relationships between surveyor and surveyed the real power bases of the authoritarian structures of modern society. Individual subject and authority are bound together in *'perpetual spirals of power and pleasure'*:

The pleasure that comes of exercising a power that questions, monitors, watches, spies, searches out, palpates, brings to light; and on the other hand, the pleasure that kindles at having to evade this power, flee from it, fool it, or travesty it. . . . Capture and seduction, confrontation and mutual reinforcement: parents and children, adults and adolescents, educator and students, doctor and patients, the psychiatrist and his hysteric and his perverts, all have played this game continually since the nineteenth century.[21]

By claiming the right to define a norm and its variations, the institutions of authority created categories of the abnormal, since extended, consolidated and ratified:

A proliferation of sexualities through the extension of power; an optimization of the power to which each of these local sexualities gave a surface of intervention: this concatenation, particularly since the nineteenth century, has been ensured and relayed by the countless economic interests which, with the help of medicine, psychiatry, prostitution, and pornography, have tapped into both this analytical multiplication of pleasure and this optimization of the power that controls it.[22]

Whatever the apparent prudishness of society and its overt prohibition of sexual 'perversions', it is in fact in sexual excess that key centres of social power lie. Formulating its questions about sexuality so as to pre-empt the answers, society has shaped it into particular patterns. We are defined by the rationality of the inquisition; in setting up its binary opposition between the 'normal' and the 'perverse', the authority that censors and censures creates the effects it deplores, and for its own purposes.

A vast number of discourses, of different kinds, go to construct our sexuality; and of these, the discourse of fiction is far less potent in its effects than that of the institutions confronted in everyday life. What it can, however, do, in its relatively free symbolic play, is articulate emerging motifs and images, making legible the latent possibilities of the real. In its own Utopian space alongside sexuality, it constructs a dream of another substance: the erotic, the body's dream of itself.

Notes

1. H.-G. de Riquetti, comte de Mirabeau, *Le Degré des âges du plaisir*, Imprimerie de la Mère des amours, Paphos, 1793.
2. Georges Bataille, Preface to *Madame Edwarda*, in *Oeuvres complètes*, Vol. III, NRF, Paris, 1971, p. 10.
3. J. Huizinga, *The Waning of the Middle Ages*, Penguin, London, 1965, p. 108.
4. Denis de Rougemont, *L'Amour et l'occident*, Paris, 1939; definitive edition, Plon, Paris, 1972.
5. Georges Bataille, 'L'Histoire de l'érotisme', written 1950–51, in *Oeuvres complètes*, Vol. VIII, NRF, Paris, 1976, p. 10.
6. *Ibid.*, p. 12.
7. Georges Bataille, *Eroticism*, tr. Mary Dalwood, John Calder, London, 1962, pp. 184–86.
8. *Les Onze Mille Verges* (uncut) is published by J. J. Pauvert, Paris. It is available in a (cut) English translation by Nina Rootes, with an excellent introductory essay by Richard N. Coe, Taplinger, New York, 1979.
9. R. Desnos, *La Liberté ou l'amour*, Gallimard, Paris, 1962, p. 104.
10. For an interesting range of feminist comment on the subject see the works by Angela Carter, Susan Griffin and Maria Marcus cited in the Bibliography. See also M. Charney, *Sexual Fiction*, Methuen, London, 1981.
11. J. Kristeva, *Desire in Language: A Semiotic Approach to Literature and Art*, Basil Blackwell, Oxford, 1980, pp. 79–80.
12. Beatrice Faust, *Women, Sex and Pornography*, Penguin, London, 1982; S. Marcus, *The Other Victorians: A Study of Sexuality and Pornography in Mid-Nineteenth Century England*, Weidenfeld & Nicolson, London, 1966; S. Sontag, 'The Pornographic Imagination', in *Styles of Radical Will*, Secker & Warburg, London, 1969.
13. Pierre Louÿs, *Trois Filles de leur mère*, Les Classiques interdits, Editions Jean-Claude Lattès, Paris, 1979.
14. Preface to reprint, Paris, 1907, of original edition ed. Brussels, 1833.
15. D.-A.-F. de Sade, *Justine, ou les Malheurs de la vertu*, Hollande, chez les Libraires associés [Girouard, Paris], 1791.
16. D.-A.-F. de Sade, *Oeuvres complètes*, Cercle du livre précieux, Paris, 1964, VIII, p. 442.
17. Michel Foucault, *The History of Sexuality*, tr. R. Hurley, Vol. I, Penguin, London, 1981, p. 21.
18. See for example David Foxon, *Libertine Literature in England 1660–1745*, rpt. from The Book Collector, London, 1964, pp. 46–47.

19. 'Sous la table', *Les Jeunes France*, Charpentier, Paris, 1883, p. 6.
20. D. Diderot, *Oeuvres*, Gallimard, Paris, 1951, p. 656.
21. Michel Foucault, *op. cit.*, p. 45.
22. *Ibid.*, p. 48.

I
Anon.

from *Les Cent Nouvelles Nouvelles* (?1464–67)

A collection of prose tales, compiler unknown, modelled on the tales of Poggio and Boccaccio, supposedly narrated by members of the court of the libertine Philippe, Duke of Burgundy. In this example, a hint of realism in the nicely observed manners and dialogue combines with an utterly unrealistic failure to distinguish between the word and the thing – the sexual act and the traditional euphemisms. The obvious affection between both couples, the sincere ingenuousness of both wives and the allusive nature of the erotic descriptions give a pastoral quality to the rivalry and cuckoldry that in other tales can take on a more bitter edge. The 'extreme indecency' and 'excessive formalism' that Huizinga picked out as the two main currents in late mediaeval sensibility are here joined together; the exact parallelism of the incidents, the joky repetition of words and phrases, emphasise the element of fiction and play.

The Miller and the Knight

Not long ago, in the dukedom of Burgundy, there was a noble knight, whose name we shall leave out of the present story, who was married to a fine handsome lady. Close by the castle where this knight lived, there lived a miller, likewise married to a fine handsome young woman. One day the knight went walking in the neighbourhood around his house, to pass the time and take some recreation. And along the river where stood the said house and the mill of the said miller, who was away at the time in Dijon, or Beaune, his eye happened to fall on the miller's wife, carrying two

jars, on her way back from the river to fetch water. He went up to
her at once and greeted her courteously. And she, being a virtuous
and well-brought-up lady, quite properly did him honour and
made him a curtsey. Our knight, observing that the miller's wife
was very buxom and comely but not over-endowed with good
sense, was struck by a good idea, and said to her: 'Well, indeed, my
dear, I see you're sick, and dangerously so.' Hearing this, the
miller's wife came closer and said: 'Alas, my lord! What's wrong
with me?' 'Frankly, my dear, it's plain to me that if you go one step
further your thingy runs a great risk of falling out. I don't think you
can have it much longer before it drops off; I know all about these
things.' The simple wife, hearing the noble lord's words, was
astounded and dismayed: astounded that milord could know and
see such a misfortune was imminent, and dismayed to hear she was
about to lose the nicest part of her body, the bit she found most
useful – and her husband too. So she replied: 'Alas, my lord, what
are you saying? And how can you tell my thingy is in danger of
falling out? It looks pretty well held on to me.' 'Steady on there,
dear,' milord replied, 'you be content with that, then; but I assure
you it's the truth, and you wouldn't be the first it happened to.'
'Alas, my lord!' she said, 'then I'm lost, ruined and dishonoured!
And by Our Lady, what will my husband say when he hears of this
misfortune? He won't love me any more.' 'Don't distress yourself
before you need to, my dear,' said milord, 'it hasn't got that far yet,
and there are some good cures.' When the young miller's wife heard
her condition could be remedied, the blood came back to her
cheeks; and summoning up all her charm, she begged milord, for
Heaven's sake! Would he please tell her what she must do to stop the
poor thingy falling out. Milord, a most gracious and courteous
man, especially with ladies, said to her: 'My dear, you're a good,
pretty girl, I'm devoted to your husband and I feel very sorry indeed
for you in that state. I'll tell you how to save your thingy.' 'Alas,
milord! I'm most grateful to you, and it would be a most meri-
torious work; I'd sooner die than live without my thingy. What
must I do, milord?' 'My dear,' he said, 'the cure for your thingy
falling out is getting it banged in again as much and as quick as you
can.' 'Banged in again, my lord? And who could do it? Who would I
have to go to, to get the job done properly?' 'I'll tell you, my dear,'
milord replied. 'Since it was I who told you of your misfortune,
which was both serious and imminent, and also of the requisite cure
to obviate the disadvantages which might arise as a consequence of

your condition, for which I'm sure you must be grateful, I am happy to further promote our new friendship by banging your thingy in again and restoring it to you in such excellent condition that you can take it everywhere in total confidence, without the slightest fear of its ever falling out, and that I can guarantee you.'

No need to ask if the miller's wife was delighted; she strained the little sense she had trying to thank milord enough. And she and milord walked together all the way to the mill, and there they set to work. Milord, most courteously, with a tool he had on him, in a very short space banged the miller's wife's thingy back in again two or three times, and she was absolutely delighted. And when the work was done, and they'd exchanged quantities of compliments, and fixed a day to work on the thingy again, milord took his leave and strode off gaily to his house. On the stated day, milord went back to the miller's wife, and exactly as related above employed himself to the best of his ability in banging her thingy in. He laboured so hard and well that as time went on the thingy was completely secure and fastened firm and tight.

The business of banging and plugging the miller's wife's thingy still had some way to go when the miller returned from his trading. He sat down to relax, and his wife came and sat beside him. And after they'd discussed a little private business his good wife said: 'Faith, sir, we're much indebted to the lord of this town.' 'Oh yes, my dear,' said the miller, 'in what way?' 'Well, it's only right I should tell you, so you can thank him, because you owe him a great deal. The fact is that while you were away milord went by our house once as I was going to the river with two jugs. He bowed, and so did I. And while I was walking along, he noticed, how I don't know, that my thingy was hanging on by a whisker and in dreadful danger of falling out. He told me so, out of kindness, and Heavens, I was astounded! and indeed, as dismayed as if everyone had suddenly dropped dead. Seeing me so distressed, the kindhearted gentleman was very sorry for me. And right there and then he told me a good remedy to save me from such hideous danger. And he did something more for me besides, that he wouldn't have done for anybody else. Because the remedy he told me – that I should get my thingy plugged and banged in again to stop it falling out – well, he did it for me himself; and it was a terrible labour for him, and he sweated over it several times, because my condition needed several visits. What more can I say? He acquitted himself so well we can never repay him. Faith, one day this week he banged it in again three or four times, another day twice, and then three times. He never let me be until I was completely mended. And he's got me so well done that my thingy is as firm and tight as any woman's in this town.'

The good miller, hearing this fine adventure, gave no indication what he felt inside but said to his wife as though he were delighted: 'Well now, my dear, I'm very pleased my lord did us this favour. And please God, when I get the chance, I'll do the same for him. But still, your condition was a bit unseemly, so mind you say nothing of this to anyone. And since you're cured, there'll be no need for you to weary milord any further.' 'You needn't worry,' said the miller's wife, 'I'll not say a word, that's just what milord said to me.'

Our miller, who was a good lad, mulled over and again in his head the courtesy milord had done him, but conducted himself so well and so wisely that the said gentleman didn't know he had the slightest suspicion how he'd deceived him, and thought he knew nothing of it. But alas! he did, and his mind and heart were all entirely concentrated on getting revenge, if he could, by paying the same or a similar trick on *his* wife. His wily brain had no rest until he'd worked out a ruse by which, he thought, if he could pull it off, milord would be paid back in his own coin.

After a while, some business came up and milord mounted his horse and took his leave of milady for a month, which made our miller not half glad. Then one day milady decided to take a bath. She had the bath drawn and the boilers heated in the house, in her private apartments. The miller knew all this, because he often visited the place. He went and took a fine pike out of his fishtrap, and went off to the castle to give it to milady. Some of milady's women wanted to take the pike from him and present it to milady on the miller's behalf; but the miller very carefully refused to let them, and said he wanted to give it to milady himself, or he swore he'd take it home again. In the end, since he was a merry fellow and practically one of the household, milady sent for him, still in her bath. The gracious miller handed over his present and milady thanked him and sent it into the kitchen to be cooked for supper. While milady was talking to the miller, he caught sight of a large, very fine diamond sitting on the edge of the bath, which she'd taken off her finger for fear of spoiling it in the water. He nabbed it so neatly that not a soul saw him. And when the next chance came he said good night to milady and her women and went back to his mill, thinking out the rest of his plan.

Milady, who'd been enjoying herself with her women, saw it was getting late and time for supper, left her bath and jumped into bed. But when she looked at her hands and her arms, she couldn't see her diamond. She called her women and asked them for the diamond, and who she'd given it to. Each one said: 'It wasn't me.' 'Nor me.' 'Nor me either.' They looked high and low, in the bath, on the bath, everywhere; but all in vain, it couldn't be found. The search for the diamond went on and on, but no one found a trace of it, which very much upset milady, because it had been lost by pure mischance and in her own chamber. It was all the more precious because milord had given it her the day they were married. No one knew whom to blame, or to ask for it back, so the whole household was in great distress. One of the women had an idea, and said: 'Not a soul came in except those of us who are already here and the miller; I think it would be a good idea to send for him.' He was sent for, and he duly came. Milady, upset, angry, and at the end of her tether, asked if the miller hadn't seen her diamond. He could keep as straight a face lying or joking as anyone else telling the truth; he denied it loudly and even asked boldly if milady took him for a thief. To which she gently replied: 'Indeed not, master miller, of course not. It wouldn't be theft if you'd taken my diamond for a joke.' 'Milady,' said the miller, 'I swear in all faith I know nothing about your diamond.' Then everyone was at a loss, especially milady, who was so upset she couldn't control herself; the tears just poured out, she was so distressed about her ring. The unhappy company considered together what they could do. One said it just had to be in the chamber, another said she'd looked everywhere and if it had been there, she'd have found it, it definitely would have shown up by now. The miller asked milady if she'd had it when she got in the bath, and she said yes. 'If that's the case, then indeed, milady, seeing that everyone has looked so hard for it, it's certainly a very strange affair. I think, though, if any man in this town could tell you how to find it, it would be me. But I don't want my methods revealed and made general knowledge, so it would be best if I spoke to you in private.' 'That won't stop us,' said milady. She dismissed her ladies; and as the women went out, Lady Jehanne, Lady Isabeau and Lady Katherine all said: 'Alas, master miller! You'll be a good man if you bring that diamond back.' 'I don't promise it,' said the miller, 'but I venture to say, if it *can* be found again, I'll tell her how to do it.'

Once alone with milady, he told her he had a strong suspicion – in fact, he was certain – that if she had had the diamond when she got in the bath, it must have fallen off her finger into the water and got stuck up inside her, because no one there would want to take it. Pretending to make a diligent search for it, he told milady to get onto the bed, which she would certainly have refused to do if it hadn't been for a good reason. And when he had her all exposed, he made as though he were searching here and there and then said: 'That's it, milady, the diamond's inside.' 'You mean you've seen it, master miller?' 'Indeed I have.' 'Alas,' she said, 'and how can we get it out?' 'Very easily, milady; I'm sure I can manage it, if you'll allow me.' 'Heaven help me, I'd do anything to get it back,' said milady, 'go on, master miller.' Milady, still lying on the bed, was put by the miller in just the same state as milord put the miller's wife when he was banging in her thingy and he made his attempt to find and fish out the diamond with just the same sort of tool. While they were resting after the miller's first and second attempts to find the diamond, milady asked whether he'd felt it. He said he had, and she was absolutely delighted and begged him to go on fishing until he'd found it. To cut the story short, the miller worked away until he'd got the fine diamond back for milady, and the whole household rejoiced. No miller ever had such honours and distinctions as milady and her women heaped on him. The good miller, in milady's very good graces after the longed-for success of his noble enterprise, left the house and went home, without boasting to his wife of his recent adventure, which pleased him more than if he'd won the whole world.

By God's grace, milord came home not long after, and was kindly received and humbly welcomed by milady. After some protracted bedtime conversation, she told him the wonderful tale of her diamond, and how the miller had fished it out from inside her; and, to be brief, gave him all the details of where, how and in what way the said miller had set about the search for the diamond. The story gave him no pleasure at all, but he said to himself that the miller had paid him back nicely. The next time he met the good miller, he gave a low bow and said: 'God save you, God save, good diamond-fisher!' To which the good miller replied: 'God save, God save indeed, good cunt-banger!' 'By Our Lady, you're right!' said the lord, 'keep quiet about me and I'll keep quiet about you.' The miller was satisfied, and never mentioned it again. And nor did the lord, as far as I know.

II
François Rabelais (1494–1553)

from *Pantagruel* (1532; text from 1542 edition)

*Cleric, physician, humanist and satirist, probably the most famous representative of the bawdy Gallic tradition, Rabelais offers a robust but complex eroticism rooted in the comedy of everyday life, the traditions of the Church, which it both sustains and subverts, and the new learning of the Renaissance. In the following extract, the lady wooed by Pantagruel's companion Panurge, torn between duty, respectability and cupidity, is a familiar object of moral satire. Mikhail Bakhtin has pointed out that the tableau of the lady and the dogs has its source in the Babylonian harlot and her attendant monsters who in popular Carnival preceded the priests in the Corpus Christi procession, the carnal parody of divine love. The apparently monstrous and sacrilegious quality of this episode is simply the accepted grotesque of a popular-festive tradition (*Rabelais and his World, M.I.T. Press, 1968, pp. 229–31). Finally, Panurge's courting speech is a brilliantly bathetic mixture of courtly eulogy, learned pastiche of classical rhetoric and forthright popular crudity.*

Following hard on Panurge's successful defeat and debunking of the pretentious English scholar, the exchange with the lady has also been seen as an attack on hypocrisy and pretension – the body, eros repressed, returning to claim its own in the humiliating but hilarious onslaught of the animals.

Chapter XXI: How Panurge Courted a Grand Lady of Paris

Having won the disputation against the Englishman, Panurge began to acquire a measure of fame in Paris. From then on, he exploited his codpiece to good advantage, and had the top section picked out with embroidery in the Romanesque style. He was highly and publicly acclaimed, someone wrote a song about him and little children sang it on their way to the shops, and he was made welcome wherever maidens and ladies met together. As a result, he became puffed up with pride and reckoned he would try to put one over on one of the great ladies of the city.

So one day, cutting out the pile of prologues and protestations habitually proffered by those lugubrious contemplative Lenten lovers, who never touch meat, he said to her: 'Lady, it were highly advantageous to the public weal, delightful for yourself, an honour for your family, and for me an urgent necessity that you be covered by a man of my breeding: and you'd better believe it, because you're about to find out.'

As soon as he had finished, the lady shoved him back from her a good hundred leagues. 'You crazy villain,' she said, 'what right have you to talk to me like that? Who do you think I am? Be off, and don't let me set eyes on you again; for two pins, I'd have your arms and legs cut off.'

'Well now,' said Panurge, 'cut off my arms and legs and I wouldn't care, as long as you and I had just one go together pulling out all the organ stops. Here's Master John Thursday' (showing her his long codpiece) 'to play you a Strip the Willow that'll shiver the marrow of your bones. He's a gallant lover, he knows how to get at all the bits and pieces and the sensitive spots in your rat-trap, and when he's done all you'll need is dusting down.'

To which the lady replied: 'Get away, you wicked creature, be off with you. One more word and I'll call for help and have you thrashed here and now.'

'Come on,' he said, 'you're not as cruel as you say, you can't be, or else your face is a great deceiver. Sooner would the earth ascend to the heavens, and the highest heaven tumble into the abyss and all natural order go awry than exquisite beauty and elegance such as yours have within it the slightest drop of malice or gall. Of course, they do say that hardly ever "Saw a man a lady fair/Who would not drive him to despair;" but that's only your common beauties. Your loveliness is so excellent, singular and divine that Nature surely placed it in you for a paragon, to show us what she's capable of when she applies all her knowledge and power.

'In you is nought but honey, sugar, manna celestial.

'It was to you that Paris should have gifted the golden apple, not Venus, no, nor Juno, nor Minerva; for never was such magnificence in Juno, such wisdom in Minerva, such elegance in Venus, as I behold in you.

'O celestial gods and goddesses all, happy shall be he to whom you grant the favour of embracing this lady, fucking her, larding her meat. And by Heaven, that happy man will be me, I can see it, she loves me already fit to burst; I know she does, and to this was I predestined by the fairies. Will you stop wasting time then, and one, two and let's be having you!'

He would have given her a kiss, but she made to go to the window and shout rape to the neighbours.

At that, Panurge departed somewhat speedily, saying as he ran off: 'Wait for me here, Lady, I'll fetch them myself, don't put yourself out.'

And away he went, not much worried by his rejection, and certainly not letting it spoil his appetite.

The next day he was at church at the time she usually attended mass.

He offered her holy water at the door, with a low, respectful bow, and then knelt down beside her like an old friend and said: 'Lady, behold, my love for you is so great that I can no longer piss or shit. I don't know what you mean to do, but if any harm came to me, what would happen then?'

'Be off,' she said, 'be off, I don't care. Let me get on with my prayers.'

'Can you,' he said, 'do me the play on *"A Beaumont le Viconte"*?'

'No,' said she, 'I can not.'

'It is,' said he, ' *"A beau con le vit monte."** So pray God grant me the desire of your noble heart, and would you mind giving me your rosary.'

'Here,' she said, 'and stop bothering me.'

So saying, she was about to take off her rosary, made of precious wood with golden paternosters. Panurge, however, promptly whipped out one of his knives, snipped it off and made off to the pawnbroker's with it, asking her: 'Do you want my blade?'

'No, no,' she said.

'Well, don't forget,' he said, 'it's at your command, body and soul, bowels and guts!'

The lady meanwhile was not pleased by the fate of her rosary,

---

*The first is a placename which, rearranged, gives: 'A prick goes up a pretty cunt.'

which she needed to keep up appearances in church, and she also thought to herself: 'This great chatterer is some fool from a foreign country. I'll never get my rosary back. What will my husband say? He'll be furious with me. I'll tell him a thief cut it off in church; he's bound to believe that, because there's still the bit of ribbon on my belt.'

After dinner, Panurge paid her a visit with a fat purse up his sleeve stuffed with counters and tokens and started out: 'Which of us loves the other more, you me or I you?'

She replied: 'For my part, I don't hate you; I love everyone, as God commands us.'

'But,' he said, 'come to the point: aren't you in love with me?'

'I have,' she said, 'already told you many times over you're not to say such things to me. If you start off again I'll show you I'm no woman to be talked to so disrespectfully. Get out of here and give me back my rosary before my husband asks where it is.'

'What,' he said, 'your rosary, Lady? By Gob I shan't give it back; but I'll give you another.

'Would you like one of well-enamelled gold in big round balls or fair love-knots, or great massive braids? Or do you want it made of ebony, jacinths, or cut garnets, with paternosters of fine turquoise or of fine cut topaz or sapphire, or magnificent rubies with paternosters of diamond with twenty-eight facets?

'No, no, that's not good enough. I know a beautiful rosary of fine emeralds studded with beads of round ambergris and a Persian pearl on the clasp as big as an orange! It only costs twenty-five thousand ducats. I'll make you a present of it, I've a purse full of money.'

As he said this, he rattled his tokens as though they were true crowns.

'Do you want a length of dark crimson velvet dyed scarlet, or a length of brocaded or crimson satin? Do you want chains, gold jewellery, circlets, rings? All you have to do is say yes. Up to fifty thousand ducats is nothing to me.'

The power of his words made her mouth water, but she still said: 'No, thank you; I want nothing of you.'

'By God,' he said, 'but I want something of you, and it'll cost you nothing and leave you no worse off. Here,' (he showed her his long codpiece), 'here's Master John Thomas looking for a home.'

He tried to embrace her, but she started to scream, though not too loud.

Then Panurge dropped the mask and said to her: 'So there's no way I'm going to get anything out of you? Fuck you then. You don't deserve the honour or the pleasure, but by God, I'll see you mounted by the dogs.'

So saying, he made off as fast as he could for fear of blows, to which he had a natural antipathy.

Chapter XXII: How Panurge Played a Trick on the Parisian Lady that Did Her No Good at All

Now the next day was the great feast of Corpus Christi, when all the women put on their most magnificent gowns and on that day the lady in question was dressed in an exquisite robe of crimson satin and a tunic of costly white velvet.

On the day of the vigil, Panurge looked all over town until he found a bitch in heat. He tied her up with his belt, took her to his room and fed her well that day and all night. When morning came he killed her, took out a bit known to the Greek geomancers, chopped it up as small as he could, hid it carefully and took it with him to the place where the lady was due to go to join the procession, as is the custom at that festival. As she went in, Panurge offered her the holy water, bowing most courteously, and as soon as she'd finished saying her prayers he went to join her on her bench and gave her a piece of paper with a rondeau, written as follows:

> For this one time that you my lady love
> Did hear my suit, your heart I could not move;
> Too harsh by far, you sent me from your side,
> Though words nor deeds did ought to hurt your pride;
> I asked you only your dear heart to prove.
> For my lament to die like stricken dove
> You needed but extend to me your glove
> And tell me: 'Dear, with me you may not bide
>   For this one time.'

> I wrong you not, to swear by God above
> My heart's afire with longing to approve
> The dazzling charms your rich gowns cannot hide;
> I ask but for the happy chance to ride
> Within your arms and all your doubts remove
>   For this one time.

As she was opening the paper up to see what it was, Panurge quickly sprinkled his preparation all over her, especially the folds of her dress and her sleeves, and then said; 'Lady, poor lovers are seldom at ease. For myself, I hope that the sleepless nights, and the pain and trouble I've suffered for love of you will be counted against my pain in Purgatory. Pray God at least that He give me patience in my trials.'

No sooner had Panurge finished speaking than all the dogs in the church came running up to the lady, drawn by the scent of the drug he had sprinkled over her. Big ones, little ones, huge ones, tiny ones all came running with members erect, sniffing and pissing all over her. It was the foulest trick ever played.

Panurge made a pretence of chasing them away, then took his leave and went into a side-chapel to see the fun. The beastly dogs were pissing all over her clothes: a tall greyhound pissed on her head, others pissed on her sleeves, and others on her hindquarters and the little ones pissed on her pattens. All the women from round about had much ado to rescue her.

Panurge laughed out loud, and said to one of the nobles of the city: 'I think the lady must be in heat, or else some greyhound's just mounted her.'

When he was quite sure all the dogs were growling round her like a bitch in heat, he left and went to find Pantagruel.

Every dog he came across in the street got a good kick and the injunction: 'Why aren't you off with your friends having fun? Go on, by the devil, go on, get away with you!'

When he got home, he said to Pantagruel: 'Pray, master, come and see every dog in the kingdom gathered around the fairest lady in the city. All hoping to get it in!'

Pantagruel cheerfully fell in with the idea, and went to see the mystery performed, which he found most exquisite and original.

But best of all was the procession. There were more than six hundred thousand and fourteen dogs to be seen gathered round her, tormenting her in a thousand different ways; and everywhere she went new dogs came running up to follow her, pissing over the road where her gown had touched.

Everybody stopped to view the sight and watch what the dogs were doing, scrambling right up to her neck, ruining all her finery. There was no cure for it but to go back to her mansion. Off she went, and the dogs straight after her, she trying to hide, and all the chambermaids in stitches.

Once she was in the house with the door barred behind her, all the dogs for half a league about came running along and pissed so profusely on the door that their urine ran in a stream deep enough for a duck to swim on. This is the stream that nowadays runs through Saint Victor, and Gobelin uses for dying his cloth scarlet on account of the specific virtue of its dog-piss, as the great Master d'Oribus once told us in a public sermon.

God help us, a mill could have ground corn with it: though not as much as the Bazacle mills at Toulouse.

III
François Béroalde de Verville
(1558–1612)

from *Le Moyen de parvenir* (1610)

In Béroalde's book, the laughter has a more sophisticated and more cynical edge. The erotic focus on the movements and gestures of the unfortunate Marcia is also a focus for competition and rivalry, and Marcia's humiliation is more real than that of the miller's wife or milady. The watchword of the whole symposium, according to Béroalde himself, is money; Monsieur de la Roche, who has most of it, is the one who controls and shapes this particular incident, and has the double erotic pleasure of Marcia's beauty and his own mildly sadistic sense of power. 'Lust,' says Sade, in Juliette, *'is the child of opulence and superiority.'*

Béroalde was canon of Tours from 1593 onwards. He also wrote the romance Les Aventures de Floride *(1594, 1601) and* Le Palais des curieux *(1612).*

Cherry-picking

The miller who lived closest to Monsieur de la Roche's castle was the first in the neighbourhood to pick some very fine early cherries and he sent them to his lord the very same day. Monsieur de la Roche happened to have with him several gentlemen from the neighbourhood; gentlemen in a small way, as you might say of the canons of Saint Mamboeuf at Angers compared with those from Saint Maurice, or the canons of Saint Venant compared with Saint Martin at Tours. (That's it; exactly right.) The miller put the cherries in a pretty little basket and gave them to his daughter to take to the master. The fair lady, about the age of an old ox, fresh and toothsome, came into the hall, curtsied to the master, who was eating dinner, and gave him the fruit from her father. 'Ha!' said de la Roche. 'They're very fine. Here,' he said to his servants, 'bring me the four finest sheets we've got and spread them on the ground.' Note, incidentally, everything he said had to be obeyed; the man was the very model of Antichrist. He's the one the preachers were calling a heretic this last Lent for flying his falcons from his tower. He was such a good shot, like my lord de Sautal, that he could aim for fun at the horse between the legs of a friend coming to dinner and get him in motion at the bend of the crossroads; and to show off his skill, when the ploughman was turning his plough he would trigger the goad with a shot, without touching the man. All for a laugh.

When the sheets were all spread out, he ordered the pretty lady to take her clothes off. Poor little Marcia started to cry. 'Well, what a good girl you are! You're determined not to laugh! When a girl's mouth is crying, her cunt's laughing. Come on then, get on with it, or I'll set all the devils in Hell on you. Look, don't annoy me, just do as I say.' The poor little thing took off her dress, then her shoes, then her cap; and then – a tricky moment – pulled off her chemise and naked as a sprite leaving her pool went scattering the cherries from side to side, up and down, over the fine sheets, at the master's orders. Her lovely hair, love's sweet snare, floated dishevelled over nature's fair masterpiece, smooth, plump and succulent, revealing with every fresh movement a thousand lovely delights. Her twin breasts, pretty bouncing handfuls, jutted out against the ivory of her throat, taking on countless different shapes depending how you looked at them. Lascivious eyes slid to her fine round thighs, enhanced with every charm beauty can give to the ramparts and gateways of love's seal; greedy glances ravished all the exquisite sights they could see.

But despite all the charms daintily displayed in this delightful spectacle, there was just one small place every eye sought with special attention; every gaze strained to the target where every man would have liked to take aim, everyone was preoccupied with that precious spot where the register of love's mysteries is kept. When the cherries had been scattered round, they had to be picked up again; and then, despite all her twists and contortions to try and hide the priceless labyrinth of desire, Marcia's poor little centre of delights was hard-pressed to find movements to screen it from view. This perfect beauty, stuff any man would ruin himself for, this body with all its charms was seen in so many delightful perspectives that it would be hard to find eyes ever more satisfied than those of the spectators.

One onlooker said: 'There's nothing so lovely in all the world; I wouldn't have missed the pleasure I've had for a hundred crowns.' Another, describing the delectation with which his imagination was filled, estimated his good fortune in seeing such a sight at more than two hundred crowns. One old sinner said the enjoyment was worth three hundred. A servant, jigging about like all the others, set his share of pleasure at ten crowns. Every single one of the masters said a hundred, or a hundred and fifty crowns, some more, some less, as their tongues followed their eyes, mentally drooling over the sight of her marble skin, roaming over her body in thoughts and words, every mind latching in imagination onto the lovely girl, with a hundred thousand beautiful fancies. Each of the onlookers had his say, naming a round sum for the delights he imagined.

The cherries back in the basket, the girl went back to the windows to put her chemise back on. Once again the onlookers stretched their eyes wide to see just one more bit of something, spying and staring as she lifted one leg, then the other, right until she was back as she had come, dressed completely from head to foot. Her lovely cherubic eyes shimmered with the fiery waves of liquid tears they had shed for shame at the adventure.

But Monsieur de la Roche had eyes in his head and was watching the fair lady, laughing deep down in his heart but listening carefully to the chatter of those little men who were talking far too much and licking their lips over what they had to say. He went on watching, remembering every word, especially the price each one set on the pleasure he had had. He even noted a humble lackey claiming a crown's worth: 'Just down a bit, that's it; all you have to do is bend down and pick them up.'

Once dressed, Marcia was seated by my lord's orders at the foot of the table and there he consoled and comforted her as best he could, serving her from the daintiest dishes. She was still angry and tearful, indignant at having exposed everything God had given her and grieved to have been seen by so many people at once, outside church. When this finally penetrated to de la Roche, he roared with anger at the whole company, like the lions on Saint John's clock in Lyons, and set to swearing his mighty evangelical oath (being

Huguenot at the time, for appearances' sake): 'God's truth' – just like thieves swear, when they profess religion – 'God's truth, gentlemen, do you take me for your jester, your servant, your paid provider of living flesh? By the twice-merited great triple horns of the greatest cuckold here, every single one of you shall pay what he said, or there won't be a single leg, head, member, gut, body, hair or shin left. Whoresbelly, you'll pay it all out right now, unless you want me to black your eyes and cut off your pricks.' (If they had cut them off, that would have been handy for the abbess of Montfleury. Last harvest-time her steward came to tell her the screw on the press had gone. She thought for some time and said, 'By my faith, if I live, I'll get a few screws in.')

Anyhow, the gentleman's words frightened the squires and they paid up what they'd said, sending out for the money or borrowing it from my lord with good notes and pledges. Between them our timid nobles coughed up into the basket about twelve hundred good solid shiny crowns. (Myself, I'd sooner shop in Paris; you can get a skirtful of flesh for twopence, and a basket of cherries for a penny.) Once the crowns were in the basket, de la Roche handed them to young Marcia, who had been biting her tongue in a frenzy of delight, knowing it was for her; and he told her: 'Here you are, my dear, take that to your father and tell him you got it showing your bum. There are plenty of people who've done it before, and still do, and never get as much; but by God, they go on trying.'

IV
Pierre de Bourdeille, abbé de Brantôme (1540–1614)

from *Les Dames galantes* (1666)

A member in his youth of the court of Marguerite de Navarre, but who fought for the Guises in the Civil Wars, Brantôme was a military man who began writing in 1584 after a riding accident. His works include a collection of Vies des grands capitaines français et étrangers *and the* Recueil des dames illustres et galantes.

A mixture of his own gossipy anecdotes and learned references to classical authors, the Dames galantes *has the air of a scientific discussion, divided into seven* Discours, *but one strongly marked by the personality of the writer: the curiosity, cynicism and salaciousness of the narrator, inviting the reader to collaboration, is an important part of the erotic effect.*

His attitude to lesbianism is ambivalent. He both applauds and abuses it, but finally decides that, kept within strict limits, it is no threat to men. On the contrary: lesbian love makes a pretty spectacle, its practitioners are amusingly vulnerable to scandal and humiliation, and it has the charm of novelty and mystery. Brantôme exploits the erotic thrill of being a superior observer (like the noble lady with her cage of weasels), of revealing private secrets, as well as enjoying the pleasures of what's seen.

On Lesbianism

I shall put another question now, something perhaps not everyone has enquired into or maybe ever thought of: that is, whether two women in love with one another, as we have seen and still do see frequently today, in bed together and engaged in what is known as *donna con donna* (in imitation of the learned Lesbian Sappho) can be said to be committing adultery and cuckolding their husbands.

It is certainly adultery if we are to believe Martial in his Epistles, Book I, epigram CXIX, where he introduces and addresses a woman called Bassa, a lesbian, and attacks her fiercely. No men were ever seen going into her house so she had got the reputation of a second Lucretia; but it so happened she had been found out. A great many lovely girls and women visited her regularly, and it was discovered that she herself served them, playing the man and the adulterer and coupling with them; Martial uses the words: *geminos committere cunnos*. In the following line of Latin, he gives the puzzle to be pondered and resolved in the form of an exclamation: *Hic, ubi vir non est, ut sit adulterium*.

'There,' he says, 'is a clear example that there can still be adultery without a man being involved.'

I knew a courtesan in Rome, a cunning old woman if there ever was one, called Isabella di Luna, a Spaniard, who conceived just such a passion for a courtesan called La Pandora, at that time one of the loveliest women in all Rome, married to one of the Cardinal d'Armagnac's stewards but still following her old trade. Isabella paid for her keep and used to sleep with her, and being a woman of loose, lewd tongue she often said in my hearing that she was making the girl a bigger whore and her husband a greater cuckold than any of the pimps she had ever had. I don't know what she would mean by that, unless she was going by Martial's epigram.

They say Sappho of Lesbos was a good mistress of this trade, not to say its inventor, and that lesbians have copied her ever since right up to our own times. In Lucian's words: the women of Lesbos are such that they will have nothing to do with men, but go with other women like men do. Women given to such practices, who have nothing to do with men but enjoy other women just as men do are called *tribades*, a Greek word derived, so I learn from the Greeks, from τρίβω, τρίβειν, which means the same as *fricare*, to rub, to frig, or to rub together, and tribades are called *fricatrices*, which is the same word in French, women who go in for frigging *donna con donna*, such as are found nowadays.

Juvenal is also referring to these women when he says: . . . *frictum Grissantis adorat*, speaking of just such a tribade who loved being frigged by a woman called Grissantis.

Our good friend Lucian has a chapter on the subject, in which he says that women should be allowed as a matter of course to have intercourse as men do, using mysterious and monstrous instruments of lechery, devoid of seed. The word *lesbianism*, that we hardly ever hear, should circulate freely and the female sex should all emulate Philaenis, who preferred making love like a man. He adds, however, that it is much better for a woman to be given to lustful desire to counterfeit the male than for a man to play the woman, which turns him into something timid and ignoble. According to that, then, a woman who plays the man can get a reputation for being braver and bolder than other women, both physically and spiritually, like some I have in fact known.

In another place, Lucian brings on two ladies discussing this kind of love. One asks the other whether such-and-such had been in love with her, if she had slept with her, what she had done to her. The other answers freely: 'First she kissed me like men do, not just with lips touching, but opening her mouth (meaning a pigeon kiss, with the tongue in the mouth); and even though she didn't have a male member and was built just like you and me, she said she had a man's heart, desires and everything else. Then I embraced her as I would a man and she set to work, kissing me, and panting . . . She seemed to be enjoying herself enormously and her way of making love was more pleasant than a man's.' That's what Lucian has to say about it.

From what I have heard, there are considerable numbers of these lesbian ladies in several towns and regions in France, Italy and Spain, Turkey, Greece and elsewhere. Wherever women are shut away and not given complete freedom, it is a very common practice; when they are aflame with passion, they say, they need the help of this remedy to cool off a little or be burnt up altogether.

Turkish women go to the baths more to indulge such lewdness than for any other reason and are much given to it. Even courtesans, who have men any time for the asking, still enjoy frigging, seek each other out and make love together, or so I have heard tell of some in Italy and Spain. In our own country of France such women are fairly common, though apparently they took it up only recently and the fashion was brought from Italy by a lady of quality whom I'll not name.

I have heard tell from the late Monsieur de Clermont-Tallard the younger, who died at La Rochelle, that when he was a little boy he had the honour of accompanying Monsieur d'Anjou, afterwards our King Henri III, into his study and working with him regularly, with Monsieur de Gournay as tutor. One day they were at

Toulouse, studying with the master in his room, and Clermont-Tallard was sitting in a corner apart. There happened to be a little crack in the wall – the studies and bedrooms were made of wood, and built in a hasty, makeshift fashion by the diligence of Cardinal d'Armagnac, the local bishop, to make it easier to receive and accommodate the King and his court. Through the crack he saw in another small room two very high-born ladies, their skirts up and their drawers down, lying on top of one another, exchanging pigeon kisses, rubbing and fondling, rolling and banging about in bawdy debauch, just like men. Their games lasted almost a good hour in which they got so tired and heated and red and sweaty, though it was extremely cold, that they could go on no longer and had to rest. He used to say he saw the same game, played the same way, as long as the court was there, but he never had the opportunity to see them afterwards, having had a favoured position there that other places didn't offer.

He told me even more I dare not write down, including the ladies' names. Whether it is true, I don't know, but he swore it was, on his honour, over and over again. In fact, it's very likely; people have always said that the two ladies in question held long love-making sessions and spent all their time at it.

I have known several other women given to such passions. I heard tell of one who was particularly good. She loved a number of women, honoured and served them better than men and made love to them as a man does to his mistress. She took them into her household, gave them hearth and board and everything they wanted. Her husband was very pleased with the situation, like a lot of other husbands I've known, very glad to have their wives engage in affairs of this kind rather than affairs with men, and less inclined to call them whores or insane. I think myself they're completely wrong; from what I've heard say, this minor exercise is an apprenticeship for the major exercise with a man.

These women get each other hot and randy but what they do doesn't reduce the heat; they need to bathe in fresh running water, which cools them off better than a still pool. So the best surgeons tell me; and certainly, if you're going to give proper treatment to a wound you don't waste time putting on salve and cleaning it round about and on the edges. You must get right down to the bottom and push your probe and swab in as far as you can.

I have seen so many lesbians, for all their rubbing and frigging, still assiduously frequenting men! Didn't Sappho, even, mistress of them all, fall in love with her beloved Phaon, and languish with longing for him? In the end, I've heard many ladies say, there is nothing like a man. The pleasure they take with other women is just a toy for practice before they get on to the real meat with the men; they only frig when there are no men to be had. If men were to be had easily, with no fear of scandal, they would happily drop their female friends and fling their arms round the good fellows' necks.

I have known in my time two lovely, noble maids of good family, both cousins, who slept together in the same bed for three years and got so used to frigging that they took it into their heads it must be a poor incomplete sort of pleasure compared with what might be got from men. They started to try it with them, and turned into excellent whores, confessing later to their lovers that it was frigging that had done most to debauch them and weaken their resistance to the other, and they hated it now; it was the sole cause of their ruin. Though mind you, when they met up with each other, or other women, they always tried a taste of frigging, to whet their appetite for the other thing with men. A noble young lady of my acquaintance said the same once, when her servant asked her one day if she ever did this frigging with her friend, who she used to sleep with. 'Oh, no!' she laughed, 'I like men too much.' In fact she went in for both.

I know a noble gentleman who one day at court, hoping to press for the hand of a very noble young lady in marriage, asked advice of one of his relatives. She told him frankly he would be wasting his time. 'Because,' she told me, 'a certain lady' (she told me her name, and I had heard her talked about) 'a certain lady will never allow her to marry.' I saw at once what the obstacle was; I knew the woman kept the girl in bed and board for her pleasure, and reserved her for her own lips. The gentleman thanked his cousin for her good advice, but accused her jokingly of speaking in her own interests as well as the other woman's, and snatching a few sly moments with the girl herself. She told me that wasn't true.

This story makes me think of men who keep whores of their own, and are so fond of them that they would not share them with prince or noble, comrade or friend, for all the money in the world. They're as jealous of them as a miser with his little barrel – though even he lets people drink from it if they ask. That lady wanted to keep the maid all to herself, without giving anyone else a share; but the girl still cuckolded her on the sly with some of her friends.

They say weasels are susceptible to this kind of passion, and their females like to couple and co-habit; in emblems, women who made love in this way used to be figured by weasels. I heard tell of a lady who herself dabbled in that passion, who always kept a few weasels and enjoyed watching the intercourse of the little creatures.

A further point is that these affairs between women take two forms. The first is frigging and (as the poet said) *geminos committere cunnos*. According to some people, this method does no harm. This is not, however, the case if the lovers resort to instruments made of . . . [sic] called instruments of pleasure, or dildoes.

I heard tell of a great prince who suspected two of his court ladies were using them, and had them watched so well that he surprised them in the act. One of them was all equipped and fitted out with a big one between her legs, neatly fastened round her body with little ribbons, so that it looked like a natural member. She was so taken by surprise she had no time to take it off; so the prince made her show him what the two of them did with it.

They say several women have died of abscesses produced in their wombs by unnatural movements and friction. I know a few of them, for whom it was a real pity. They were noble and lovely maids and ladies, who would have done far better to keep company with noble gentlemen whose love-making doesn't kill women but makes them live and flourish, as I hope to show elsewhere. In fact, I've heard some surgeons say that to cure that kind of disease the best thing is to clean them out inside with the natural male member, which is much better than the pessary with special fluid that doctors and nurses use. Yet there are still many women who insist on having these artificial devices, despite the problems they so obviously often create.

When I was at court, I heard a story of how the Queen Mother one day during the disturbances ordered a search of all the rooms and boxes of the people living in the Louvre, not excepting the ladies and young girls, to see whether there were any hidden weapons, possibly even pistols. There was one lady whose box the captain of the guard found fitted out not with pistols but four huge well-made dildoes, which gave everyone a good laugh and her tremendous embarrassment. I know the young lady. I think she is still alive, but she never looked well. All these instruments are extremely dangerous.

There is also the story of two court ladies who were so much in love and so hot for each other that wherever they were they couldn't stop themselves exchanging at least a couple of kisses, or flirtatious signals which gave them a scandalous reputation and the men who saw them considerable food for thought. One was a widow and the other married. One high festival day, the married woman had made an elaborate toilet and put on a gown of cloth-of-silver. Their mistress had gone to evensong, so they went into her withdrawing-room and began to frig on her commode with such rough, impetuous passion that it broke under them. The married woman, who was underneath, fell over backwards in her fine cloth-of-silver dress, right into the ordure in the pan. She was so completely covered with filth that all she could do was wipe herself off as much as possible, tuck up her skirts and hurry off to her own room to change her dress. But she was still seen and smelled as she went by, she stank so much. Those who heard the story found it highly amusing. Their mistress, who made the same use of the commode, heard it too, and laughed heartily. Their passion must have been overwhelming for them not to wait for a decent time and place and save themselves scandal.

Excuses are usually found for young girls and widows indulging in these empty, frivolous pleasures. It's much better that they should dissipate their heat by such indulgence than go with men and get pregnant and dishonoured, or destroy their fruit, as many have done and still do. They say they offend God less and are not such whores as if they went with men: there is a considerable difference between throwing water into a vase and just wetting it round the edges. I'll go along with them. I'm neither their censor nor their husband. Husbands may not like it – though I never saw one that wasn't delighted that his wife had a crush on a woman friend, and wished heartily it was the only kind of adultery she might ever indulge in. It's perfectly true that such intercourse is quite different from intercourse with men, and whatever Martial says, it doesn't make them cuckolds. A mad poet's text is hardly gospel truth. And as Lucian says, it is a fine thing for a woman to be virile, or a real amazon, or lubricious in this way – but not for a man to be effeminate like Sardanapalus or Heliogabalus, or others of that ilk. The more a woman is like a man, the more valiant she is. And after all this, I leave it to the public to decide.

V
Michel Millot

from *L'École des filles* (?1665)

Nothing is known of the author, whose name appears on various editions as Mililot, Milot, Mililorme and Helot. The work was one of the earliest to be translated from the French for the English market (see Foxon, op. cit.). In the form of a lively dialogue between two cousins, it offers an initiation into the language and techniques of love-making.
  See the Introduction for further discussion.

A Night of Bliss

SUZANNE: I've told you already, surely. You just have to do as he tells you.
FANNY: I'm sorry, cousin; I just don't know anything at all. While we're waiting for him to come, will you tell me what your lover does when you're in bed together, so I won't be such a novice when mine tries to do the same with me.
SUZANNE: Of course I will. The first thing to know is that the pleasure of putting a prick in a cunt is all the better for being spiced with hundreds of different passionate caresses. There was one time I remember when my lover tried nearly all of them on me in a single night; I've never seen him in such spirits as he was then.
FANNY: But when he comes to you, what does he say, and what does he do?
SUZANNE: Usually he sets about it something like this. To start with, he comes at night by a little hidden staircase, when every-body's in bed, and he usually finds me in bed, tucked up for the

night, and sometimes even asleep. He wastes no time; he gets undressed, puts a lighted candle by the bedside and then stretches out beside me. He takes a few minutes to get warmed up and then he has a think and says: 'Are you asleep, my love?' – and stretches his hand out over my belly – 'I've had such a wearying day I can hardly move.' So saying, he tells me all his troubles and puts his hand on my breast and fondles both breasts to his heart's content, telling me what he's being doing all day. He goes on and on at my tits, when he's done with one, he goes to the other, then he does both, and sometimes he says: 'God, love, I'm lucky to get this served up every day.' Then I can feel him turning onto his side as the fancy suddenly takes him, and sometimes I say: 'Oh, love, leave me alone, I want to go to sleep.' He doesn't seem to hear me, he puts his hand on my belly, and when he finds my nightdress he pulls it up and puts his hand on my mound and twists and pinches it for a while with his fingers. Then he puts his mouth on mine and slips in his tongue, then he goes and touches my buttocks and my thighs, and then he goes back to my belly, or sucks one of my tits. Then to have his fill of pleasure, because he likes looking, he throws off the sheet and the blanket, and if my nightdress is in the way he makes me take it off, and then he takes the candle and looks me all over. Then he makes me take hold of his thing, and it's all stiff, and sometimes he grabs right hold of me and rolls me all over him, first on top and then underneath, and makes me touch his prick, and between his thighs, and then his buttocks, then comes back again kissing my eyes and my mouth and calling me his dear love, his dear heart. After that he gets on top of me, puts his great stiff prick in my cunt and rides me till his spunk runs down in my womb.

FANNY: What was that other word beside 'ride'? I've forgotten it.

SUZANNE: You say, he fucks me.

FANNY: Do you like it?

SUZANNE: What do you think! Now there are several different ways of putting this thing of his in mine, as I've found out going with him. Sometimes he does me underneath, sometimes on top, or else on my side, or across, or in front, kneeling, or from behind, like taking an enema, sometimes standing up, sometimes sitting down. Sometimes when he's in a hurry he throws me on a form or a chair or a mattress, or whatever he gets to first. Every way of doing it gives him a different kind of pleasure: the different positions he puts me in make his thing go in further, or not so far, or it sits at different angles inside mine. The fuss and bother isn't always so bad, and to be honest it's what makes the fun.

Sometimes, if we meet in the daytime and there's no one else there, he makes me rest my hands on a form and bend over, and pulls my dress up behind, right over my head. When I'm like that he can look and gaze to his heart's content, and in case anyone comes in unexpectedly he doesn't take down his breeches, he just pulls his prick out of his flies, comes and shows me and then goes to the door to listen if anyone's coming, and then signals me not to move, comes over and shoves it round by my bum and into my cunt. He's told me Lord knows how many times that he likes it better doing me on the sly like that than any other way.

FANNY: Well, cousin, there must be a lot of pleasure in this, with so many different ways to do it. I can already picture all the ones you've told me, and if it's just a case of finding different ways of putting a prick in a cunt for the pleasure to be got out of it, I think I could soon think up others beside what you've told me, anyone at all could dream up new ones. But we shouldn't start that now. I'd just like to know what happened that night with your lover when you had all those different kinds of pleasure with him.

SUZANNE: Ah! Well, that particular stroke of good fortune was yesterday. Listen, I'll tell you the thousands of foolish lovers' tricks only true lovers play. First of all, my lover hadn't been to see me for two nights and to my annoyance part of the third had already gone with no sign of him. At last I saw him come into the room, carrying the little muffled lantern he always brings to see by, and with sweets and preserves under his cloak to make our mouths water.

FANNY: I needn't ask if you were pleased.

SUZANNE: First he put his parcel down, and finding me still in my petticoat, because I hadn't gone to bed, he pulled it up straight away and without a word threw me on the bed, put it right into me, gave me a feel of his great hard prick and in less than six thrusts I was generously drenched in love's liquor.

FANNY: So it's when this liquor comes you feel best, and all this wriggling about is to get it out?

SUZANNE: That's right. When he'd finished, I got straight into bed while he got undressed and I'd no sooner started to close my eyes (there's nothing like that for making you sleep) when I felt him alongside me, covering me with passionate kisses and pushing his prick into my hand. I forgot right away I'd wanted to go to sleep.

FANNY: How long does it take their tool to stand up again after it's fallen down? How many times can it go into a cunt in one night?

SUZANNE: Devil take you with all your interruptions! Look, it depends on the people involved, and they're more passionate sometimes than others. Sometimes you get men who can do it twice without coming out, which is very exciting for the girl. Some men say they can do it seven or eight times, or even ten or twelve; but that's not credible, and five or six decent ones are enough to satisfy a woman. There are some who can only do it two or three times, and are very quick or very slow in coming. Mind you, those who do it least produce more fluid than the others and give and feel more pleasure. Still, whatever's the case with one man or another, a girl always gets a lot of satisfaction from such a little thing. What the girl looks like makes a big difference too, and can mean one or two times extra. Habit spoils everything and the boy gets fed up when he has to do it every day, so it's not bad going if you do it once every night and once again every morning. Now with your interruptions I don't know where I'd got to.

FANNY: You were where he got you when you were asleep and put his stiff prick in your hand.

SUZANNE: Yes, now I remember. As soon as I felt how stiff he was, I gave up the idea of going to sleep and returned his caresses, while he called me his dear heart and his dear love, and we rolled over and over together, arms and legs entwined, going so well that the blanket fell right off. It wasn't cold, so we didn't stop to pick it up, in fact, we were getting hotter and hotter, so he took off his shirt and made me take off my slip and he bounced around on the bed to show me how stiff his prick was. Then he asked my permission to play to his heart's content and scattered hundreds of rosebuds all over the floor and sent me to pick them up, all naked, in the middle of the room, making me turn from side to side and contemplating by the light of the fire and the candles posted round the chamber all my different postures as I bent down or stretched out to collect them. He rubbed my whole body with essence of jasmine and then rubbed it on himself; we got back on the bed and turned twenty somersaults for the fun of it. Then he had me kneel in front of him and looked me over everywhere, his eyes ecstatic. He praised my belly, then my thighs, then my breasts, then my swelling mound, firm and plump, he said, putting his hand there now and again, and I won't say I didn't like all his little games. He turned me round with my back towards him and looked at my shoulders, then my buttocks, then made me put my hands down on the bed, mounted me like a horse, and told me to gee up. He stayed up there for a while and then dismounted, not sideways, but backwards (he wasn't afraid, he said, of my kicking him), and in one single movement he trailed his tool down between my cheeks and pushed it in my cunt. At first I wouldn't go along and said I wanted to get up, but he begged, prayed and pleaded so hard that I took pity on him. I got back down again, and he took great pleasure in putting it in and pulling it out all of a sudden, enjoying watching it go in and out, and cousin, it made a noise like a baker thrusting his fist into the dough and then pulling it out all at once, or children ramming a paper wad into their toy guns and then pulling the stick out.

FANNY: Good Lord, you're shameless, both of you. Did *you* enjoy that as well?

SUZANNE: And why not? When you're in love, it's just nice fun and games, that works you up a bit and passes the time pleasantly, as well as making it better afterwards.

FANNY: Oh, well then, go on, if you don't mind.

SUZANNE: Finally, when he was tired of tickling and teasing, we went to the fireside, still naked, and he made me sit by him in a chair and fetched from a corner of the room a bottle of Hippocras and some preserves, which he gave me to eat, and I felt wonderfully refreshed. While we were eating, he'd slipped down beside me in a humble, suppliant attitude, coaxing me as if he'd never seen me before, telling me of his torment, and how he would die for love of me, with the sweetest words you can imagine. So I pretended to take pity on him, opened my thighs, naked as I was, and he, with his prick in his hand, dragged himself on his knees between them, saying all he wanted was to put it somewhere safe. He took care of that straight away, and then, instead of moving any more he kept me sitting on it and we went on eating, discussing everything we picked up, and when it was half-eaten we passed it from mouth to mouth. When we were tired of this position, we started on another, then another, and so on, and so on, and he gazed at every part of me, and it was as though he'd never done it before and he'd never grow tired of it. Then he thought of something, took a glass from the table and filled it with Hippocras, and made me drink first. I emptied it completely, and he refilled it at once for himself and did the same. We repeated that two or three times, until our eyes were sparkling with passion and radiating lust for battle. We left off the banqueting; he returned to his caresses, took me under the arms and lifted me up, and when I was on my feet he made as if to mount me in that position, wriggling down towards me while I wriggled up to him. Our arses were both going as though he already had his prick in my cunt. Seeing he couldn't get anything in because of the awkwardness of our being on our feet, he said that at least what he was doing would teach me to move my buttocks in time when we finally coupled: a pair of cheeks moving in time backwards and forwards at the right moment adds extra spice to the pleasure of sex. He taught me several other things as well that he said he liked before and during love's revels. What else can I tell you? All we were short of was a mirror to watch our positions in. Failing the mirror, he showed me all the parts of his body, which were very shapely, and invited me to fondle them; he took as much pleasure in my touching him as he had done in touching me. He'd never put as much preparation into mounting me as he did that time; I told him so, and then asked him to bring it all to climax. He was weary himself of kissing, fondling, fumbling and rummaging, so he listened to me this time and we decided the moment of satisfaction could wait no longer. I took hold of his shaft and led him to the foot of the bed, lay back and pulled him on top of me. With my own hands I put his prick inside up to the hilt; his thrusts made the bed creak, and I thrust back with all my strength. We were both pushing and writhing, and could get no more in however much we wriggled our bums. I enjoyed the feel of his balls beating rhythmically against my cheeks. At last he leapt against me with pleasure, and said he was going to do one last thrust and I would be completely ravished. I told him to hurry up, and we said to each other a score of times: 'Hurry up, my love, dear heart, when are you going to come?' Then he started coming, and gave me the signal by embracing me tight and thrusting his tongue right in my mouth. I thought that was it, and then he squirted love's liquor into me more than six times, in little jerks, and each one made me faint and die all over again. I came with him, and cousin, if you want an idea of what we felt, you'd have been in the seventh heaven just seeing him choking and writhing on top of me until we were finished.

FANNY: I believe you, cousin, and not only that, your description makes me feel just as excited, and if you want my opinion, I'd much sooner have the conclusions to these affairs than waste time on all the complicated preliminaries you've been telling me about.

SUZANNE: No, it's just the opposite. You're always sure of getting the conclusion, so what you have to work on is the quality of the pleasure: without the preliminaries, it would be far too quick.

VI
Jean-Baptiste de Boyer, marquis d'Argens (1704–71)

from *Thérèse philosophe* (c.1748)

Novelist, memoir-writer and philosophe, *chamberlain to Frederick II of Prussia, d'Argens' works also include the* Lettres juives *(1736).* Thérèse philosophe *has also been attributed to Diderot and to Darles de Montigny, who was employed in the French War Office, and who served eight months in the Bastille for the imputed authorship.*

This eighteenth-century classic earned Sade's whole-hearted approval for its mixture of eroticism and (anti-clerical) philosophy. Thérèse, the first-person narrator, is a positive and attractive character with a lively, ironic, observant and self-critical wit, able to talk fluently and at length on the enlightened principles that finally save her from superstition and death by sexual frustration. She attacks religious hypocrisy (nicely caught in the ambiguities of Father Dirrag's discourse on surrender to the divine will), the ascetic denial of nature's impulses, and human willingness to be deceived. The text has some slight resemblance to Diderot's La Religieuse, *but the balance is quite different; Thérèse's philosophy is subordinate, a frame for the central erotic drama, like the keyhole and Eradice's carefully draped chemise. The text focuses on the flagellation and initiation of Eradice, with the effects intensified by the quality of the observer – pruriently naïve, and with a scientific eye for detail. The episode selected here is based on a real incident.*

Holy Ecstasy: The Scandal of Father Dirrag

Let's get back to my story. As I said, when I was twenty-three my mother took me away from the convent, at death's door. My whole body was wasting away, my skin was yellow and my lips pallid: I looked like a living skeleton. In short, I was near killing myself with piety by the time I got back to my mother's house. A skilled doctor she sent to the convent had recognised the cause of my illness straight away. That divine fluid whose function is to stimulate us to physical pleasure, the only pleasure with no bitter taste, that fluid whose discharge is as necessary for certain constitutions as that of the fluid that results from the food we eat, had escaped from its proper vessels into ones where it ought not to be and had thrown the workings of my whole body into disarray.

My mother was advised to find me a husband, which, they said, was the only thing that would save my life. She broached the subject gently but I was still full of my religious prejudices and told her bluntly I would rather die than offend God by entering such a contemptible condition, which he only tolerated out of his great benevolence. Nothing she could say would move me. My weakened constitution left me no love at all for this world and all I could think of was the happiness I had been promised in the next.

I went on performing my devotional exercises with all possible fervour. I had heard a great deal about the famous Father Dirrag. I expressed a desire to see him. He became my spiritual director and Mademoiselle Eradice, his most tender penitent, was soon my best friend.

You know the story of these two famous characters, dear Count, so I won't repeat here everything that is public knowledge and rumour. However, an unusual incident that I witnessed might amuse you and help convince you that although it's true that in the end Mademoiselle Eradice knew quite well what she was doing when she yielded to the hypocrite's embraces it's also certain that for a long time she was taken in by the holy lecher.

Mademoiselle Eradice had become very close friends with me. She told me her most intimate thoughts and the likeness in our characters, our religious devotions and perhaps also our hot-bloodedness made us inseparable. We were both virtuous, longed to be saints and had a tremendous desire to work miracles. She was so completely gripped by this passion that she would have suffered every imaginable torment, steadfast as any martyr, if she had been persuaded it would help her raise a second Lazarus; and it was Father Dirrag's chief talent to make her believe what he liked.

Eradice had told me several times, with a certain vanity, that

Father Dirrag only opened his heart fully to her and no one else. In the private talks they often had in her room he had assured her she had very little further to go to reach sainthood. God had told him so in a dream, in which he had clearly seen that she would soon be working great miracles if she continued to be guided by him through the necessary degrees of virtue and mortification.

You find envy and jealousy in every calling and among the devout, perhaps, more than most.

Eradice saw I was jealous of her good fortune, so much so that I didn't appear to believe what she said. I was indeed especially surprised by what she told me of her private talks with Father Dirrag because he had always avoided anything of that kind with me when we met in the house of another of his penitents, a friend of mine who had stigmata like Eradice. I expect my miserable face and yellowish skin hadn't struck the Reverend Father as a restorative likely to arouse the needful appetite for his spiritual labours. I was spurred to rivalry: no stigmata, no private talks for me! I was piqued, and made a point of showing I didn't believe her.

Eradice, obviously upset, offered to let me see her good fortune with my own eyes the very next morning. 'You shall see,' she said heatedly, 'the force of my spiritual exercises and the degrees of penitence by which the good Father is transforming me into a great saint and you'll have no more doubts about the ecstasies and transports that come out of them. I hope,' she added, somewhat more gently, 'that my example will work in you its first miracle and give you strength to free your mind completely of material things by the great virtue of meditation, and set it on God alone!'

At five o'clock next morning I went to see Eradice, as agreed. I found her at prayer, with a book in her hand. 'The holy man is about to arrive,' she said, 'and God with him. Hide in this little anteroom and from there you'll be able to see and hear how far divine goodness is pleased to extend in favour of an unworthy creature, with the pious assistance of our Director.'

A moment after there came a soft knock at the door. I slipped into the anteroom and Eradice took the key. A hole in the door the size of my hand, covered with an old loose-woven tapestry from Bergama, gave me a free view of the whole room without risk of being seen.

The holy Father came in. 'Good morning, dear sister in God,' he said, 'the Holy Spirit and Saint Francis be with you!'

She was about to throw herself at his feet, but he raised her up and

made her sit beside him. 'I need to go over with you,' said the holy
man, 'the principles which must guide you in every action of your
life. But tell me first about your stigmata. Is the one on your breast
still the same? Let me see.'

Eradice prepared herself at once to uncover her left breast, below
which was the mark. 'Ah, sister! Stop! Cover your breast with this
handkerchief' (holding one out). 'A member of my order may not
look on such things; all I need to see is the wound imprinted by Saint
Francis. Ah! There it is still. Good,' he said, 'I'm very pleased. Saint
Francis loves you still: the wound is crimson. I took care to bring
with me the holy remnant of his cord; we shall need it at the end of
our exercises. I have already told you dear sister,' he went on, 'that I
distinguished you out of all my penitents, your companions,
because God himself clearly distinguishes you among his holy
flock, as the Sun is distinguished from the Moon and the other
planets. For this reason I have had no hesitation in revealing to you
His most hidden mysteries. I have told you, dear sister, you must
forget yourself and *let God have His way.* All God wants from men is
their hearts and minds. In forgetfulness of the body lies the way to
union with God, to sainthood and the capacity to work miracles.

'I can't hide from you, my little angel, that in the course of our
last exercise I noticed that your mind was still fixed on the flesh.
How can you be half-hearted in your imitation of those blessed
martyrs who were whipped, racked and burned but felt not the
slightest pain, for their imaginations were so filled with the glory of
God that every shred of their intellect was bent on that divine
object?

'The mechanism is certain, beloved daughter. We are feeling
creatures, and all our ideas of physical good and evil, like those of
moral good and evil, come to us by way of the senses. Whenever we
touch, hear or see an object, spirit particles flow through the little
cavities of the nerves that carry the message to the soul. If you have
enough fervour to concentrate all the spirit particles that are in you,
through the strength of your meditation, on the love you owe to
God, and fix them all on that object, there will be none left to tell
your soul of the blows your flesh is about to receive: and you will
not feel them. Think of the hunter, his imagination occupied with
tracking down his prey, feeling neither the brambles nor the thorns
that tear him as he penetrates the forests. Will you be weaker than he
is, when your goal is a thousand times more important? Will you
feel the light blows of the whip if your soul is fixed and concentrated

on the happiness that awaits you? This is the touchstone that helps us work miracles: such must be the state of perfection that joins us to God.

'Let us begin, dear daughter: perform your duty well and you may be sure that with the help of the cord of Saint Francis and your meditations this saintly exercise will end in a torrent of unspeakable delights. Kneel down, my child, and uncover the parts of your flesh that provoke God to anger. Their mortification will make your spirit one with His. I say again, *forget yourself and let God have His way.*'

Mademoiselle Eradice obeyed instantly, without a word. She knelt down on a prayer-stool with a book in front of her; then, lifting her skirts and her chemise to her waist, she revealed a pair of cheeks white as snow, perfect ovals, supported by a pair of admirably proportioned thighs. 'Lift your chemise higher,' he said, 'it's not right; yes, that's it. Now put your hands together and lift your soul to God; let your mind be filled with the thought of the eternal bliss He has promised you.' Then the Father pulled up a stool and knelt on it, behind her and a little to one side. He lifted up his robe and tucked it into his belt. Underneath was a long thick bunch of rods, which he gave his penitent to kiss.

As I watched closely to see how the scene would turn out, I found myself filled with holy dread and a kind of indescribable trembling. The priest ran his burning eyes over the cheeks displayed before him. As he gazed, I caught his murmur of admiration: 'Oh, what a lovely bosom! What delightful breasts!' He bent down, stood up, bent down again, muttering a few verses from the Bible. His lascivious eyes missed nothing. After a few moments, he asked his penitent if her soul had entered into contemplation. 'Yes, most Reverend Father,' she answered him, 'I can feel my spirit departing from my flesh and I beseech you, begin the holy work.' 'That is sufficient,' answered the priest; 'your spirit will be contented.' He recited a few more prayers and the ceremony began with three blows of the rods, laid fairly lightly on her behind. The three blows were followed by the recital of a verse and then three more blows a little harder than the first.

After five or six verses interspersed with this kind of diversion, imagine my surprise when I saw Father Dirrag unbuttoning his drawers and loosing a fiery dart exactly like that fatal serpent which had earned me the reproaches of my former director! This particular monster had grown as long, fat and firm as the Capucin had predicted; I trembled at the sight. Its rosy head threatened Eradice's cheeks, which had turned a magnificent crimson; and the Father's face was all inflamed. 'You will now,' he said, 'be in the highest state of contemplation; your soul will be free of your senses. If my daughter has not disappointed my most holy expectations, she will see, hear and feel nothing more.' And at that same moment the tormentor hailed a storm of blows on all the parts of Eradice's body that were uncovered. She still said nothing; she seemed motionless, insensible to the dreadful strokes. All I could make out was a convulsive movement of her buttocks, rapidly clenching and unclenching.

'I am pleased with you,' he said, after a quarter of an hour of this harsh discipline. 'It is time you began to enjoy the fruit of your labours. Do not listen to me, dear daughter, but let God guide you. Set your face to the ground, and with the holy cord of Saint Francis I shall drive out all impurity still within you.'

The good Father then placed her in an attitude that was indeed humiliating, but which was also the most convenient for his purposes. Never was there a finer presentation: her cheeks were parted, and the twin road to pleasure revealed in its entirety.

After a moment's contemplation, the hypocrite moistened with saliva what he called the *cord* and uttered a few words in the tones of an exorcist labouring to drive the devil from a demon-ridden body. His Reverence then began his intromission.

I was so placed that I couldn't miss a single detail of the scene: the windows of the room where it was taking place were opposite the door of the antechamber I had been locked into. Eradice had just been made to kneel down on the floor, her arms folded on the step of the prayer-stool and her head resting on her arms. Her chemise, carefully lifted right up to the waist, offered me in half-profile her buttocks and a very handsome back. This lewd prospect was the focus of the Reverend Father's attention. He too had knelt down with the penitent's legs between his own, his drawers lowered and his dreadful *cord* in his hand, muttering a few incoherent words.

He remained for a few moments in this edifying attitude, sweeping the altar with his blazing eyes, apparently undecided what kind of sacrifice he should make. There were two holes offered and his eyes devoured both. It was a difficult choice to make. One of them was a very dainty morsel for a man of his cloth. However, he'd promised his penitent ecstatic delight, so what was he to do? Several times he risked aiming the head of his instrument at his favourite portal, knocking gently. In the end, prudence defeated inclination. In all justice I have to admit that I saw his Reverence's rosy rod take the canonical way, after he had daintily opened its crimson lips with the thumb and forefinger of each hand.

He began his labours with three hearty thrusts that got it nearly half in – at which point the Reverend Father's apparent calm turned into a kind of madness. Heavens, his face! Imagine a satyr, lips foaming, mouth wide open, grinding teeth, panting and bellowing like a bull. His nostrils were swollen and flaring, his hands held out two inches above Eradice's rump, where he was obviously afraid to rest them for support, and his outstretched fingers twisted and clenched like a roast capon's foot. His head was down, his glittering eyes fixed on the labours of his doughty peg, rigorously controlling its comings and goings so that when it pulled back it never left its sheath, and when it pressed forward his belly never touched the buttocks of his penitent – who might well, if she had thought, have managed to guess what the so-called cord was fastened onto. What admirable presence of mind the man had! I noted that about a thumb's thickness of the holy instrument stayed outside the whole time and had no part of the maid.

I saw how every time the Reverend Father's rump moved backwards, pulling the cord out of its resting-place up to the head, the lips of Eradice's privy part fell open, bright crimson, delighting the eye. I saw how when the Reverend Father in an opposite motion thrust forward, the same lips, now invisible except for their cloak of short black hair, swallowed the dart up so tight that it was hard to say which of the two actors owned the peg that seemed to fasten both together without distinction.

What an interesting operation! What a sight, dear Count, for a girl of my age with no knowledge of such mysteries! A host of different fancies raced through my mind, but I couldn't settle on a single one. All I can remember is that twenty times over I almost threw myself at the knees of the famous director to beg him to give me the same treatment as my friend. An impulse of devotion? Or desire? I simply can't tell.

Back to our acolytes. Father Dirrag's movements were getting faster; he could hardly keep his balance. He was so positioned that from head to knees he formed an S, whose belly moved to and fro horizontally at Eradice's buttocks. The part of Eradice that acted as the channel for his peg was the centre of his labours, and two great warts hanging between His Reverence's thighs were apparently standing witness. 'Is your spirit content, my little saint?' he asked with a kind of sigh. 'I can see the heavens opening, sufficient grace sweeps me away . . . ' 'Oh, Father,' exclaimed Eradice, 'I can feel the starts and pricks of heavenly delight! I rejoice in celestial bliss, I feel my spirit entirely detached from all material things. Drive out, Father, drive out all impurities within me. I can see the an . . . angels, push harder, then . . . go on, push . . . ah, yes, good . . . Saint Francis! Don't abandon me, I feel your cor . . . cor . . . cord . . . I can't bear it, I'm dying . . . '

The Reverend Father, also feeling the imminence of sovereign delight, stuttered, pushed, puffed, panted. Eradice's last words were the signal for retreat. I saw the proud serpent, humbled, creeping, quit his hiding-place, covered in foam.

Everything was quickly put back into place, the holy Father dropped his robe and tottered to the prayer-stool Eradice had just left. He pretended to fall to prayer, ordering his penitent to get up, cover herself and come and join him in thanking the Lord for the favour she had just received.

Well, what can I say, dear Count? Dirrag left, and Eradice un-locked the door of my room and threw her arms round my neck. 'Oh, dear Theresa!' she said. 'Rejoice in my felicity! Yes, I have seen Paradise opened, and shared the bliss of the Angels! So much delight, my dear, for a brief moment of travail! By the virtue of the holy cord, my soul was almost entirely freed from matter. You saw where the good director put it in me. Well, I assure you, I felt it penetrate right into my heart. A very little fervour more, and I swear I would have gone for ever into the home of the blessed.'

Eradice went on at vivacious length, leaving me in no doubt of the reality of the supreme bliss she had enjoyed. I was in such a state I could hardly find words to congratulate her; my heart was in violent tumult, so I kissed her and left.

How much food for thought here on the way the most respect-able social institutions can be abused! . . .

All Europe has heard of the adventure of Father Dirrag and Mademoiselle Eradice and everyone has had something to say about it. But not many people have really heard the truth of the tale, which became a political issue between the Jansenists and the Jesuits.

VII
Denis Diderot (1713–84)

from *Les Bijoux indiscrets* (1748)

Long neglected, Diderot is now generally recognised as the most important of the Enlightenment philosophes, a many-sided genius who not only edited the Encyclopédie *but also wrote major works of creative fiction. His* Supplément au voyage de Bougainville *(1796) presents a new sexual ethic based on tolerance, materialism, anti-authoritarianism and 'nature'; his novels,* Jacques le fataliste *(1797) and* La Religieuse *(1798), argue for individual responsibility and against repression.*

This earlier and lighter work is in the tradition that exploits sexual embarrassment and titillation for entertainment and subversion. The Sultan Mangogul, eager to find out about the intrigues of his Court ladies, has obtained a ring that enables their 'jewels' ('the most sincere and best-informed part of them') to speak. The following episode is a short digression in the story.

The Sultan's Vision

It was while all the jewels were chattering away that further trouble arose in the realm. This was caused by the tradition of the *penum*, the little piece of cloth laid on the dying. The old rite ordained that it should go on the mouth. Certain reformers claimed it should be placed on the behind. Spirits had grown heated. The protagonists were about to come to blows when the sultan, appealed to by both sides, gave permission for a symposium of the most learned of their leaders to be held in his presence. The matter was discussed in depth. Tradition, the sacred books and their commentators, were invoked. There were weighty reasons and powerful authorities on both sides. Mangogul, in his perplexity, reserved judgement for a week. When this term had expired, the sectarians and their opponents appeared again before him.

THE SULTAN: Pontiffs and priests, please be seated. Fully alive to the importance of the point of discipline which divides you, ever since the conference that was held at the foot of our throne we have been praying constantly for guidance from on high. Last night, at the hour when it pleases Brahma to commune with his beloved ones, we had a vision. It seemed we heard a conversation between two most worthy gentlemen, one of whom thought he had two noses in the middle of his face and the other two holes in his arse; and this is what they said. The first to speak was the gentleman with two noses.

'Putting your hand to your behind all the time is a ridiculous habit . . .'

'That's true . . . '

'Can't you get rid of it? . . . '

'No more than you can get rid of your two noses . . . '

'But my two noses are real; I can see them and touch them; and the more I see and touch them, the more convinced I am that I've got them, while in the ten years you've been feeling yourself and finding your arse just like anyone else's you ought to be cured of your madness . . . '

'Madness! Come on, you with the two noses; you're the one who's mad.'

'Don't let's argue. Let's get on: I've told you how I got my two noses. Tell me the story of your two holes, if you can remember it . . . '

'Remember it! It's unforgettable. It was the thirty-first day of the month, between one and two o'clock in the morning.'

'Look, not again!'

'Just hold on a minute, I'm afraid . . . no. If my arithmetic is correct, there's exactly what there should be and no more.'

'You amaze me! Well then, what happened that night? . . . '

'That night, I heard a vaguely familiar voice shouting: "Help! help!". I looked and saw a terrified, dishevelled young creature rushing towards me. She was being chased by a rough, surly old fellow. To judge by his getup and the tool he wielded, he was a carpenter. He was in breeches and shirt. His shirtsleeves were rolled up to the elbow, his arms were sinewy, his complexion dark, his brow wrinkled, his chin bearded, his cheeks puffed out, his eyes sparkled, his chest was hairy and he had a pointed cap on his head.'

'I can see him perfectly.'

'The carpenter had almost caught the woman, who was still shouting: "Help! help!" while he was chasing after her, saying: "There's no point running. I've got you; no one's going to say you're the only one who hasn't got one. By all the devils in hell, you'll have one like everyone else." At that very moment, the poor wretch stumbled and fell flat on her belly, screaming louder than ever: "Help! help!" while the carpenter went on: "Go on and shout all you want; you're going to get one, a big one or a little one; I'll answer for that." And at once he lifted up her petticoats and exposed her behind to the air. White as snow, fat, firm, round, plump and chubby, it was the spitting image of the behind of the sovereign pontiff's wife.'

THE PONTIFF: My wife!

THE SULTAN: And why not?

The gentleman with two holes added: 'In fact it *was* the pontiff's wife, I can remember her now. The old carpenter put one of his feet on the small of her back, bent down, put both hands just below her buttocks on the place where the legs and thighs bend, pushed both her knees up under her belly and lifted up her arse so effectively that I could look it over at my ease, which I quite enjoyed, even though there was this weak voice coming out of her skirts: "Help! help!". You're going to think me a harsh soul, a man of no heart, but there's no call for a man to make himself out better than he is, and I admit to my shame, that at that moment I felt more curiosity than pity and was thinking less of helping than looking.'

At that point the high pontiff interrupted the sultan once more, and said: 'My lord, am I by any chance one of the two parties to this conversation? . . .'

'Well, why not?'

'The man with two noses?'

'Why not?'

'And am I,' put in the leader of the innovators, 'the man with two holes?'

'Why not?

'The villainous carpenter had picked up the tool that he'd put down. It was a brace. He put the tip in his mouth to wet it; he pressed the handle hard against his stomach, leaned over the wretched woman, who was still shouting: "Help! help!" and made

ready to drill a hole where there ought to be two and there wasn't
even one.'
THE PONTIFF: Then it's not my wife.
THE SULTAN: 'Suddenly the carpenter broke off the operation,
struck by a thought, and said: "What a fine job I nearly made of it!
But it would have been her own fault. Why doesn't she co-operate
with a good grace? Madam, bear with me a moment." He put down
his brace and took out of his pocket a pale pink ribbon. With the
thumb of his left hand, he fixed one end to the tip of the coccyx,
folded the rest into the shape of a gutter, pressed it down between
her buttocks with the blade of his other hand, and drew it round in a
circle right to where the lady's stomach began. She, still shouting
"Help! help!", wriggled, struggled, thrashed around from right to
left and threw out the ribbon and the carpenter's measurements,
while he said: "Madam, it's not time to shout yet; I'm not hurting
you. I couldn't possibly do it more gently. If you don't look out, the
job will be all over the place, and you'll only have yourself to blame.
Everything has to have its own place. There are certain proportions
to be observed. That's more important than you realise. In a
minute, there'll be no curing it, and then you'll really be sorry." '
THE PONTIFF: Did you really hear all that, Sire?
THE SULTAN: As well as I hear you now.
THE PONTIFF: And what did the woman do?
THE SULTAN: 'It seemed to me,' the speaker went on, 'that she
was half-convinced; and I assumed from the distance between her
heels that she was beginning to resign herself. I couldn't hear what
she was saying to the carpenter; but he answered: "Now that's what
I call reasonable! Lord, what a business it is to get a woman to do
anything!" Having taken his measurements somewhat more peacefully, Master Perforanus stretched his pale pink ribbon over a
folding ruler and, pencil in hand, asked the lady: "How do you want
it?"
    ' "I don't understand."
    ' "Ancient proportions, or modern ones?" '
THE PONTIFF: Blessed be the profundity of the decrees that come
from on high! The whole thing would be lunatic, if it weren't
revealed. Let us submit our reason and worship.
THE SULTAN: 'I can't remember what the lady said, but the
carpenter replied: "Truly, she's lost her wits; it'll look like nothing
on earth. People will say: Who's the donkey who drilled that
arse? . . . "

' "No more of your verbiage, Master Perforanus," said the lady, "do it as I say."

' "Do it as I say! But look, Madam, everyone has his reputation to look after . . ."

' "I want it like that, and I want it there, I tell you. I want it like that, just like that . . ."

'The carpenter was in fits of laughter, and do you think I could keep a straight face? Perforanus drew the lines on the ribbon, put it in place, and then expostulated: "Madam, it's impossible; it's beyond all common sense. Anybody who sees that arse won't need to be any kind of expert to laugh at you and me both. Everyone knows there has to be a gap from there to there, but no one's ever made one that size. Too much is too much. Do you really want it? . . ."

' "Yes, I do, so let's get it over with," said the lady.

'Straight away Master Perforanus took his pencil, drew on the lady's buttocks the lines that corresponded to those he'd drawn on the ribbon and drew the square, shrugging his shoulders and muttering to himself: "What a sight it'll be! But if that's how she wants it." He picked up his brace again, and said: "You want it there?"

' "Yes, there; get on with it . . ."

' "Oh, come on, Madam."

' "Now what's the problem?"

' "Problem? It's just not possible."

' "And why not, pray?"

' "Why not? Because you're shaking, and clenching your buttocks. I can't see my square and I'm bound to drill too high or too low. Come, Madam, be brave."

' "It's easy for you to say that; show me your brace; oh my God!"

' "I swear it's the smallest in the shop. While we're chattering on here I could have drilled half a dozen. Come on, Madam, loosen up a bit; good; a bit more; fantastic; again; and again." In the meantime I could see the sardonic carpenter softly bringing his brace closer. He was just about to . . . when I was seized by rage and pity together. I struggled; I tried to rush to the victim's aid; but my arms were strapped tight, and I couldn't move them. I shouted to the carpenter: "You vile creature, you villain, stop!" My shouts were accompanied by such violent struggles that the bonds holding me suddenly snapped. I hurled myself at the carpenter and took him by the throat. The carpenter said: "Who are you? What have you got against me? Can't you see she has no arse? Know who I am; I am the

great Perforanus; I make arses for people who haven't got any. I
have to give her one, it's the will of Him who sent me; and after me,
there will come another more powerful than I, who will not have a
brace; he will have a gouge, and with his gouge he will complete the
restoration of that which she lacks. Depart, infidel; or by my brace,
or by the gouge of my successor, you too shall be . . . "
    ' "Me?"
    ' "Yes, you . . . " At that very moment, the instrument in his
left hand started to whirr through the air.'
    And the man with two holes, who you've been listening to all this
time, said to the man with two noses: 'What's the matter? You keep
moving away.'
    'I'm afraid with all your waving about you're going to break one
of my noses. Go on.'
    'I can't remember where I was.'
    'You'd got to the instrument that the carpenter was whirring
through the air . . . '
    'He thumped my shoulders with the back of his right arm, with
such fury that I was knocked onto my belly; and the next thing I
knew my shirt was pulled up, there was another behind in the air,
and the fearsome Perforanus was threatening me with the point of
his tool, saying: "Beg for mercy, scoundrel, beg for mercy, or I'll
give you two . . . " The next minute I felt the chill tip of the brace.
Horror seized me; I woke up; and ever since, I've been convinced I
have two holes in my arse.'
    'The two speakers,' added the sultan, 'then started jeering at one
another. "Ha, ha, he's two holes in his arse!"
    ' "Ha, ha, it's so you can stick your two noses in it!" '
    Then, turning gravely to the assembly, he said: 'And you, pon-
tiffs and servants of the altars, you too are laughing! What is more
common than to think one has two noses on one's face, and to laugh
at the man who thinks he has two holes in his arse?'
    After a moment's silence, his brow grew calm again and he
turned to the leaders of the sect and asked what they thought of his
vision.
    'By Brahma,' they replied, 'it's one of the most profound that
Heaven has ever vouchsafed to any prophet.'
    'Do you understand any of it?'
    'No, Sire.'
    'What do you think of the two speakers?'
    'They're both mad.'

'What if they took it into their heads to become leaders of factions, and the two-hole arse sect started to persecute the two-noses? . . . '

Pontiffs and priests lowered their eyes, and Mangogul said: 'I want my subjects to live and die in their own way. I want the *penum* to be applied to the mouth or the behind, as each one prefers; and don't bother me with any more of these impertinences.'

The priests withdrew; and at the synod held a few months later, it was declared that the vision of Mangogul should be added to the sum of canonic books, which was none the worse for it.

VIII
Claude-Prosper Jolyot de Crébillon (1707–77)

from *Tableaux des moeurs du temps dans les différents âges de la vie*

The original is undated, but the date of printing has been set at 1750–60. The work has also been attributed to the tax-farmer Le Riche de la Popélinière, but the style – especially the lively, realistic language – seems very much that of the author of Les Égarements du coeur et de l'esprit *(1736) and* Le Sopha *(1745).*

'Delightful artistry' and 'horrifyingly shameless', according to one critic, the work takes the rivalries, competitions and intimidations of the eroticism of contemporary society and turns them into harmless play. The innocence of the children in the convent, with their complicitous authorities, is also a quality of the grown-up adulterous wives who figure later in the book, with their no less complaisant husbands; innocence flavoured with corruption provides idyllic light relief for the worldly aristocrats locked in the salons Crébillon so well evoked. 'Little games like that keep us cheerful and stop us feeling how tedious it is to be shut in.'

A Convent Childhood

AUGUSTE: Well, that's how the fancy for such things comes to take us, and how it took me. The more I saw, the more I wanted to see. Two years ago, before you came, we had a different mistress, who was the reason why I got into the habit. She was strict, and often whipped people; and always in public, in front of all of us, and in the middle of classes. Scarcely a day went by without someone catching it. You saw her bottom, quite likely a pretty one; then you saw someone else's; and then you ended up showing your own. We got so used to it that all the boarders had the taste for it; whenever we got together, we would pull up our skirts, or even whip one another. I've even seen some who would just as soon be whipped by a friend as whip her. There was one, who's been married for a year and plays the fine lady nowadays, whom I whipped more than thirty times, because she wanted me to, because her bottom had got used to it, because it had become a need for her, and when I whipped her very hard she would shout for me to do it again and get even more excitement and pleasure from it. I'll tell you honestly, I do enjoy all that immensely, and I would never have got over it if you'd left the convent without going through my hands. As for the rods, we don't, of course, use birch; we use reeds, or twigs of lavender like that one. We've almost all got them, and you can see they don't hurt.

THÉRÈSE: Have you played this game for some time, then?

AUGUSTE: Me? The whole two and a half years I've been in the convent. Shall I tell you about my welcoming party?

THÉRÈSE: Oh, yes, dear Auguste, please do.

AUGUSTE: I had been brought up to begin with by my grand-mother, in perfect simplicity and deepest ignorance. When the good lady died, my mother, who still passed for a pretty young thing and had no great wish to have a fourteen-year-old daughter around, put me in this convent, about this same time of year, in midsummer. The convent seemed very strange at first: I saw the big pond, but nothing else. I attended the exercises like the other boarders, whom I didn't know. There were big ones, not so big, and quite small.

Two or three days later, the whole household was celebrating the feast of Saint John, and we were allowed to walk where we liked that afternoon in the gardens. I was out there like everyone else, not expecting anything, when one of the biggest girls, called Miss Hélène, who was walking with four others, left the group, came over to me and said: 'Miss Auguste, Mother Tutor is unwell and has just gone up to her room, but since you are new here she says you may walk a little while longer, as long as you stay with four or five big girls like us, and don't leave us. Mother Tutor also gave me one or two other things to tell you and the young ladies with me. So come with me . . .'

I made a deep curtsey, thanked her for her kindness, and followed her. We joined the four others and all six walked together.

At the end of the avenue, Miss Hélène led us through a little gate, that was only latched, and we found ourselves where the gardener kept the animals: it was a little corner of the field with hay still on the ground, probably cut the day before. Miss Hélène closed the gate after her, fixed the latch so it could not be lifted and said to me: 'Now, little Auguste, let's settle down here, and do as we show you.' Straight away I saw Miss Hélène collect up a pile of hay, make a big bundle, and the four others do just the same. So did I, and seeing Miss Hélène sitting on her pile of hay and the four others about to do likewise in a circle, close in front of her, I sat in the circle too, without any idea what it was all about . . .

'Young ladies,' said Miss Hélène, 'Mother Tutor has told me to take her place here with her full authority. Think of me as the assistant teacher and do as I say . . . Let us see if you have remembered the last lessons she told you to learn by heart . . . Auguste,' she said, 'stand up and come here.' I stood up; it took just three steps to reach her; she took my hand and held me standing between her legs. 'Auguste,' she went on, 'recite the fifteen proverbs of Solomon you had to read out the day before yesterday, and were told to learn for today.' 'Yes, teacher,' I said, 'I know them, honestly.' 'Let's see then, let's see,' she said, with a threatening look that intimidated me so much I could not remember the first one. 'You're a liar!' she said, 'you don't know them . . .' 'I'm sorry!' I cried in confusion . . . 'Well then, say them quickly,' she said . . . I simply couldn't manage it. Seeing this, Miss Hélène scolded me for my lies and insolence and said I would have to be punished . . . I had no idea what would happen next. I was bewildered and embarrassed in front of this so-called teacher, with the four other young ladies sitting behind and all around me, not moving and not saying anything. I was dressed like all of them, for the heat: all I had on was a short little dress and a light petticoat that was soon lifted, as well as my chemise . . . I started to cry; she dropped them and said: 'All right then, since it's the first time I'll punish you in secret, without the other girls seeing . . .' So saying, she pulled me still closer, slipped her hand under my chemise and straight away I felt it on my bottom. I was almost dead with shame, heaving huge sighs and even shedding a few tears . . . Her hand ran all over my behind, then moved on to my belly, then she went lower down and made to push in the tip of her finger. That caused me such a sudden, extraordinary thrill that I wriggled and cried out . . . 'What, little girl,' said the teacher, 'trying to resist, trying to rebel! . . .' She seized me bodily, between her legs, with a look of anger that frightened me so much that I started to cry in earnest. Apparently my tears moved her, because she let me go at once, saying: 'That will do for the first time. Go back to your place.' I went back with speed to my bundle of hay.

She turned at once to another of the four: 'Now, Miss Rosalie,' she said, 'come here; it's your turn. Recite the deeds of Charlemagne in the first three years of his reign.' Rosalie gave her the account at once, so well that the teacher had nothing to reprimand her for . . . Suddenly she broke in: 'Why are you always chattering in the refectory, instead of listening to the reading?' . . . 'Well, Mother,' answered Rosalie, 'because I just want to . . .' 'What an answer!' the other said, 'I'll teach you to speak to me properly! . . .' And the teacher took both her hands and made first of all to lift up her skirt. 'Oh, Mother,' said Rosalie, 'don't shame me in front of my friends, they'll laugh at me . . .' The teacher made just a half-turn to the right, still holding Rosalie, and put her over her knee ready for a whipping. We couldn't see anything because the teacher, with her back to us, was stopping us. I began to feel a little more cheerful and wipe away my tears; Rosalie, more than fifteen years old, bigger than me and very pretty, was getting just the same treatment as I had . . . I watched carefully to see what would happen to her . . . I listened hard, but heard nothing . . . Miss Agathe, sitting beside me, was more curious; she got up and tiptoed to have a good look at what was going on. The teacher turned her head and saw her standing behind. She immediately caught her by her dress and said: 'Come here, you insolent little thing, I'll teach you to be curious . . .' She let go of Rosalie, who went back to her place . . . She took hold of Agathe and held her so we couldn't see her in just the same way . . .

The teacher had still not said anything to Miss Victorine and Miss Clairon; she seemed afraid to, because they were both very grown-up and beautiful . . . They both got up at the same moment, went to her and said: 'Mother, we know our lessons perfectly, and are ready to recite them if you want. But it's getting late, and you promised we could play for quarter of an hour before we went back to the house . . .' 'Right, agreed,' said the teacher, 'all forgiven and forgotten; let's all get in a circle, a bit closer, everyone; let's play a little game, and I'll be in it . . .'

We got in a circle, all six close together . . . and I swear, Thérèse, that I still didn't understand a thing of what was going on . . . 'Let's play a forfeit game,' said the teacher . . . 'Yes, that's a good idea,' they said . . . I just fell in with everything without a word . . . 'Go on then,' said the teacher, 'let's play word games . . . You've to repeat one after another what I say to you . . . You, Victorine,' she said, 'since you're the nearest . . . Mr Cutfunk went to see Mrs Funcut, and Mrs Funcut went to see Mr Cutfunk.' 'I bet I can get it right,' said Victorine, 'Mr Fuckcunt' . . . 'A forfeit,' cried the teacher, 'a good one!' Victorine needed no pressing; she handed over her watch. 'Your turn, Miss Clairon,' said the teacher . . .

Clairon mixed it up just the same . . . a forfeit: she gave her purse . . . Then it was Rosalie's turn, she got the beginning right and the end wrong . . . a forfeit: she gave her scent-bottle . . . Then it was Agathe's turn, and she was so excited she couldn't say a word . . . a forfeit: she gave her toothpick holder . . . I made every effort to remember the words and managed to recite them without a mistake . . . 'Oh!' exclaimed the girls, 'Auguste got it right. Now it's her turn to give us another one; and this time, please, Mother, you've to play.' 'All right,' she said, 'but I'm not giving a forfeit if I get it wrong . . .' 'And why not, pray? You're only a boarder like us, you're Miss Hélène, pretty Hélène, and that's all! Play now, or we'll all gang up on you . . .' 'All right, all right,' said Hélène, 'come on, Auguste, what have we got to say?' 'I only know a little word game that isn't very hard, that my governess taught me; you have to say it three times very quickly. Listen: "I'll pick up a few pink bricks when I'm big." I was standing next to Rosalie, who said it all three times without a mistake; Victorine did the same, and Clairon and Agathe. But the teacher, Miss Hélène, failed completely . . . a forfeit: one of the diamond studs in her ears. All the forfeits were put together to one side and covered with a handkerchief for drawing by lot.

Agathe drew them out, and I was allowed to set the conditions for getting them back; I had to do it before every turn. 'What has the first one that comes out to do?' they asked. I started giggling, but I was frightened to say it; I was beginning to enjoy playing with them, but I was shy and afraid of making them cross . . . I made up my mind, and I said: 'Well, you said I could, so I order the owner of the first forfeit drawn to come out of the circle . . .' 'Oh, no,' they shouted, 'you can't; everything's got to be in the middle, in that little space.' 'Right,' I said, 'I order her to let me give her a kiss and ask her to be my friend . . .' Agathe drew Rosalie's forfeit . . . I got up, and so did she; I gave her a kiss, she gave me four back, and we sat down again . . . 'That's not ordering people,' said Rosalie, 'it's just nothing. Will you let me do it instead?' 'Certainly,' I said. 'Now let's see,' she said, 'I order the owner of the second forfeit to show whether she's got any hair yet . . . under her chin . . .' It was little Agathe's forfeit, she drew her own favour . . . And straight away she lay down, pulled her skirts up to her chin and showed us her white thighs and a tiny bit of hair, hardly anything . . . And you can imagine, in that position, anyone who wanted to could fondle her.

THÉRÈSE: Heavens, what strange goings-on.

AUGUSTE: I thought so too . . . But listen . . . There's more. Rosalie said next: 'I order the owner of the third forfeit to get up, make her neighbour lie down . . . pull her clothes up . . . pull up her own . . . get astride her . . . and lie on her, if she feels like it . . .' That was Clairon's forfeit, sitting next to Victorine, so she pulled up her skirts . . . then her own . . . straddled her . . . and then lay right on top of her for a little while . . . Next Rosalie said: 'I order the owner of the fourth forfeit to get on her knees and come and rub us all nicely, under our chemises, on the bit she knows is itchy . . .' That was Victorine's forfeit, and she was next to me, because I was between her and the so-called teacher . . . And there was Victorine on her knees in front of me . . . kissing me first, then pushing me back on my bundle of hay . . . tickling me . . . and making me so excited my cheeks went really red . . . After me, she turned to the teacher and did the same to her . . . then the next, and the next . . . She went round the whole ring on her knees, with everyone letting out shouts of laughter so that I did the same, and the laughter was surprising but it was fun as well . . . There was only one lot left to draw, Miss Hélène, who was waiting impatiently . . . 'I order,' said Rosalie, 'the owner of the fifth forfeit, if it's the teacher's, as I should think it will be, since there's only hers left, I order her to take Miss Auguste . . . make her lie down nicely there . . . in front of us, on her belly . . . lift up her dress, her petticoat and her chemise, come behind her, very humbly, on her knees, hold her buttocks in both hands and kiss her for every smack she gave her without us seeing . . . send Auguste back to her place . . . then go round on her hands and knees and show herself to all of us, three times round the little circle, so everyone can pay her back what she's owed . . .' 'That's far too many things!' cried Miss Hélène . . . 'No it's not,' said the others, 'and you're not as strong as we are, even if you are the biggest, and perhaps the nicest and the shapeliest; and that's exactly why we're going to see how you do as you're told . . . Come on, hurry up and don't miss anything out . . .' The ceremony had as much to do with me as Miss Hélène, but I complied with a good grace: I didn't struggle against anything . . . She took me . . . made me lie down in the middle of the circle . . . lifted up carefully my dress, my skirt and my chemise . . . came up to me on her knees . . . fondled my behind in lots of different ways . . . took my bottom in her hands . . . and kissed it twenty times . . .

I went back to my seat, eager to see what she would do next . . . She stayed on her knees a moment, then came on all fours and stopped first in front of Victorine, sideways on . . . Victorine pulled her as close as she could . . . she pulled up grown-up Miss Hélène's skirts . . . pushed her skirts and petticoats over her head . . . exposed her fine arse . . . and it was very fine indeed . . . touched and fondled it . . . smacked it in lots of different ways . . . As soon as that was over, her skirts and petticoats down again, she offered herself in the same posture to Clairon, who caressed and rubbed her bottom in the same way and then put her skirts and petticoats down again, so the next girl could have the pleasure of lifting them as she liked . . . It was Rosalie, whom Miss Hélène had whipped on the hay bundle at the beginning of the scene, and who was longing to pay her back . . . Rosalie pulled Miss Hélène nearer . . . She turned her a little to one side so it was easier . . . she pulled her chemise higher than anyone else, and fastened it with two pins . . . and then she tickled her in front, thrashed her behind and smacked her heartily . . . Leaving Rosalie, she came before Agathe, who seized her bodily . . . and enjoyed herself just as much . . . Finally, she was in front of me, still on all fours . . . her arse completely exposed . . . I put my left arm right round her to hold her tight . . . then . . . I spent a short moment thinking about what I had before my eyes . . . and in my power, the naked buttocks of tall, pretty Miss Hélène, our so-called teacher, who had taken advantage of my innocence to treat me like a child . . . 'Oh, you'll pay for that!' I said . . . I took hold of her . . . pulled her tightly to me with my left hand . . . with my right hand I caress her belly . . . fondle and pinch her buttocks . . . rub them . . . smack them . . . she moves under me . . . my face burns red . . . I'm burning in an ecstasy of pleasure . . . I slap her with both hands . . . my sheaf of hay comes apart . . . I fall with my nose in her rump . . . I kiss her . . . I want to kiss her buttocks . . . I bite them . . . and she was furious . . . 'Biting!' she said . . . she took me . . . pulled up my skirts . . . whipped me hard . . . Clairon joined in, fondling and whipping us both . . . along came Agathe, pulling up Clairon's skirts as fast as she can and doing the same. Victorine threw herself on Agathe . . . Rosalie on Victorine . . . Each one held her own partner and did what she wanted with her . . .

Shortly afterwards we got up: then we straightened our clothes to go back into the house, and all the girls said to me: 'Auguste, you belong now; you're one of us; now you know as much as we do.'

THÉRÈSE: Auguste, I'm amazed, and I can't get over it; who could have imagined such madness, such libertine behaviour, in a house like this?

AUGUSTE: Libertine, if you like, I don't mind . . . and then, what harm does it do? None at all. In fact, it means we can be fond of one another and have fun without anyone knowing, and little games like that keep us cheerful and stop us feeling how tedious it is to be shut in.

IX
André Robert Andréa de Nerciat
(1739–1800)

from *Félicia, ou Mes Fredaines* (1775)

Like Crébillon, Nerciat presents contemporary salon society with the image of itself it would like to see: a frivolous, amoral but fundamentally harmless eroticism combined, in his case, with an ethic of moderation in passion and even a certain affectionate sensitivity for the feelings of others. Félicia, her feet set firmly by her guardians Sylvino and Sylvina on the path of pleasure (granted her licence by the appropriate authorities), proceeds to initiate the well-born young man picked up on the road. This is an eroticism that even in its language tests conventions to their limits but refuses to break them: both Félicia and Sylvina gloss a frank and practical sensuality with euphemism, allusion and precious conceits.

An army officer and supporter of the ancien régime, Nerciat emigrated during the Revolution and was imprisoned by the Revolutionary armies. He was also the author of Monrose, ou le libertin par fatalité *(1792),* Les Aphrodites *(1793) and* Le Diable au corps *(1803; attributed).*

First lessons

Part III Chapter II: The Story of Monrose. His Strange Misfortunes

We were very eager to know who was the charming young man we had chanced to carry off. Of his own accord, he forestalled our curiosity and with a considerable display of assurance, but without impudence, opened his heart to us, more or less as follows: 'You

must think it very strange, ladies, that I slipped into your company
in this way without having the honour of your acquaintance; and
although you caught me in such bad society, please believe that I am
not like those villains I was with. I am a poor wretch without
resources. I know I am a gentleman, but I have never seen any
member of my own family. I was given from my childhood into
paid hands, and I left a wretched elementary school to go straight
into a college. A meagre allowance was paid for me regularly. I have
been badly cared for and badly taught, humiliated and beaten: and
there in brief, ladies, is the image of my existence. Though I look
tall, I'm only fourteen years old; but a harsh life has made me
precocious and I seem more advanced than is usual for my age. For
some time I've already been thinking and working things out for
myself, and I even feel capable of making my own way, now that
my boldness has lost me the little money I got from my unknown
relatives. I am called Monrose, but it's only a nickname: the
Principal of the college told me so. He has my papers, and he is the
only one who knows my origins and my name.'

The interesting youth was about to stop there, but we insisted on
knowing how he had happened to fall into the company of those
soldiers and what he intended to do with himself.

'Ladies,' he answered with a blush, 'I ran away from school and
on my honour no power on earth will ever make me go back there. I
have nothing more to say. The secret of my flight is one that cannot
be revealed.' Our impatience doubled. We pressed Monrose to
speak. He put up considerable resistance, but finally yielded to our
entreaties and added the following sad postscript to his story,
blushing and changing colour:

'Ladies, I doubt if there is a more wretched condition in the world
than that of a child taken away from its mother and father and
handed over to schoolmasters. Those villains, with their grim faces,
hard hearts and vile souls, have persecuted me continually. Born
proud and hot-tempered, I have had to suffer more than others.
Increasing the burden or the boredom of my tasks, cutting down
my food and my sleep, depriving me of recreation and the company
of my friends were daily acts of injustice from these loathsome
monsters. How happy I would have been if I could have made them
loathe me in turn, and if my fatal destiny had not led me to
encounter in their affection for me the most unbearable of my
torments.

'About six months ago my need for a friend led me to pick out

one of my classmates whose brilliant academic achievements had
earned him the favour of all the masters. I had a great deal of respect
and affection for Carvel, which was the boy's name; and I intended
to learn from this young man, who met with general favour, the art
of mollifying the tigers who until then had done nothing but tear
me to pieces. My obvious desire to be friends with Carvel seemed in
fact to bring round the Principal: he seemed pleased to see that we
got on well. We were in the same class; I soon shared with him the
good graces of the form-master, and for a moment I thought my
unhappiness was about to be ended. Soon however certain advances
from my new friend and certain approaches from the master made
me take fright. For some mysterious reason I was getting praise and
caresses; I sensed some plot was being hatched against me. Shortly I
discovered that Carvel owed some of the favour he was in to his
ways of paying court, which I felt unable to imitate . . .

'My doubts finally became certainties. Our master was the
Principal's close friend, and Carvel a close friend of them both.
Enough of a blind eye was turned to our conduct for us to find ways
of sleeping together fairly often. Carvel, a practised libertine and
older than me, began to take liberties and teach me obscene little
tricks that I picked up quite easily and for which I developed a kind
of liking. But I see, ladies, that I'm wrong to speak so openly: are
you laughing at me?' (We were in fact smiling.)

'No, my pretty friend,' answered Sylvina, 'we find you very
interesting, diverting, charming. Go on.'

'Gradually, the enthusiast pushed his lessons further and
further . . . Finally, one night, he waxed eloquent on the excellence
of certain pleasures . . . But the mere description of them made me
feel an immediate dreadful repugnance . . . He tried in vain to make
me more amenable to his suggestions, supporting them with
practical illustration, and I became very angry. He calmed me as
best he could and I forgave him, but we agreed there would be no
further talk of the disgusting subject, although he assured me, to
justify himself and to seduce me, that the Head and the form-master
were the people he had got it from and that I could quite well let him
do to me what such important people saw no difficulty in doing to
him.

'There is no point, ladies, in going into much further detail.
Carvel, of course, was only acting under the direction of the
masters. He was dedicated to their interests, under orders to
debauch me so I could then be used for their infamous pleasures.

Caresses, prayers, threats, violence – the villains then tried everything to achieve their aims. Soon they were divided by terrible
jealousy, each convinced that I preferred his rival; and I was the
constant victim of the rages of one or the other. I broke irrevocably
with the despicable Carvel . . .' (Sylvina, entranced: 'He's
delightful!')

'Finally, the night before last the Principal summoned me to his
room at bedtime on the pretext of making peace with me, took me
in his arms and asked me to forget the past. I said I would. He
overwhelmed me with caresses and gave me fruit, preserves and
wine. I tasted everything, unsuspecting. We talked intimately for
more than an hour . . . then the loathsome man suddenly dropped
his hypocritical mask, rushed on me like a mad wolf and tried to
force me into yielding those so-called favours, using all the weight
of his massive male frame . . .

'His robe was already over my head and I was down on the bed
with my face against the covers, scarcely able to breathe. He had
one leg round both of mine, holding them in a tight grip; and with
his free hand, the monster had already cut the fastenings of my
breeches and uncovered . . . At that very moment, the enraged
form-master, who had probably been on the watch for some time,
threw down the door, smashing the bolts, and dragged me with
some difficulty from the hands of the madman driven distracted by
passion, who couldn't let go. I made my escape while the two
savage beasts were locked together in paroxysms of rage. In a
moment, the whole house was in an uproar. My sole aim was to get
away; I managed it thanks to the general confusion, and the gates by
chance were unlocked.

'I left the town at once, my only property the clothes you see on
my body and a few coins that I spent at my first halt. I covered a
considerable distance without stopping for breath, and met up with
these soldiers, who were on the same road as me. We got to know
each other, and they suggested I join up. Poverty was at my heels,
and I didn't hesitate. We had already drunk the King's health
together, and this evening I was to sign my enlistment papers.'

Chapter VII: Good Things Sometimes Come in Sleep

There was no time to lose; I knew that if I gave Sylvina time to train

my handsome child, I had lost him. Love inspired the following
stratagem.

On the night of the day we had seen Monsignor and his nephew, I
got up quietly and went to wake Monrose, who was sleeping as
peacefully as could be imagined. However, I set to persuading him
that I had heard frightening snores coming from his room and run
in for fear he was suffocating. The sudden interruption of his sleep
made him in fact slightly agitated. I told him that was a result of the
state he had been in in his sleep; I slipped my arms round him; I held
him tight to my breast, with signs of lively anxiety. The young man
overwhelmed me with his gratitude; his lips reached out automati-
cally to kiss the twin globes where I held his breathing face. Oh
nature, what a marvellous teacher you are!

Very soon I felt two tender arms fasten around me and make
trembling efforts to pull me closer. 'Monrose,' I said, overwhelmed
with emotion and desire, 'if you were afraid of feeling ill again . . . I
could stay with you. Would you be shocked if . . . You worry me
terribly . . . I can't leave you in such a critical state . . .' 'You are so
kind, and so beautiful, my lady,' he answered, beside himself, 'I feel
very well, but I wish I were ill enough to need your precious care.'
'Tell me the truth, Monrose, weren't you at least having a bad
dream?' 'No, on the contrary, to be honest, I was dreaming . . . I
don't like to tell you, it's too stupid.' 'Tell me, my dear. I insist on
knowing.' 'Well, then . . . I was dreaming that . . . you were the
Principal of the college, and you looked lovely, even with the robe
and square hat . . . and you asked me . . . you know what, but so
sweetly that I didn't have the heart to refuse you. I wasn't angry, in
fact I was very sorry when I woke up . . . imagine how surprised I
was when I found myself in your arms.'

I didn't have a robe or a square hat and my intentions were not
quite the same as those of the father supervisor, but in other respects
Monrose had dreamed the exact truth. I fell into fits of laughter and
could not help giving him kiss after kiss. I was half lying on the bed;
I gradually slipped under the blanket and finally found myself by
the side of the delightful youth.

I saw at once that he was good material. What he lacked in
quantity he made up for in quality. Monrose was not surprised to
feel my hands running over him; his friend Carvel had taught him
the mysteries of pleasure and more besides, but he had not yet got
very far, as I could tell by the sudden jerk of his hand, pulling away
as soon as it felt a different shape, the absence of what he apparently

thought common to both sexes. I caught the over-timid hand in its flight and brought it back to the spot. 'As you see, dear Monrose,' I said, kissing him passionately, 'I am not your Principal.' 'I don't know where I am,' he replied, in some embarrassment. At the same time one of his hands was exploring with interest this new region and the adjoining parts, which were less foreign to him, while the other was enjoying the satin feel of my breasts . . . He was breathing heavily, consumed with desire but still ignorant of its object and how to satisfy it . . . His new discoveries had confused him completely.

I revelled in his delightful bewilderment. 'Well, Monrose,' I said, 'you've nothing to fear from me. I can't do foolish things to you.' 'No, I'm afraid not,' he sighed, 'but if Carvel had been you, or you really had been the Principal, I couldn't have resisted the desire to do some, and let you do some to me, because I think it would be to our mutual advantage.' 'Well then,' I said, beside myself with passion, 'since unfortunately I can't take advantage of your goodwill, you'd better do what *you* want.'

Poor Monrose was even more at a loss. His desire had only one object, but even that he could only speculate about. And I completed his despair by being in a position that thwarted his intentions as much as it favoured mine. 'Come into my arms,' I said, 'and perhaps someone will do a miracle for us.'

Chapter X: The End of Monrose's Novitiate

He obeyed enthusiastically. I was in ecstasy, feeling the slight weight of my young lover on my burning body. He was shivering, with no notion how to pull himself together. For a long time, I held him tight, devouring him with my kisses, my mouth sucking frantically at his beautiful lips, lavishing on him passionate confessions of love. My precious pupil let me take the lead, waiting in silence to see what would come of it. I was beside myself. I made to . . . an obstacle arose. The poor boy's confusion had a cruel effect on love's goad, which turned cold in my hand . . . Such a dreadful setback inflamed my desire to madness, I summoned up all the tricks I knew . . . The spell was soon broken, and I was quick to take advantage. I applied the remedy I had been languishing for. Monrose learned his first lesson like a good boy. I took hold of those plump cushions whose charms make us forget nature's shameful purposes, and pressed him hard against me until certain delightful movements finally enlightened the fortunate Monrose. I felt the moment when Venus received her first offering, and we both yielded to pleasure at the same time.

That was how I frustrated Sylvina's lascivious designs, thwarted her of a precious flower she was about to pluck, and revenged myself for having had to share d'Aiglemont and Fiorelli. That was a humiliation that rankled and might perhaps have turned into hatred, but for the infinite kindnesses my rival had so long shown me and for which I was so grateful. I am not afraid to admit to pettiness; women will know that it's how they react themselves and men will not blame me for attitudes that prove what importance we attach to winning them.

The sensations I felt were delightful, and I was surprised at the tremendous contrast between the satisfaction a man gets when he makes a girl into a woman and what a woman feels when she receives the first fruits of an apprentice in love. With Monrose, I had just enjoyed ecstatic pleasure; what a night poor d'Aiglemont had had with me when it was my first time!

Monrose, intoxicated by what was for him such a novel feeling, was afraid to interrupt my amorous reverie. He stayed in the exciting position I had put him in. I had to speak to him to get him to break his silence. 'What do you think of it, my dear?' I asked, with a kiss. 'Give me time to find the words, if there are any, to convey what I've just experienced.' 'Monrose, are you cross with me for disturbing your sleep?' 'Oh, my lady,' he exclaimed, with passionate caresses, 'could you really think me so ungrateful?' 'Truly? You won't wish me ill like you did your friend Carvel? or the Principal?' 'How wicked you are to tease me about something so humiliating. But let me tell you what I think. The pleasures that that evil Carvel never stopped talking about can't possibly be the same as those I've just enjoyed with you. Why didn't I feel the same desire for them? When we played about together at night, why did Carvel have to use all his skill before he could arouse one faint spark of the desire that the first of your caresses stirred into flame? I think the satisfaction he vaunted must be as much inferior to this as it is different in form.'

While Monrose was arguing so sensibly, I was surreptitiously beginning to take advantage of his position again. My kisses closed his mouth. He was already doing it better, and I admired his intelligence. However, trying too hard to do well, he did rather badly, and I had to put him back on the right track. Thereafter I was perfectly pleased with him, and he must have been pleased with me. Spinning out his satisfaction with all my skill and experience, I only gave myself up to my own pleasure when I saw he was near the decisive moment.

So Monrose's talent for love was no less precocious than his bravery and wit. Having acquitted himself so well in this fresh trial, he became all the dearer to me. We swore secrecy to one another; and for fear we might sleep too long and be caught together, I went back to my own bed. I fell deeply asleep in the tranquillity of perfect bliss.

Chapter XV: Intrigues of which the Handsome Monrose Is the Object

His night's efforts had turned my delightful pupil slightly pale. The sweet languor of pleasure was written in the blue rings under his eyes; he was entrancing. I advised him though to say he felt slightly unwell, so as to forestall any jealous suspicion from Sylvina. The visible change in Monrose's complexion did not in fact escape her. She expressed lively anxiety. I did the same, and we got through safely.

I reproached myself, however, for having initiated so early a boy to whom the knowledge he had just acquired could prove fatal. He was very passionate; I was afraid he might succumb to some hot-blooded woman incapable of using him sparingly and whose wishes he would not be able to refuse. I could envisage a future where he could easily become an agent of his own ruin, and soon run to all the excesses that his charms and merits would so easily permit. I was sorry to think that this fine plant might wither and die before reaching maturity; that for having known pleasure too early, Monrose might give himself over to passion and frustrate the great designs that nature must certainly have for such a perfect creature. In order to check the progress of an evil which would have been my fault, I decided to require Monrose to submit himself entirely to my wishes. I approached him the very next day, pretending to attach the greatest importance to what had happened, and made the following speech, having prepared the ground by a few preliminary sophistries.

'It was something more than chance, my dear Monrose, that presided over the relationship that has formed between us; and you seem yourself inclined to think that a strong bond of mutual attraction destined us for one another from the start. There are therefore certain duties you owe me from which you cannot be released, even though, by a strange and happy chance, our affair began at the point where others usually finish. One of the first laws of love is not to share one's affections. You belong to me; you must sacrifice to me all offers of pleasure you may receive. It will be up to me to permit or prohibit in this respect what I think proper. You must also allow me to grant or refuse as I wish whatever desires you intimate to me. Your sex was meant to earn the favours of mine; you will enjoy those I grant you all the more if they are a reward for your efforts and the proof of my satisfaction.'

Monrose promised everything I said I wanted. He was in love; his innocent heart was full of that initial fervour that makes a lover incapable of selfishness and mistrust. He did not notice that while binding him with commitments I made none for myself, and he swore a thousand oaths at my feet, with all the enthusiasm of passion and respect.

Fair ladies craving for pure adoration, take your men at Monrose's age, if you want to breathe just for a moment such delicate flattery. But only a moment, do you hear me? Very soon these open, sensitive hearts succumb to the general infection: and you become the fools of those you thought you were fooling. They grow tired of flattering the illusions of your pride. Your admirers laugh and run away. You are left behind consumed with regrets and covered in ridicule.

Monrose was acting in good faith; and I for my part was not interested in adoration. It has never pleased me; I have always wanted brief love and long friendship. But I've already given my reasons. Not all women who set out to deceive have such delicate ones. Let's get back to the subject.

It was not long before Monrose had secrets to tell me. Whenever he was alone with Sylvina, she tried hard to provoke him. She had got into the way of giving him the most libidinous caresses and behaving as uninhibitedly with him as if he belonged to the same sex. Her favourite ruse was to call him in in the morning to read by her bed. He would get a glimpse of an arm, a breast; she would feel hot and push back her covers, or else there would be a troublesome flea; the zealous Monrose would be asked to hunt it down. First it was here, then there, and the clever insect could never be found, especially if it was lucky enough to retreat into certain advantageous positions which the shy hunter always respected.

One day, and I still laugh when I think of it, one of the little creatures must have been running wild; Sylvina had had no profit at all from the reading. After a long chase, the wily beast had gone to ground . . . you know where . . . and the poor boy had fallen for the old story! 'But isn't that odd? Monrose? . . . There . . . just there!' She drew the reader's pretty hand to it, choosing the biggest finger to declare cruel war on the flea. Directed to a most sensitive spot, the finger set to work and was soon praised for its skill. 'Marvellous,' said Sylvina, swooning . . . 'I think, I do think, you're killing it . . . A bit more . . . Just a little more . . . Make sure the cursed creature never comes back.'

Not to put too fine a point on it, I listened in on this excellent scene. Suspicious of these readings, wanting to know where Monrose had got to and whether or not he was deceiving me, I had slipped through the dressing-room into the little blind passage it's now the fashion to have around most elegant beds – an invention that can't be praised enough for the pleasures it provides and the dangers it prevents. From this vantage point I saw every detail of the famous hunt. I left my post only to go and vent my laughter somewhere else; and then, fearing things might go further, given such a convenient opportunity, I took it on myself to go in and open the shutters wide. This put Sylvina in a very bad mood, although it was already later than her usual time for getting up.

Chapter XI: In which Sylvina Is Caught in an Unusual Trap

Monrose proved his honesty by his haste to come and tell me his new adventure. Not only was his story accurate but he also had the good faith to confess to me that he had felt violent temptation and had it not been for the oaths he had sworn to me could not have borne such a difficult trial without asking for relief. So far I had put off making the fair lad happy for the second time, although he had constantly begged me to. I realised it was time to be kind to him and arranged a meeting for that night, as a well-earned reward. He was so beside himself that I thought he had lost his mind.

This time it was in my bed that we enjoyed our games and pleasures. Twice I made the passionate Monrose taste the height of ecstasy and reached it myself several times over . . .

We spent the rest of the time working out how he should behave in future with Sylvina. Her caprice would have to be satisfied. I thought it ought to be sooner rather than later and gave the following instructions to the handsome boy.

The next morning he was to go himself and offer to read to her. She was bound to accept. This time he would let his attention wander during his reading . . . sigh . . . she would ask him what was wrong . . . he would hum and haw a little . . . Finally, he would let slip how much he desired her (there was no point talking about love), complain of his sufferings . . . She would take the hint . . . She would ask him if he had any idea how his pain might be relieved, and he would innocently beg to be told . . . and she would ask nothing better. Having just left my embrace he would be tired, so he would not perform very well; that was probably enough to turn her off him, at least for a while. Monrose gladly fell in with the plan. His intentions were so honest that he tried to insist before he left me on getting into a state where I could have no doubts of him at all; but I thought it better to leave him something to put up some sort of show with, just in case. We parted more pleased than ever with one another. But I did find it rather funny that unlike other lovers in our situation, making countless protestations of fidelity, we were planning quite the opposite; and I was demanding and receiving as an offering what is supposed to be love's most serious crime.

I took care to hide myself in the same place as before. Everything happened just as I had foreseen. Sylvina was delighted with the declaration and the request. She asked Monrose to bolt the door, told him to undress, and took him into her bed.

'Poor child,' she said, no doubt at the sight of what she was about to put to the test, 'well, that's not much is it? So you want to eat your corn before it's ripe? . . . Let's see, anyhow . . . Kiss me . . . Come here, on top of me . . . Though I really don't see . . . Are you never any different? . . . I must say, it's hardly flattering . . . Come on, let's try . . . Heavens, my dear, I'm beginning to give up hope . . . Calm down . . . it's only your shyness . . . How can I possibly intimidate you when I'm being so accommodating? Look . . . let me take that pretty mouth of yours . . . Do you feel how my heart breathes out in my kisses? . . . No, I won't give up . . . My own desire shall *make* nature give you the strength; I'm absolutely determined . . . It's so unfair to her to refuse it . . . I'd sooner die than fail, it's too shameful.'

All that signified that Monrose was still no use for anything;

however, a moment later I could tell things were taking a turn for the better. 'Not before time,' she said, 'and not without a lot of effort . . . All right then, my precious, the rest is easy.'

After that all I heard was the passionate writhing of the lascivious Sylvina, who seemed to be doing all the work herself. 'It's forcing nature,' she said, when it was all over. 'As you see, Monrose, you aren't yet ready for love. I'm ashamed to have been so accommodating, and I hope you will keep it absolutely secret and do your best to forget it. I hope particularly that if you ever ask me such a thing in future it won't just be out of mere curiosity. Leave me now, I need to go to sleep.'

Poor Monrose came in his embarrassment to find me in my apartment to which I had returned, in tears of laughter over what had happened. His shamefaced looks doubled my mirth, which cast him into total despair. But his affection for me soon won out against the little prick to his self-esteem, and he laughed himself at his adventure. We congratulated each other enthusiastically on having disposed by our ingenious stratagem of an obstacle which would have been fatal to our pleasures.

X
Pierre-Ambroise Choderlos de Laclos (1741–1803)

from *Les Liaisons dangereuses* (1782)

An artillery officer not aristocratic enough to win his proper promotion, Laclos eventually became secretary to the Duke d'Orléans and a major figure in the Orleanist faction in the early days of the Revolution. A relative outsider, he draws the love-play of aristocratic society as a vicious and violent struggle for power: a battlefield or a theatre where individuals superior in reason and will direct from behind the scenes the activities of the unfortunates who fall victim to passion. Rivalry is intense; there is no affection, only ruthless destruction and cold contempt.

In this episode, Valmont has just seduced Cécile, fresh from the convent and would-be betrothed of his own protégé Danceny, as a diversion from his own long-term campaign to seduce the virtuous Madame de Tourvel. Both he and Cécile immediately communicate the episode to the Marquise de Merteuil, Valmont's rival in libertinism.

The erotic focus here is outside the text, in the Marquise's – and the reader's – reception of the letters. Despite his protestations of triumph, Valmont, in writing, constitutes himself as a spectacle for his rival, conceding her the dominant position.

The Seduction of Cécile

Letter 96: The Vicomte de Valmont to the Marquise de Merteuil

I wager that since your adventure you live in daily expectation of my compliments and praise; I don't even doubt that my long silence has put you a little out of temper with me: but what do you expect? I have always thought that if nothing remained but to applaud a woman, one could leave that safely to her and attend to something else.

However, I do indeed thank you on my own account and congratulate you on yours. And just to make you completely happy, I'll even agree that this time you've surpassed all my expectations. After that, let's see if for my part I've at least partially fulfilled yours.

It isn't Madame de Tourvel I want to talk to you about; you don't like the slowness of that particular development. You only like affairs all done and dusted. Protracted scenes bore you; but I've never tasted the like of the pleasure I'm getting from what you might call heel-dragging.

Yes, I like to watch and observe this prudent woman, setting out without realising it on a road of no return, a swift, dangerous slope that carries her along despite herself and forces her to follow me. Once embarked, terrified at the risks she's running, she tries to stop but can't keep herself from falling. Her efforts and her ingenuity can make her steps shorter, but each one still has to follow the next. Sometimes, afraid to look danger in the face, she closes her eyes, lets herself go, abandons herself to my attentions. More often, fresh fear spurs her to new efforts; in fear and dread, she thinks she must make one more try to go back; she exhausts all her strength in a painful effort to scale a tiny distance; and some magic force promptly puts her back even closer to the danger she tried vainly to flee. Then with only me left to guide and protect her, instead of heaping reproaches on me for her inevitable fall, she beseeches me to try to delay it. Fervent prayers, humble supplications, everything that fearful mortals offer the deity, I receive from her; and you want me to turn a deaf ear to her pleas, destroy with my own hand the cult she offers, and use to destroy her the power she invokes to sustain her! Oh, at least give me the time to watch these touching struggles between love and virtue.

I'm amazed! Do you think that a spectacle that makes you rush into the theatre and applaud with frenzy, is any less gripping in reality? You listen with enthusiasm to the feelings of a pure, tender soul, afraid of the happiness she craves, who goes on fighting even when her resistance is ended; must the man who inspires such feelings be the only one who fails to appreciate them? Yet these are exactly the delightful pleasures this heavenly woman gives me daily to enjoy; and you reproach me for enjoying their sweetness! Ah, the time will come only too soon when, fallen and degraded, she'll be no more to me than an ordinary woman.

But I forget, telling you about her, that I didn't intend to tell you about her. There's some strange power draws me to her, brings me back again and again, even while I'm insulting her. Let's forget the dangerous thought of her; let me be myself again, and talk of something more amusing. Your pupil, in fact, who's now become mine, and here, I think, you will recognise the old Valmont.

For a few days now, getting kinder treatment from my pious sweetheart and as a result less interested in her, I had noticed that little Volanges was in fact very pretty; and that if it was somewhat foolish to be as much in love with her as Danceny, it might be no less foolish of me not to seek with her the amusement that my isolation required. Also, it seemed fair that I should get some reward for the trouble I was going to on her behalf; I remembered besides that you'd offered her to me before Danceny laid any claims; and I reckoned I had good cause to claim a few rights over a property he only owned because I'd refused and relinquished the title. The little lady's pretty face, fresh mouth, childish looks, and her very awkwardness fortified my wise reflections; I decided to act accordingly and the enterprise was crowned with success.

You will already be wondering what device I used to supplant so quickly the lover she worships; what seductions work best with that age and inexperience? Save yourself the trouble, I used none. While you were skilfully wielding the weapons of your sex, to triumph by subtlety, I conquered by authority, rendering to Man his inalienable rights. I knew I could get hold of my prey if I could once get to it, so the only ruse I needed was for getting close; and even that scarcely deserves the name.

I took advantage of the first letter I got from Danceny for his lovely lady. I let her know I had it by means of our agreed signal and then instead of applying my skill to handing it over, I bent all my efforts to not finding a way. I pretended to share the impatience I provoked, and having caused the ill, prescribed the cure.

The young lady has a room with a door opening onto the corridor; the mother, naturally, had taken the key. I merely had to acquire command of it myself. Nothing easier to organise; all I asked was to have it for a couple of hours, and I could answer for getting a duplicate. Correspondence, interviews, midnight meetings, all then became simple and safe; but would you believe it? The

Illustration by Gustave Doré for the
Oeuvres de Rabelais, *Garnier, Paris 1873.*
'How Panurge Played a Trick on the Parisian Lady.'
Reproduced by kind permission of Éditions Garnier, Paris.

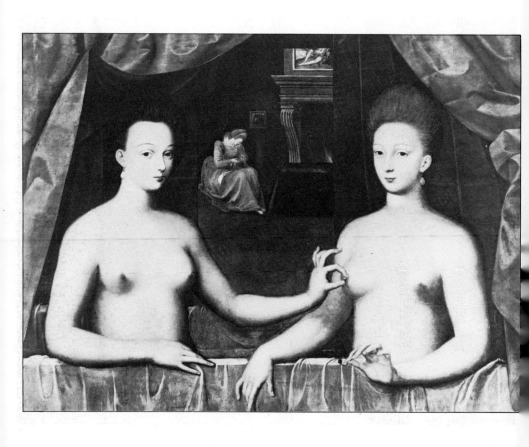

École de Fontainbleau:
The Duchesse de Villars and Gabrielle d'Estrées in the bath. *Circa 1595.*
The Louvre, Paris.

François Boucher:
Girl on a couch. *1752.*
Aeltere Pinakothek, Munich.

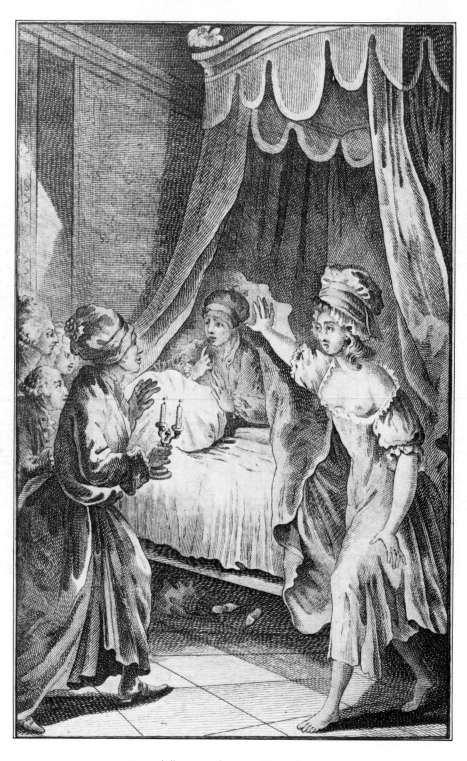

Original illustration from Restif de la Bretonne,
L'Année des dames nationales *(1791-94):*
'Maid of Thionvillète Defiled by Her Vile Husband.'
Reproduced by kind permission of the Syndics of Cambridge University Library.

Jean Auguste Ingres:
Roger and Angélique. *Circa 1820.*
The Louvre, Paris.

Gustave Courbet:
Woman with a parrot. *1866.*
The H. O. Havemeyer Collection, The Metropolitan Museum of Art, New York.

Gustave Moreau:
The Apparition. *1876.*
The Louvre, Paris.

Félicien Rops:
Ancient Priestess. *1894.*
Reproduced by kind permission of Éditions Graphiques Gallery, London.

timid child took fright and refused. Another man would have been devastated; I only saw the chance for an even more piquant pleasure. I wrote to Danceny to complain of her refusal, and handled it so well that the foolish fellow left no stone unturned to obtain – demand, indeed – of his timorous mistress that she agree to my request and hand herself over entirely to my discretion.

I must admit, I took considerable satisfaction in changing roles and having the young man do for me what he is counting on me to do for him. The notion doubled, in my view, the value of the escapade: and so as soon as I had the precious key I made haste to put it to use, and that was last night.

Having made sure all was quiet in the castle, armed with a veiled lantern, and dressed appropriately for the time and the occasion, I paid my first visit to your pupil. I had had all the necessary preparations made (by the lady herself) to effect a noiseless entrance. She had just fallen asleep, and was dreaming as soundly as one does at her age; so I got right to her bed before she woke up. I was tempted at first to go further and try and pass myself off as a dream; but fearing the effects of surprise and the consequent noise I decided instead to wake the pretty sleeper carefully, and managed in fact to forestall the scream I feared.

I calmed her first fears; then, not having come there for conversation, I risked a few liberties. She can't have been at all well taught in her convent how many and how diverse are the perils to which timid innocence is exposed, and all it has to guard against surprise: for as she turned all her attention and her forces to fighting off a kiss, which was only a feint, she left everything else undefended; and how could I help but take advantage! I changed my line of attack, and at once took position. At that point we were both nearly lost; the little thing, absolutely beside herself, tried to scream in earnest; fortunately, her voice was swallowed up in tears. She also hurled herself at the bellpull, but I was quick enough to catch her hand in time.

'What are you trying to do,' I said, 'ruin yourself for good? What difference does it make to me if anyone comes? Who is going to believe that you didn't invite me in? Who else but you gave me the means of getting in? This key I got from you, that I could only have got from you, will you tell them what it's for?'

This short harangue calmed neither her sorrow nor her anger but it got her to submit. I don't know if I had the note of eloquence; I definitely didn't have the gestures. One hand busy holding her down, the other making love – what orator could claim to be inspired in such a situation? If you picture it correctly, you'll agree it was at least favourable for attack; though I, of course, know nothing about anything, and as you say, the most naive of women, a schoolgirl, can handle me like a child.

This particular one, in the middle of her tears, realised she had to make up her mind and come to some kind of compromise. Her prayers fell on stony ground, so she had to move on to concessions. You think, no doubt, that I sold my key position dear: no, I promised everything for a kiss. It's true that once I had the kiss I didn't keep my promise: but I had good reasons. Had we agreed it would be taken or given? We bargained a while, and agreed on a second; and that one I was definitely to be given. So guiding the timid arms round my body, and pressing her more passionately with one of mine, the sweet kiss was indeed given; given very well, to absolute perfection; so much so that Love itself couldn't have done better.

So much good faith deserved a reward, so I granted her request at once. The hand withdrew; but by some mysterious chance I found myself in its place. You think once there I made a point of being quick and lively, don't you? Not at all. I've learned to enjoy the slow approach, I tell you. Once you're certain of getting there, why rush the journey?

Seriously, I was pleased to be able to observe for once the power of opportunity, and here it was stripped of all extraneous assistance. Not only that, it had to overcome love, and a love that was strengthened by modesty, or shame, and reinforced particularly by the bad temper I had given grounds for and of which she gave ample evidence. It was opportunity, nothing else; but there it was, on permanent offer, present and waiting – and love, unfortunately, was absent.

To confirm my observations, I had the wicked notion of using only as much force as could be resisted. If my delightful opponent, taking advantage of my obliging nature, seemed about to escape me, I simply held her in check by that same threat whose happy effect I had already tried. Well! With no other effort on my part, Danceny's loving lady, forgetting all her vows, first gave in and finally gave consent. Not that after the first moment the tears and reproaches didn't make a joint come-back; I don't know if they were real or feigned, but as always happens they stopped as soon as I busied myself with giving them new occasion. Finally, after

weakening and reproaches, reproaches and weakening, we parted
company fully satisfied with each other, and equally agreed on this
evening's appointment.

It was already dawn when I got back to my room and I was worn
out with tiredness and exhaustion. I sacrificed both, however, to
my desire to be at breakfast this morning: I adore morning-after
faces. You couldn't possibly imagine what this one was like. She
carried herself so awkwardly, and such difficulty she had in
walking; eyes permanently cast down, and so puffy and blotchy!
That round face grown so long! I've never seen anything so funny.
And for the first time her mother, alarmed by the transformation,
showed quite an affectionate interest! And Madame de Tourvel was
there, fussing around her! Oh, *those* attentions are just on loan;
there'll come a day when there'll be a chance to pay them back, and
that day isn't far off. Goodbye, dear friend.

. . . Castle, 1 October 17★★

Letter 97: Cécile Volanges to the Marquise de Merteuil

Oh good heavens, Madame, how wretched I am, how unhappy!
Who will comfort me in my trouble? Where can I turn for advice in
the tangle I am in? That Monsieur de Valmont . . . and Danceny!
Oh, no, the thought of Danceny fills me with despair . . . How can
I tell you? How can I say it? . . . I don't know what to do. But my
heart is brimming over . . . I *must* speak to someone, and you are
the only person I can, or dare, confide in. You have been so kind to
me! But don't be now; I'm not worthy: what am I trying to say? I
don't want you to be. Everyone here has been nice to me today . . .
they've all made me feel worse. I know so well that I didn't deserve
it! Scold me rather; scold me severely, for I'm very bad: and then,
save me; if you won't tell me what to do, out of your kindness, I
shall die of grief.

I must tell you then . . . you can see, my hand is shaking, I can
hardly write, my face feels on fire . . . oh, it's the red of shame.
Well then! I shall endure it; it shall be my first punishment for my
wickedness. I shall tell you everything.

You must know first that Monsieur de Valmont, who until now
had been passing on to me Monsieur Danceny's letters, suddenly
found it too difficult; and he said he wanted a key to my room. I can
assure you that I didn't want that: but he went and wrote to

Danceny, and Danceny said that was how he wanted it too; and it hurts me so much to refuse him anything, especially since he's so unhappy now I'm away, that I finally agreed. I didn't dream what a dreadful thing would come of it.

Yesterday, Monsieur de Valmont used the key to come into my room while I was asleep; I was so far from expecting it that he frightened me out of my wits when he woke me up; but he spoke out straight away, so I recognised him, and I didn't call for help; and then the first thing I thought was that he was perhaps bringing me a letter from Danceny. Far from it. Scarcely a minute later he tried to kiss me; and while I was struggling, just as you would naturally expect, he did it so cleverly, I wouldn't have wanted that for anything in the world . . . but he wanted a kiss first. I had to, because what could I do? And I had tried to shout, but I couldn't and besides he made sure to tell me that if someone did come he would know how to make it out it was all my fault; and indeed that would have been very easy, because of that key. And then he still didn't go away. He wanted a second; and I don't know what happened with that one but it put me in a terrible confusion; and afterwards it was even worse than before. Oh, honestly, it was very wicked. And then . . . you won't make me say the rest; but I am as wretched as anyone can be.

What I feel sorriest for, but I still ought to tell you, is that I am afraid I perhaps didn't fight as hard as I could have. I don't know how that happened: certainly, I don't love Monsieur de Valmont, quite the opposite; but there were moments when I acted just as if I did love him . . . You can imagine that that didn't stop me saying no to him, all the time: but I knew very well that I wasn't doing what I was saying; and it was as if I was doing it in spite of myself; and then, I was very confused! If it's always as hard as that to defend yourself, you must need a lot of practice! Certainly Monsieur de Valmont has ways of saying things so that you don't know how to answer him: anyway, would you believe that when he went away I felt as though I was sorry he was going, and I was weak enough to say he could come back tonight. That makes me more miserable than all the rest.

Oh, but even though I promised, I do assure you I shall stop him coming. He was no sooner out of the room than I realised it was very wrong to promise him that. I cried all the rest of the time. It was especially Danceny that made me so sorry! Every time I thought of him my tears came so fast that I was suffocated and I went on thinking about it . . . and you can still see now what happens; my paper is quite soaked through. No, I shall never forgive myself for this, if only because of him . . . I just couldn't bear it any more, and I couldn't sleep a wink. And this morning when I got up and looked in the mirror I was frightened, I looked so different.

Mama noticed as soon as she saw me and asked me what was wrong. I started crying on the spot. I thought she was going to scold me, and that would perhaps have made me less sorry: but not at all! She was very gentle with me! I didn't deserve it. She told me not to be so sad. (She didn't know what I had to be sad about.) I would make myself ill. There are times when I wish I were dead. I couldn't bear it. I threw myself into her arms sobbing, saying: 'Oh Mama, your little girl is very unhappy!' Mama couldn't help crying a bit, and that only made me sorrier: fortunately, she didn't ask why I was so unhappy, because I wouldn't have known what to say to her.

I beg you, Madame, write to me as soon as you can and tell me what I must do: for I haven't the heart to think of anything and all I can do is cry. Please forward your letter through Monsieur de Valmont; but if you write to him at the same time, please don't talk as though I've told you anything.

I have the honour to be Madame your very humble and obedient servant, and affectionate as always . . .

I daren't sign this letter.

. . . Castle, 1 October 17**

XI
Honoré-Gabriel de Riquetti, comte de Mirabeau (1749–91)

from *Le Libertin de qualité* (1783)

One of the great Revolutionary orators and statesmen, Mirabeau was also a celebrated libertine who spent much of his youth in prison as a result of lettres de cachet *sought by his family. His best erotic writing came out of the Vincennes prison, including his tender letters to his mistress (*Lettres à Sophie*), the* Erotika Biblion *(1783), an erudite collection of sexual practices drawn from Ancient and Biblical history, and the novel from which the following extract is taken (first published as* Ma Conversion*).*

This episode is something of a smoking-room tale, in the style of Maupassant's 'Marroca' (below), with the virile narrator comically telling the tale of his own embarrassment. The narrator here is cleverly subverted: as venal, hypocritical and pretentious as the female enemy and despite his bluster terrified at the threat posed by sexuality to his pride and his pocket.

Marriage à la mode

I was in debt; my creditors, honest Jews, came to see me with their gallows-faces. I took a noble resolution; I decided to put my head in the noose and get married. 'Ah! you're going to settle down in the end.' End indeed; I never meant to die so young!

I knew a scheming old woman, a senior much-respected marchioness, a well-known matchmaker. I went and told her how I was fixed, stressing I was in a hurry. 'Right then,' she said, 'do you want a pretty one?' 'God, it's all the same to me; I want her for a wife; I'm not going to be bothered about her face, and I'm not getting her for other people to look at.' 'Does she need to be rich?' 'Right, as rich as possible.' 'Witty?' 'Yes, yes, if you like, get on with it.' 'I've got just what you want. Do you know Madame de l'Hermitage?' 'No.' 'I'll introduce you. She's one of my friends; her daughter is eighteen, very rich, and of excellent character.' (Bugger me, she's an ugly old cow! . . .) My kind duenna went off at once to make the first approaches, get me fixed up and tell them how marvellous I was. She wrote me a short note that evening, and two days later we went to see my future mother-in-law.

Madame de l'Hermitage sets herself up for a thinker and a wit. All our modern demi-gods and Apollos visit her salon in search of dinners, to be paid for with fatuous remarks. In the antechamber, I breathed in a perfume of antiquity that ravished my sense of smell; the old woman had told me to pile on the admiration. I went into a huge square drawing-room, where I found the mistress of the house; she looked like a witch, with a body of a skeleton and the bearing of an Empress. She bored me to death with lengthy compliments; I answered with a plethora of bows; I looked round for my intended . . . Bloody hell, they're going to keep you guessing! What the devil! Her mother has to look me over first and it's not done, is it, to expose a girl to the eyes of her future possessor?

The duenna and the mother started on the big words and the old stories. In the meantime I looked over the drawing-room. The walls were covered with antique flower-bordered tapestries. Cassandra and Polixenes were both there, with King Priam, and quantities of Trojans and perfidious Greeks, each one with a scroll coming out of his mouth for ease of conversation. From the ceiling there hung a huge seven-branched lamp, gilded bronze, left over from Nebuchadnezzar's banquets. In the four corners were ancient lacquered tripods, bearing antique urns and truncated pyramids found in the ditches of proud Nineveh. There were tables of Paros marble, standing on granite pillars, loaded with Greek and Latin busts and a massive medal cabinet. The mantelpiece was a good eight feet high and topped with a metal mirror, set in a huge filigree frame; no doubt it once belonged to fair Helen. The armchairs were apparently based on the Queen of Sheba's, covered in tapestry, tightly stuffed to keep you sitting up straight, but magnificently gilded . . . Those, friend, were the furnishings that met my eyes. For the rest, everything else indicated to my practised eye a wealth of riches that tickled my fancy, and I was already working out how I would change all this rubbish for the fine inventions of modern luxury. I waxed lyrical over every item, I expressed my admiration in the authoritative tones of the connoisseur; my praise found favour, and the duenna and I withdrew.

As we left, she told me that my appearance and my serious, sedate air (by God, I hadn't let slip one single smile) and particularly my excessive politeness had made a good impression, I would probably be invited to dinner for Thursday, which was their reception day, and I would see Mademoiselle Euterpe then . . . Bugger me! There's a fine name: I'm devilish afraid my charmer is going to turn out yet another antique.

I got my invitation; the dinner matched the furniture, and I saw my Euterpe . . . Good God! What a pretty wife-to-be; a craggy piece, damned if she wasn't built after a monkey; and indeed, her dear mother told me she was the living image of Monsieur de l'Hermitage. Short, fat and stumpy; a greeny-yellow complexion; little deep-set eyes with blue rings right down to the middle of two puffy cheeks; hair hanging half-way down her forehead, an enormous mouth stuck with cloves, a black neck and then . . . what a relief, a jealous gauze veiled something that stuck up like the very devil. By God, it was a pity she hadn't also covered up two paws as ugly as any servant ever washed. To finish off, Mademoiselle Euterpe pouts and grins to order, and it makes her all the uglier . . . It was even worse when she started to talk. God, a serving wench is nothing compared to her . . . 'God's death! Marry that!' I said to myself. 'It's pretty hard!' 'Well, suppose you didn't marry her?' 'Here, friend, forty thousand francs' interest to start with, and the same to finish; it's not to be sneezed at; she's got fine cash-box eyes, and all I've got is a fine prick she won't see much of.' My creditors are on my heels, and the sacrifice has to be made.

After dinner, Mademoiselle Euterpe planted herself by her dear mother; I went and cooed and gurgled a few love-notes to which she deigned to turn a kindly ear; and to cut a long story short, we were married in a fortnight, and I got twenty thousand francs' income by the contract. So there I was, Euterpe's husband. The mother gave her beloved daughter her blessing and the kiss of peace; my chaste wife went and got between the sheets, her heels tucked up to her bum, like modest girls do. Some of the wedding party were in adjacent rooms; the young men especially, who thought it was a great laugh, complimented me on my future happiness, wished me good luck, and waited in ambush. I planted myself next to my sweet wife, who was weeping great tears. 'Madame,' I said, 'the condition of marriage, to which we are now committed, is a *hard* one, a *narrow* path, but one that leads to happiness; there's no rose without thorns, and as your husband, it falls to me to pull them off. The Creator united us so our two halves could make a whole. To make his work more solid, he has given man, master of his wife, a certain peg . . . Have a feel.' (I put her hand on it, and the death's head pulled her paw away as if she were terrified.) 'This instrument has to find its proper hole, and the hole is in you; so allow me to find it and stuff it up . . .' I seized my Christian spouse with vigorous arm; she squeezed her thighs tight together; I inserted a knee as a wedge, she throws a few punches by way of resistance; finally, she lets on that she's hurting, straightens her legs, lifts up her bum, and I bang on the door . . . Bloody hellfire, I'm done for! 'What's wrong?' 'Why, you villain! Horns two feet long! . . .' I'm choked with fury . . . she's already standing wide open! 'You bitch, you stinking carrion! and you were defending the breach . . . Bloody whore! . . .' I belted her one; she scratched me, set to screaming, I swore and hit her again; her mother came, frothing with rage; I jumped out of the bed and was off. My friends, lined up outside, asked with malicious solicitude if I felt ill, did I want a glass of water . . . I wanted the devil out of there! . . . A moment later, my mother-in-law came out, and said in senatorial tones: 'My son, I know what is wrong.' 'You do, by God! So do I, only too well.' 'It's absolutely nothing; the very same thing happened to me on my wedding day.' 'What a bloody family!' 'Calm down, she's only a child and she doesn't know what it's all about, she'll get used to it; go back to bed with her, and try to be gentle.' My choking fury had stopped me interrupting so far, but at that gentle invitation I burst out: 'Back to bed! Let the bastard who's started her finish her off . . . Bugger me! she's big enough for a mare or a donkey.' Madame de l'Hermitage frowned at this. 'My son, I see now, you can't manage it.' 'Bugger me, madame, manage it! By God, there's no effort needed, you could drive a coach and four through her.' The old witch lost her temper; I nearly threw her out of the window, and left the damned place for ever.

Rage, despair! Me, the terror of husbands, the pearl of fuckers, there I am sporting the fashionable headgear . . . Haw, haw, what a green 'un! What a green 'un, caught good and proper by a slut, caught by an ugly old monkey! Where can I run, where can I hide? . . . They'll kill me with all their lampoons.

There was more to come. Next day, a man in black asked to speak to me. With a flourish of bows, he drew a small document to my attention . . . 'Sir, there is some mistake.' 'No, sir,' said the man of the law. 'But who is it from?' 'From the high and mighty lady Euterpe de l'Hermitage, your legitimate wife.' 'What, that villain! Bugger me, if you don't get out of here . . .' He was already out, and no doubt still running . . . Well! The bitch was serving me with a summons to give her her conjugal rights or else, they kindly informed me, there would be a request for a separation. I ran off to my solicitor; I got his advice, and we fought the case for three months; my ears rang with the ridicule; finally I was forced to give up ten of the twenty thousand pounds' income assigned me by the marriage contract and declared the father of an individual (a little monkey, I presume) the bitch was carrying – not her first, either.

In fury and despair, I left for foreign parts, renouncing for ever the accursed country where I risked confronting so many disagreeable sights.

Fate, you're bloody hard! Why should I suffer your strange whims? So these are the fruits of my fine resolutions! All my plans coming down to Moses' headgear! Leave me alone, be off with you, hateful dreams, figments of my bilious imagination . . . No, ladies, you won't get my head between your accursed thighs, I'm having no more horn-bearing vapours coming at me from married twats. Beggar my *conversion*! It's revenge I'm after, and I'm going to screw everything in nature. I'll have whole virginities (if there are any) sacrificed to my rod; I'll people palaces, countryside and cities with whole legions of cuckolds; I'll usurp the rights of our good mother Holy Church. I'll have every prelate's whore, every priest's mount, in every possible way (to keep them in the habit) until Satan's fatherly arms receive my bachelor's soul, and I can go and fuck the dead!

XII
Le marquis de Sentilly

from *Le Rideau levé, ou l'Éducation de Laure* (1786)

Like Thérèse philosophe, *this is also a first-person narrative in a convent setting, closely linked to the thematic and formal conventions of the 'mainstream' eighteenth-century novel, but this time in the tradition of sensibility. Laura is writing her life story for the benefit of the novice Eugénie, whose seduction she engineers in the second episode. In the first, she describes her own seduction by the adopted 'father' whose death she is mourning in the convent.*

The book has also been attributed to Mirabeau, but the tone is too sentimental, pretentious and cliché-ridden for this to be convincing.

Nothing seems to be known about the marquis de Sentilly.

Laura Deflowered

All daylight was barred from the room. There was a bed draped in blue grosgrain set in an alcove surrounded by mirrors. The rays of four lamps set in the corners and dimmed with blue gauze focused on a little cushion of flame-coloured satin placed in the middle, the stone on which the sacrifice was to be consummated. Lucette swiftly exposed to view all the charms with which nature had endowed me; for sole adornment, she decked her willing victim in flame-coloured ribbons, which she tied above my elbows and onto the girdle with which, like a second Venus, she marked my waist. My head, crowned only with its own long hair, had for sole ornament a ribbon of the same colour that held the hair in place. Of my own accord I threw myself onto the altar.

I had worn many fine clothes before, but I felt far lovelier clad in my beauty alone; I looked at myself in the mirrors with satisfied indulgence and a strange contentment. My skin was dazzling white; my little breasts, still so young, rose in front like two perfectly round half globes, set off by two little flesh-pink buds; a light down shaded a pretty, plump, swelling mound, slightly parted, allowing a glimpse of a clitoris like a tongue-tip between two lips, inviting pleasure and delight. A slim well-moulded waist, a dainty foot topped with a slender leg and a rounded thigh, pink-cheeked buttocks, shoulders, neck, a delightfully curving back and the freshness of Hebe! No, Cupid himself, had he been of my sex, could have rivalled none of my charms. In such language, Lucette and my father vied with one another in my praises. I was lost in a dizzy ecstasy of pride. The better pleased I was with myself, the more pleasing they thought me and the more delighted I was for the father so dear to my heart to enjoy to the full everything I could offer. He examined and admired me; his ardent hands and lips turned their attentions to every part of my body; the two of us were as passionate as two young lovers beset by obstacles, about to enjoy at last the reward of their patience and their love.

I was full of an eager desire to see him in the same condition as myself; I urged and insisted; and very soon he was. Lucette helped him out of all his clothes; he laid me down on the bed, my buttocks resting on the cushion. I held in my hand the sacred blade that was shortly to sacrifice my maidenhead. This prick, like a bee's sting, that I caressed so passionately, was so stiff that I knew it would pierce right through the rose he had so carefully preserved and tended. My imagination was aflame with desire; my little pussy, all afire, was thirsting for the dear prick, and I led it straight into the path. We held each other glued in a tight embrace, devouring one another with our mouths and tongues. I could tell he was trying to be gentle; crossing my legs over his buttocks and pressing hard, I gave an upward thrust that pushed him as far in as he could go. The pain he felt and the cry that escaped me signalled his triumph. Lucette, slipping her hand between us, began to fondle me, while her other hand tickled my arsehole. The mingled pleasure and pain, the flow of blood and semen, lifted me to unspeakable heights of pleasure and desire. I was swooning, dying; my arms, legs and head flailed in all directions; I was so intensely alive that I lost all sense of existence. I gave myself up to the delight of such extremes of sensation, almost unbearable. What a wonderful state that is! Soon I was taken from it by fresh caresses; he embraced me, sucked me, felt my breasts, my cheeks, my mound; he lifted my legs in the air for the pleasure of examining my arse and my cunt from another angle and seeing the ravage he had wreaked. Soon the prick I was holding and his balls, stroked by Lucette, went firm and hard again; he came back inside me. Now the passage was eased we felt nothing but ecstasy from the moment he entered. Lucette, still attentive to our pleasure, renewed her caresses and I sank into the same voluptuous apathy I felt before.

Proud of his victory and delighted by the sacrifice my heart had made, my father took the cushion from underneath me, stained with the blood he had caused to flow, and hugged it to him like a trophy, with the devoted enthusiasm of the fondest lover. Then he came back to us: 'My dear, lovely Laura, Lucette enhanced your pleasures; would it not be fair to let her share them?' I flung my arms round her and pulled her onto the bed. He took her in his arms and set her beside me. I pulled up her skirts and discovered she was soaking wet: 'How excited you are, dear girl! I'd like to repay you a part of the pleasure I've had.' I took my father's hand and slipped one of his fingers inside her; he pushed it in and out, while I caressed her. She soon fell into the same ecstasy I had just emerged from.

Oh, dear Eugénie, what a delightful day that was! I confess, my dear, it was the loveliest day of my life and the first day I experienced the highest delights of sexual pleasure. I still remember it with a shiver of satisfaction impossible to convey, but also with cruel anguish in my heart. Why must a memory that gives me so much pleasure and joy also provoke the bitterest regret! Let's set aside for a moment the image that gives me such pain.

The room was full of soft warmth; I felt so comfortable in the state I was in that I refused to put anything on; I was giddy and gay; I insisted on dining clad only in my own charms. Lucette, attentive as ever, had taken the precaution of keeping the servants well away and drawing a heavy veil in front of their prying eyes. She was good enough to bring in and set out herself all we needed, and closed the doors carefully behind her. I wasn't satisfied until I had her just as we were; I pulled off all her clothing; I thought she looked charming. We sat down to eat. Sitting between the two of us, my father was the object of our caresses and paid them back to each of us in turn. The mirrors reflected the delightful scene; our attitudes and graces were varied by the witty inventions inspired by a fine wine; its brilliant colour added entirely new shades; we soon felt the effects of its virtues and our mutual caresses. Our cunts were inflamed; his prick had regained all its stiffness and resilience. In such an eager, animated state, we had no wish for the pleasures of the table; we flew in haste to the bed. On that day, which was entirely mine, I was once again plunged into the delights of supreme pleasure; he lay on my left, his thighs under mine, which were lifted up; his prick stood proudly at the gate. Lucette climbed on top of me with my head between her knees; her pretty cunt was before my eyes; I parted it, tickled it, and caressed her cheeks, stuck up in the air; her belly brushed my breasts, and her thighs lay between my arms. Everything about us stirred and animated the flames of desire; she pulled open the lips of my little pussy, which was bright red; I asked her to insert the sponge so that my father could enjoy me without fear of consequences and come inside. My cunt was painful and sensitive: it hurt when it was touched; but though the sensation was painful I endured it in the hope of soon having more pleasant ones. Lucette guided my father's prick into the path she had cleared of danger, that was now all flowers. He thrust and pressed in with eager haste, she frigged me and I did the same for her, while his finger in the maidservant's cunt performed the same movements as his prick did in me. This diversity, our positions, the multiplicity of objects and sensations in the preliminary moments of pleasure vastly increased its delight. We felt its approach; it seemed almost to slip from our grasp, like the brilliant flash of lightning that vanishes from sight, but at last we savoured it to the full in a delectable moment of annihilation whose entrancing sweetness words cannot express. We were growing tired; Lucette got up and went to put everything in order, and as soon as she came back we got into bed in one another's arms, where we spent a night that we thought preferable to the most glorious day.

Alas, dear Eugénie, why does imagination always so far outstrip reality . . .

The End of a Convent Education

I cared for nothing; I was completely lifeless; I hardly knew I still existed, except in my grief. I felt I needed a friend, but dared not hope to find such a one as I wanted. It was then I felt most keenly how much I missed Lucette. I thought she could never be replaced; much less did I imagine I would find her like under the mask that veils you. You offered me without disguise your temperament, your moods and your heart, together with your pretty face; for some time I studied it, and all my observations concluded in your favour; your trust and friendship inspired mine.

I repaid your confidences with my own and found in your arms the consolation you longed to give me. I still remember with satisfaction the night you said to me: 'Laura my love, my dear friend, I have good cause to know how acute is your suffering; but if by sharing my own with you I can help dull your overwhelming pain, I can at least enjoy the happiness of seeing your grief diminished.' You judged correctly that if I could keep so closely reserved the secrets of my own heart, I would also respect yours; and you were not mistaken. I can still hear your voice: 'Listen, dear, I am in love, as deeply in love as any woman can be, and it's my cruel misfortune to be clad in a religious habit. Honey-tongued, deceitful nuns surrounded my youth and inexperience with walls and bars and enticed it into their hellish prison. I am tortured by my ignorance, by my vows, by prejudices of all kinds; my desires are the executioners and I am the victim. At night, sleep flees my eyes and tears take its place; by day, all seems barren and burdensome; my mind is always elsewhere. Can you picture the state I am in? You at least are free, and need not fear to yield to your lover those charms I have seen and can touch.'

The hand you laid on my breast made me tremble. 'Ah, dear Eugénie,' I said with feeling, 'there's the origin of my despair! I have lost the lover I worshipped, death has taken him from me. Oh Heaven, if only he were here! But he is, yes, here he is in my arms!' I was holding you in a tight embrace, victim of my own delusions. Alas! As I ran my hands over your charms, their nature brought me back to myself; a certain absence broke the spell of my imagination and the illusion it had created; but in its place your attractions inspired my tongue with all the praise you so richly deserved. Your bosom, your waist, your cheeks, your thighs, your mound, your skin – I admired them all. 'What pleasure for your lover and for you,' I exclaimed, 'if he could hold you in his arms as I hold you in mine!'

You longed for knowledge and instruction, but you hesitated; you tried to ask questions, but you didn't dare. I could see what you wanted; and at last you plucked up courage to ask if I knew what those pleasures were, and if they were indeed so great. I confessed that I did, and I drew a portrait that enchanted you, even though you still couldn't imagine them. 'You must try them yourself,' I said. 'What, gone seventeen and still ignorant of these things? If you like, my dear, I can at least give you a taste of their keenest delights.' Curiosity and desire, awakened by my caresses, kindling the fires of lust in every part of your body, induced you to agree. I forgot my own sorrow in my eagerness to console you in my turn and dispel the darkness of your ignorance. You lent yourself to my lessons. I parted your thighs and stroked the lips of your little pussy, whose roses had scarcely begun to blossom. I didn't dare press in my finger; you weren't advanced enough to know that the initial pain would increase your pleasure. I soon found the throne of delight, and under my caresses your charming clitoris plunged you into ecstasies you could hardly believe. 'Heavens, dear Laura, what supreme delight!' Then it was your turn to mistake me for your lover; I was covered with your kisses; your hands wandered all over my body. You tried to repay me the service I had just done you, but my heart, still too grief-stricken, was unwilling, and I stopped your hand. Soon I took you in my arms again, and with renewed caresses taught you more about that first moment that leads to the climax of pleasure. You were excited and easy to persuade. 'Well then!' you said to me, with that delightful vivacity that suits you so prettily; 'Do what you like with me.' I took hold of your little pussy again and plunged in the finger of one hand while I fondled you with the other. The mingled pain and pleasure made the experience even more delightful; and I, dear tender friend, was the lucky mortal who plucked your virginity, that rare, exquisite flower!

I could be more free with you now that you had discovered and experienced the charms of pleasure. I was ready now to open my heart entirely, to lead you along all its pathways, and to tell you in brief the story set out here in all its detail.

Pleasure and my hand were able to free you from the shackles of ignorance and the prejudices it breeds, but what a struggle I had to overcome your resistance on all other points! Fear of pregnancy no longer made you tremble; I had cured that with my story and my own experience. Your lover was already indebted to me for your first steps towards his happiness and your own fulfilment. But: 'Alas!' you told me, 'All the doctrines that cradled me as a child, up to the present day, the vows dictated to me, my veil, the convent bars around us, everything tells me no!' But your love and my help and advice disarmed your prejudices and overcame all obstacles. Dear Eugénie, you owe to me the calm of mind and the company you now enjoy. In every way, your lover's triumph is due to me; in every way, my friendship has been of service to you both.

First, however, I insisted on meeting this Valsay so dear to your heart, to study his way of thinking and to see whether he deserved your love, trust and favours. These tasks, as you know, were not accomplished in a single day. Women of finely trained judgement can penetrate men's hearts with a delicate, refined and certain touch, despite all their deviousness and duplicity and the veils behind which they try to hide. I was pleased, though, with de Valsay; I found enough in him to feel certain that I could without fear of risk do all that was necessary to satisfy your desires, assist your inexperience and banish your fears. It was fortunate that I was there in the convent to serve as a pretext for his passion while working in both your interests, because without my help your shyness and weakness would never have been overcome. Think back to that day when after some considerable time your suitor began to press you with ardent insistence to make him happy. I did all in my power to support him; you fought against it, although you wanted to. You opposed him with what you thought were compelling arguments; you presented him with obstacles that in your eyes were insurmountable; I felt sorry for you. I was sorry too for him, and made no secret of it; you were both, I could see, in a fever of passionate desire. The moment seemed propitious, and I was intoxicated by the idea of making you happy. 'Well then!' I said to you, 'I shall dispose of all your difficulties. Valsay, if what I'm about to do to make you happy makes you think ill of me afterwards, you're an ingrate and don't deserve your reward.'

I closed the parlour doors on our side, despite feigned objections; your lover did the same on his. I took you in my arms, drew you to the grill, and lifted your veil; he took hold of your breasts, kissed your lips and sucked the tongue you finally yielded to him; and then in a raging thirst of desire slipped his hand under your skirts to find and grasp your mound. I pressed you against him, and I embraced you too; you couldn't get away from me, nor pull your arms out of mine; and finally he had the skill and the satisfaction to lift your skirts and take hold of your sweet little cunny with all its fresh, youthful charms. His caresses inflamed you with the fire of passion with which he was already consumed; he cursed the pitiless bars that kept us apart and stood in the way of his enjoyment. I was aroused, and beside myself! 'What!' I said to your lover, 'So lacking in ingenuity! Ah, Valsay, true love makes child's play of such things. I

think I must love dear Eugénie more than you do; I shall prove to
her that my love makes all things possible and that nothing can stop
me from procuring her satisfaction; I shall oblige you both. If she's
left to her own devices, you're lost.' You finally gave in. I made you
climb on the bar supporting the grill with your hands on my
shoulders, while I held you up. Valsay lifted up the black habit that
set off the white splendour of your delightful cheeks; he touched
them, kissed them, and paid them all due honour. Your little
cunny, framed in one of the diamonds of the grill, was a living
picture that held him spellbound. He kissed it a hundred times and
then, eager to crown his happiness, slipped inside you while I put
my own hand between your thighs and caressed you. The pleasure
we sought to invoke with our caresses suddenly took hold of you;
you seized my breasts, kissed me, devoured me, and came! Valsay,
about to do the same, had the prudence to withdraw; his passion
expired between my fingers and spread over my hand like lava from
a volcano. I left you both to yourselves.

You contemplated the jewel I had so often described to you, took
it in your hand and caressed it, but without the facilities I procured
for you you couldn't make use of it again. When you came back to
me, you complained bitterly; but you didn't dare ask me to assist
again your lack of expertise. I was aware how much you wanted me
to; you begged and urged me not to leave you again. Cruel friend,
asking me to observe your happiness and pleasures when mine were
lost forever! My good-nature and my affection for you induced me
once more to offer you fresh assistance. My offers delighted you
and you overwhelmed me with kisses and caresses. I reminded you
then to take care and make use of the sponge and you swept me off
to be present at your ecstasy and the enjoyment of your happiness.

You showed me the god that Valsay bore, the god you adored,
and played with, and whose presence I had felt that very first time.
Every day you invented new follies; you showed him my breasts
and my most hidden secrets; I lent myself to your playfulness; you
made him touch them. What a state of excitement you put me in
between you! I whispered as much to you, and out of treacherous
compassion you revealed my secret. You wanted me to enjoy your
lover and him to receive my favours; you pressed me to grant them
to him; you wanted to lift me up to the place where you had been.
Your admission, your eagerness and his desire, of which you set
visible evidence in my hands, all incited him to press his suit. But I
continued to resist; your prayers, his solicitations and even the fire

coursing through my veins could not bring me to it. No, dear Eugénie, no, you hope in vain for his victory, for I shall never consent. You are wrong to reproach me, for my motives are neither dislike nor indifference; Valsay destroys the one and is incapable of inspiring the other. Your friendship alone is enough for me. After the loss I have suffered, I am renouncing forever all intimate relations with men, and I shall be firm in my resolution. You must by now be convinced of this; for notwithstanding your own pleasures, the caresses you exchanged and those I myself received, although I saw and touched your most intimate parts, and though your transports of passion stirred and confused my senses I have not allowed myself to be persuaded. I was satisfied and content when at night you held me in your arms and calmed the flames you had lit that day.

XIII
Pierre-Sylvain Maréchal
(1750–1803)

from *Contes saugrenus* (1789)

Lawyer, librarian, journalist, novelist and militant atheist, Maréchal was famous for the 'popular, crude, filthy, belligerent and negative anti-clericalism' (C.-A. Fusil, Sylvain Maréchal, ou l'Homme sans Dieu, *Plon, Paris, 1936) fully evinced in the following short story. The tale of the Fairy Kyrie-Eleison, joining Voltairean irony to Rabelaisian obscenity, deflates the sexual pretensions of the powerful with a compendium of all the traditional jokes, euphemisms and puns.*

Maréchal's other works include the obscene Almanach des honnêtes femmes pour l'année 1790 *and a sentimental novel,* La Femme-Abbé *(1801).*

Perpetual Motion, or the Magic Gallery

> Every woman is made up of two parts: one the heart, or if you prefer, the soul; the other the body, or a certain something you can probably put your finger on better than I. The two parts are often in conflict. One sometimes won't have this or that but the other always wants it, and there's the source of their arguments. The part I'd rather not name, a haughty piece, hard to put down, is the one that normally wins the day – especially when it's not been getting enough to do.
>
> Vergier

Chapter 1

In the year 30998 before the Chinese era, Europe was governed by the Fairy Kyrie-Eleison.

'Ah!' exclaimed my Lord Archbishop. 'How fortunate we are not to have lived in those times, when neither Moses nor Christ had yet turned up, and everyone was necessarily damned.'

'Forgive me, your Excellence,' was my reply, 'there was no devil either.'

'That's a point,' the holy man answered, 'that hadn't occurred to me.'

This fairy was the richest and most powerful princess you could possibly imagine, but she wasn't at all happy. Tormented day and night by a certain itch in a certain spot, she had in her young days travelled Spain, Italy, France and Germany; she had visited every monastery and slept in every barracks, hoping to find a cure for her sickness, but it only increased as the days wore on. She had invented machines to fill the gap while her doctors were busy getting their strength back; but all in vain.

After many useless efforts, giving up hope of a complete cure, she resolved to take every day as much medicine as she could get, to have at least some relief for her pains. She carried out her resolution faithfully until she reached the nine-hundred-and-sixty-ninth year of her life and then she began to grow old.

Who would have thought the poor fairy would feel her illness much more in her declining years than she had in her youth? Such is the nature of the disease that it generally attacks a woman in the change of life with far more violence than a tender young sprig. The worst part of the whole business was that the poor fairy could no longer find doctors to offer her the least little cure. She was reduced to having the affected part rubbed night and day by her ladies-in-waiting and all that did was make the itch worse. A number of surgeons who tried out of pity to give her relief saw the instrument of the operation shrink in their hands until it was no further use: the local priests cried miracle, clearly recognising the finger of God. Other surgeons, tempted by the huge rewards promised by the fairy for a modicum of relief, tried their chances, first taking the precaution of turning her on her belly so they couldn't see her drab face and blindfolding themselves so they weren't forced to look at an arse that was very nearly as wrinkled and skinny. Even with all this attire, they had no success. As the instrument approached the part in question it was, so to speak, blunted by the roughness and hardness of the postern and straightway drooped its head. In short, these new champions met the same fate as those who had gone before.

Nothing is more natural in men than to envy others a pleasure they can no longer enjoy. This envy, together with the spirit of revenge which is equally natural in women, inspired in the bellicose fairy, her mind and brain seething away in search of monstrous new ways to vent her anger, one of the most cruel, horrible plans ever devised. She didn't stop to think it might not be the easiest thing in the world to pleasure a woman with weepy eyes and leathery skin, however much of a fairy she might be. She was determined to stop any man from giving any woman the relief denied her. We shall see now how she carried out her terrible design.

Chapter 2

One fine morning as Cardinal Crimson was about to do honour to a pretty penitent he had in his bed, he suddenly saw vanish from his hands the huge sprinkler with which he was about to spray her with holy water.

Pure respect for religion had led the pious fairy to begin her revenge with a man of the Church.

The holy Cardinal cried miracle. 'Well!' said the distraught beauty, 'If God wants to work miracles, why doesn't he work nicer ones? That's a miracle of a very stupid kind.'

'The decrees of Providence are impenetrable,' answered the priest, himself shocked by the strange adventure.

Alas! From that unhappy moment, the Lord Cardinal distributed no more holy water, having lost his sprinkler.

Abandoned by all his penitents, his life was more wretched than the lowest of his curates.

The same morning, Master Lozenge, king of the dandies, was about to thrust his little stick into his lady's sheath when it suddenly vanished out of sight. From that fatal moment, there was no dandy more foppish nor foolish than he. The same jokes which moments before everyone said were delightful found no favour; people called him boring company, a poor wit, a ruffian; he was cast off by good society and refused admittance to the gallant gatherings where once he had shone.

The poor gentleman was in despair at the loss of his delightful mascot, without which he no longer had the wit or the happy talent to please society.

Captain Swashbuckler had just lowered his pike against a crusty-eyed marchioness when he suddenly realised the devil had carried off his weapon.

The marchioness rummaged vainly in every nook and cranny of her hero's breeches. Alas! all to no avail: she got nothing.

'Hell and damnation!' cried the furious bully boy, 'It's total defeat. Devil take it! What misery to lose alongside an old marchioness what I've hung on to through a hundred battles and skirmishes.'

Master Fat-tub, who had slipped out of his wife's bed to bear his paunch to that of his humble serving-girl, lost between her sheets the only part of his body that still had some facility of movement.

From that fatal moment Fat-tub, deprived of his joist, never moved again and never thought another thought, having lost the only organ he could think with. His wife, finding her husband's drawers empty, quickly consoled herself for the accident with two raw lads: taken together, they made as much as her late husband.

As for Master Fat-tub's losing all his wits, she never noticed that at all.

Then there was a Recollect friar wearing himself out to little purpose over an old magistrate's wife who was cracked as a skiff in need of a refit. He was the first to notice the accident that befell him, but he didn't dare admit it; monks get so embarrassed.

The lady, wondering at the scant success of his efforts, said: 'Brother Elfin! I think you're making fun of me; really, it feels just as if you'd left your roll at home.'

The monk, as astounded by his strange loss as the fat dame wriggling under him, pleaded he must have been ambushed: but alas! Madam was still not satisfied.

Stripped of his only claim to fame, the monk, who was a great braggart, became a model of humility. Brother Chubby's convent (so he was called) soon felt the effects of this dreadful mishap. Once frequented by ladies whose wisdom and piety was of the highest repute, it now found itself abandoned, and lost all the alms once so freely bestowed on it.

Master Pot-belly, Mayor of France, suffered a like reversal while he was with the Queen.

The Court poet, Master Sweety, most tender and platonic of

lovers, had so far forgotten himself with a chambermaid that he mistook her for Pegasus and climbed on. Poets are so absent-minded! Ah! From that moment on, he was free to be as platonic as he liked.

But the really annoying thing was that the poor poet, stripped of his pen, could write no more of those delightful poems at which ladies blush for modesty and smile with pleasure.

In a few days his misfortune was practically universal. The effect was as miserable as can be imagined. The Empire was desolate. The wits cracked no more jokes. Monks had no more penitents. Even the doctors at the University would have become more stupid than before, if such a thing had been possible.

What else was to be expected? What can a man do, stripped of the part with which he thinks and acts!

Men of the Sword, the Law and the Church were wretches and scoundrels. The women said so publicly.

Those who were still men took care to keep well away from females of any kind, since they stopped being men as soon as they tried to make use of their manhood. There was such a famine that there wasn't a kitchenboy in the whole of the land so ugly that he couldn't have had the loveliest and highest-born of ladies.

However, as a faithful historian, I can relate to the honour of France that all the men preferred to keep what they'd got in their breeches sooner than sleep with all the duchesses in Paris. Morals have changed a lot in our time.

The more the men practised abstinence, the longer their bows stretched, but if they released them they were lost. Women, as we know, always have their eyes on that spot and their desires grew ever more inflamed. A few of the hardier ones were so forward as to force the men to lose their precious jewels – the greatest deprivation a man can ever experience, since to own one is his greatest claim to merit.

It was the excesses of female lust that forced men to conceal certain swellings from the ladies' eyes. That's why they took to wearing long tunics down to the knees, that were still being worn only fifty years ago in several countries in Europe.

It was also at this period when frequenting women was so dangerous that men began to use boys: a custom widespread since in Greece and Rome and still very fashionable in the city on the seven hills.

It was then that women first thought of relieving one another and doing without masculine assistance in their pleasures; a discovery which afterwards was much enjoyed by Sappho and in our day is still much used by pious women and nuns.

It was also at that time that women took to keeping monkeys and pet dogs; a strange taste, which has nevertheless persisted to the present day.

The distress of the State was great. It could however have gone much further without the Government paying the slightest attention, had not the King, coming back from the hunt, lost his spear while sticking a certain two-legged animal which was walking in the royal park waiting for his return.

To speak plainly, it was one of the King's mistresses, who brought down on him the same misfortune as everyone else.

As soon as the disaster struck the King, he called his council. After a debate of several hours which revealed nothing that couldn't have been said in a minute, it was decided to send ambassadors to Asia, to the great magician Pantaristokai-Tachistoprattore who ruled the other half of the world.

In those days all they knew was Europe and Asia. Even so the scholars of the time stated with total confidence that the Globe could only possibly consist of those two parts and pronounced with surprising assurance on its dimensions which they thought they'd got measured. It is true that they were disproved by subsequent generations, just as the scholars of our times will be disproved by their successors.

But what does it matter? The learned gentlemen enjoyed the admiration of their contemporaries; so what do they care for posterity?

Chapter 3

The ambassadors arrived in the courtyard of the palace of the great magician, who knew as much as he'd learned, and did as much as he could, and were granted an audience at once. They set out the situation so succinctly that after having listened to them for four hours the magician still had no idea what was going on. That was because the King had chosen for his important embassy the greatest speechmakers in his council, who were so keen to display their eloquence that they hadn't time to talk of the object of their journey.

But the rumour of the misfortune devastating France had reached the magician, and finally, with astonishing sagacity, he guessed what the envoys might want.

'Am I right in thinking, gentlemen,' he asked, after they had finished their speeches, 'that you've come to get back objects lost by you yourselves, your most Christian King, and the greater part of his humble subjects?'

The ambassadors were unending in their admiration of the profound wisdom of the magician, which had penetrated to the depths of their breeches, which were, in fact, empty.

The King, being a wise prince, had deliberately chosen ambassadors with a vested interest in the success of their mission. This is what every sovereign should do if he wants his business properly taken care of, and what no despot *can* do, since his interests are always separate from those of his citizens.

The ladies of Pantaristokai-Tachistoprattore's court had contrived to discover the wretched condition of the newcomers. The matter became public; so one can easily see how the magician knew what he did.

A noble soul, he was not only sorry for the sad state of the French but at the same time promised a cure.

He himself took the envoys into his storerooms, where the greatest marvels met their gaze.

There were philtres to inspire Kings with love for their subjects. The ambassadors wondered why all the bottles of this excellent specific were dirty and still stoppered.

'That,' they were told, 'is because no Monarch has yet drunk any.'

There were big bottles inscribed: 'Female modesty': but unfortunately there was nothing in them.

Financiers' honesty, scholarly moderation, and theological reason were supposed to be in other bottles, also empty.

The fullest bottles were those that contained the arrogance of fops, the pride of priests, the jealousy of authors, the follies of religion, flirts' embraces and the lust of pious women.

'There's a talisman,' said the magician, showing them some magic symbols, 'for giving wit; but no one wants it, everyone thinks he's got plenty.'

'Here's another,' he went on, 'to prove conclusively to scholars that they know nothing. They don't want that either. It's understandable; what could they do with a talisman that would only teach them what fools they are?'

Then he showed them the intolerance of priests, represented by a torrent of blood streaming into a huge bottomless basin, held in the claws of stupidity and despotism, the two immortal monsters.

Said the enchanter: 'That blood will flow until men regain their primitive rights, throw out their earthly tyrants, and rid themselves of their foolish fear of the eternal tyrant they've made up for themselves.'

The representatives caught sight of an enormous cage divided into a hundred thousand little kennels separated by iron grills, each with a monkey inside.

'Those are the different religions,' said the magician: 'they are all apish antics. No one knows which ape is the oldest, or which of all those before you is the greatest ape. But it's a problem whose solution is utterly unimportant for humanity. If men had any sense, they would throw the whole cage into the sea of forgetfulness.

'Without the iron grills that you see there, these bloodthirsty animals would tear out each other's throats,' went on the worthy master of the storerooms. 'They may be apes, but they're cruel as tigers and cunning as foxes. They often get through the grills to deal each other deadly blows.'

Around the cage, all the time, fluttered will-o'the-wisps and little sprites with grotesque faces.

'Those are opinions, hypotheses and prejudices,' said the enchanter: 'They're what the apes play with.'

Having showed the envoys all these rare things, he took a wand out of a cupboard and gave it to them, saying they should present it to the Fairy Kyrie-Eleison, who had in her palace everything that had been lost in France. He added that the fairy would be appeased by the gift and its marvellous virtue and allow every man to take his own again, so everyone would be happy.

The stick had the form of a priapus: but the rod was so long and thick virtuous Greece had not for a long time seen its like. Its virtue, said the old man, was that as soon as the fairy put it in the place where the problem was, it would start moving and go on for ever and ever. 'That's what the fairy needs, and what every woman needs. Until men invent this machine they will never be able to rely on the virtue of their women. It's the Perpetual Motion machine,' he added, 'all of your engineers are obsessed with it, and I've finally invented it after several centuries' study. Oh, your scholars are fools! They think they can make discoveries that require uninterrupted observation of nature over centuries, when they live only a few moments. And even in that short space they can't make their observations uninterrupted. Take off the time they need to eat, sleep, reproduce, recuperate, intrigue, jockey for positions, etc., etc., and how short is the time left them to think!'

Having humbly thanked Pantaristokai-Tachistoprattore for the care he had deigned to take for their well-being, the ambassadors took the liberty of asking him whether he had any more of these instruments; if he had, they begged him to grant them at least one more for the Queen, another for the ladies-in-waiting, and another for their wives.

The magician replied that he had only the one he had just gratified them with and he couldn't make more even if he wanted to, since nature took several centuries to produce such a wonder. Also, the wand he had given them would only work in the fairy's chasm: such was the will of fate. 'But say I had more,' he added with a smile, 'do you think I would be cruel enough to give them you? And would you be stupid enough to take them? These devices would bring disorder into your State. The women who had them wouldn't even lend them to their best friends, for they would always be needing them themselves. They could do without you completely, so they would treat you worse than they do now, when they sometimes remember you can give them pleasure. Those who didn't have them would be at the throats of those who did, and there would be a thousand times more hatred and envy amongst women than there is today.'

The representatives were men of such penetrating and subtle wit that they could understand anything when it was put to them as clearly as that. They appreciated, then, the arguments of Pantaristokai-Tachistoprattore, took straightway their leave, and hastened to bring joy and consolation back to their country.

Chapter 4

The rumour of the happy success of their mission preceded the ambassadors. The King and the people ran to meet them: and the King ordered the wand to be carried by two men on a pole, like the bunch of grapes the Israelites were later to bear, and to be offered immediately to the fairy.

They marched to her palace. She, being informed of the nature of the visit, received the envoys with all civility and tried out the wand in the presence of the King, the high Council and the clergy.

As soon as the mystic rod was inserted in the spot, the fairy was so tickled by it that she closed her eyes with delight and wriggled her behind with such violence that the sofa where she lay groaned under her.

There was no doubt now that what Pantaristokai-Tachistoprattore had promised was true. The witch, entranced by the fine gift, ordered her genies to fling open the gallery where she kept the treasures she had stolen from Frenchmen.

The fairy no longer envied others a pleasure she was now sure of enjoying for eternity. She had read in the stars that this was the true *perpetuum mobile* that the great magician Pantaristokai-Tachistoprattore had invented, and she thanked Fate for having cured her.

When the gallery was opened, the first object to meet the on-lookers' gaze was a relic set in gold, greater and lovelier than all the others.

Cardinal Crimson seized on it, thinking it was his, but his despair was terrible when that very evening, trying to initiate a young novice, he couldn't manage it, the relic being too big to fit into the cap of a little virgin nun.

By an unfortunate error, Brother Chubby got the Cardinal's cutlass. He went to the magistrate's wife to repair the wrong he had done to her; but alas! In her gaping chasm the lady could hardly feel such a tiny jewel.

By a like mistake, Lozenge got Swashbuckler's blade, chipped in several places; it had already been in far too many battles. What a humiliation for the fop, to take out that scarred spear in front of a dainty Countess.

The Captain was no less unhappy with the dandy's scented jewel, which had fallen to his lot. He preferred his own much-scarred thing, which had already fought so many campaigns, and was more experienced that the moppet of that young fool.

A tax-collector suddenly found himself with no foreskin, having stuck on himself a Jew's thing.

The poor Jew was thrown out of the synagogue because the tax-collector's, which he'd got, wasn't circumcised. There was only the foreskin's difference between the tax-collector and the Jew.

The poet Sweety absent-mindedly picked up the relic of a Turk: a mistake that did much damage to the poet's platonism.

The King girded on the Mayor's property and the Mayor claimed the royal sceptre.

'Oh, no!' exclaimed the Queen, 'that's my husband's!' and after that unfortunate mistake, the Mayor never dared appear at Court again.

The Kings's mistresses, who were well acquainted with the Mayor, recognised at once the equipment the King was wearing: but understandably they pretended not to notice.

Master Fat-tub, who had been given the tiny root belonging to a fourteen-year-old pageboy, had no idea how to get on with such a little bit of nonsense. It was hardly visible under his paunch, and his lady wife, used to her lads' exploits, was as badly off as he.

The disorder rife in this unhappy nation is impossible to describe. It suffered as much for the cure that had been brought as from the first catastrophe.

The great magician Pantaristokai-Tachistoprattore, who prided himself on his speed and efficiency, hadn't foreseen this problem. The King found himself forced to send a second mission to beg his help with the second disaster.

The magician, a little ashamed at not having foreseen a mishap he could easily have envisaged, gave the envoys an ointment, saying that anyone who put it on his eyes would be able to see clearly, so each would recognise his own.

He ordained at the same time that everyone should assemble on a great esplanade, where all the relics would drop off as soon as they were touched by the hand of a virgin, who should also speak certain words he gave them written out on a talisman; the eyes of the men then being opened, everyone could stick on again what belonged to him. He added that if that didn't work there was no other way of getting things back into the right place.

No sooner had the envoys brought back this message than new troubles divided the Empire.

The married women, jealous at not being entrusted with the disenchantment, and also afraid the men might be stripped for ever of their manhood if they parted with it a second time, refused to let the magician's advice be carried out.

After they'd been persuaded to agree, no one could find the virgin without whom there could be no operation.

People's first thought was for the little nuns; but alas! The monks had had them all.

Then it was the village girls: but the priests had been stripping all the villages.

In the towns no one even bothered to look for such a rare bird. If it were possible, town girls would lose their virginity before they were born.

After a long and difficult search they finally unearthed a virgin ten years old.

The people were summoned. Little boxes had been knocked up, where the women could stare and wink from behind their fans at the fresh miracle that was about to take place. But alas! A fat canon, first to come up for disenchantment, his eyes devouring the girl who was going to remove his equipment, the property of a Capucin gatekeeper, couldn't resist his lust. He violated the little girl in full view of the whole gathering before she could pronounce the words laid down by the magician.

As I said, she was the only virgin they could find. Once she was deflowered, things had to be left as they were; and that is the cause of the great disproportion still found among men as regards that particular part.

Every day, you see dwarfs amply provided with that which makes us pleasing to the fair sex and giants who are badly endowed. You see big noses that promise a lot and never perform.

Oh my friends! If the accursed canon had restrained himself but a little, you would not suffer such inconveniences.

And after that, surely we're right when we say that all the evil on earth is from the priests?

XIV
Nicolas-Edmé Restif de la Bretonne (1734–1806)

from *Le Palais-Royal* (1790)
L'Année des dames nationales (1791–94)
L'Anti-Justine (1798)

The next three extracts present a single sensibility in three very different styles.

Les Filles du Palais-Royal *(1790) is a relatively sober set of anecdotes purportedly based on on-the-spot interviews and observation. Restif sees himself as a new Petronius, charting the abuses of the* ancien régime *and bringing hitherto neglected subject-matter to public attention; whores too are French citizens, corrupted by the aristocracy, and about to be saved by the Revolution (*Le Palais-Royal, Vol.II, Introduction*). Despite its simple language and interest in practicalities, this is still an idealisation of the prostitute's existence; it is, however, less wild than the Utopian set of administrative proposals for State-regulated prostitution offered in 1769 in Restif's* Le Pornographe.

The tale of the Maid of Thionville, taking prostitution into the family, also has a documentary basis: the unhappy marriage of Restif's own daughter. The violence close to the surface of Restif's sensuality is here attributed to the son-in-law, as well as the desire to violate his daughter-figure, which is only made explicit in the angry and apparently gratuitous final disclaimer. The situations are melodramatic but the language, an uneven mixture of the crude and the sentimental, gives a paradoxical illusion of realism.

L'Anti-Justine *explicitly offers incest, as an antidote to the sadistic cruelties of* Justine *and with the daughter, Conquette, a far from unwilling victim. The desire to brutalise and humiliate the victim is again shifted to the*

*son-in-law and also, this time, to the traditional villain – the monk
Foutencul, who later tears to pieces the prostitute substituted for Conquette
and feeds her to his religious community. With the morality of true melo-
drama, the evil monks perish in agonies of syphilis. This is the pornographic
fantasy writ large, intense and highly personalised, with a confessional
frankness that privatises the clichés, down to Conquette's 'fuckable foot'.*

from Le Palais-Royal *(1790)*

17th Whore: Sophie

I looked hard for Dorine. I didn't see her, but I had the unexpected
luck to meet up with Elise. She said she had to go and collect her
child. I assured her she was such a beautiful woman that it would be
my privilege to walk along with her.

At that moment six girls appeared, the ones I mentioned in my
Preliminary Remarks under numbers 18, 19, 20, 21, 22, 23. They
were so striking that I was rather annoyed to have encumbered
myself with Elise. But that was want of foresight. The six nymphs
made just a moment's appearance, went inside again at once and
didn't return.

I asked Elise if she knew them. 'They're the *Houris!*' she replied. I
offered her the usual six francs for a half-hour's conversation. The
fair lady agreed to the bargain. But she insisted on having her child
with her: 'If not for your sake,' she said, 'then for mine. I want to
look respectable.' I observed that this was vice paying homage to
virtue. She admitted it. Then, since I knew her, I ventured a few
reproaches on the way she behaved with children. She cut short the
conversation then, and offered of her own accord to tell me over six
evenings the stories of the six girls we had just seen, including the
black and the mulatto. I was delighted and promised her six francs
for each session. She went to get the child, which I offered to carry,
and she began her story.

'The biggest, the dark-haired one, is called Sophie. She is sixteen
years old. There are thirty-six girls in the house, administered by a
strange woman whom her friends call Madame Ogret, though in
public she has another name. This woman taught geography and
had a lot of pupils. She was once married, and her four daughters
live with her. Her husband managed to have the marriage annulled
and is now married and living with another woman.

'As soon as Madame Ogret found herself designated his concubine, she gave up her teaching and came to live by the Palais-
Royal with her four daughters, Sophie, Angélique, Adèle and
Zéphire, who in all probability have four different fathers. (The
lady was known for her gallantry.) She told them what she intended
to do. The four girls burst into tears, threw themselves at their
mother's feet, and begged her not to turn them into prostitutes.
"That's my intention," said Madame Ogret, "but we can come to
some agreement." The bargain she struck with them was that they
would never have to carry an episode through to the end. For that
purpose, Madame Ogret took a number of whores into her house,
and her clientele has expanded so much that she now has twelve
living in, as well as the six you've just seen, and eighteen outside
(I'm one) who come when she asks them.

'Sophie isn't the oldest; that's Angélique. But Sophie is considered senior because of her figure and her particular attractions.
That child has been wretched all her life. Before he had the marriage
annulled, her father, who was a libertine, had let his wife go to a
journalist-editor priest, who had fallen in love with her, and to save
money had taken on a fat whore out of one of our brothels who used
to be a cook, and who cost him less than his wife brought in. He
kept two of the children, Sophie and Adèle. His wife had
Angélique, the eldest, and Zéphire, the youngest. The priest,
wanting to look respectable when he walked out with Madame
Ogret, used to hold Angélique's hand and have Zéphire carried by a
nanny . . . But let's get back to Sophie.

'From the age of six or seven, which is what she was then, she was
delightful. Monsieur Ogret's fat cook–concubine was a whore. He
knew that, and in fact, since he was terrifyingly ugly he'd chosen a
whore thinking she'd present fewer obstacles. But how could he
have foreseen what happened? There were days when he regularly
went out to dinner with the priest who had hired his wife, or various
managers of small theatres. People knew what time he would get
back. Fat Gillette took advantage of this to carry on her trade in her
master's house. She would go out, "pick up" a man, and bring him
home. At first she used to send the children out. But gradually she
came to neglect this precaution, and even made a point of dressing
them up. One day, one particular libertine declared Sophie delightful, and caressed her . . . Gillette realised then what a profit she
could make out of the two children . . . She coined in the money,
until Sophie's mouth became infected and the doctor had to be

called. The parents then made enquiries and learned from the neighbours of Gillette's strange behaviour! . . . She was put in prison, the
father went off to the provinces, all the children stayed with their
mother, and the priest was a good father to them. Unfortunately he
died. Ogret came back, took advantage of the new divorce law to
put an end to his marriage, which didn't look very sound, and
married again. The mother had been teaching geography since the
priest died; she found things too difficult, and made the decision I
told you of.

'Once her mother had set up her new establishment, Sophie
remembered the trade she'd been set to as a child. She backed up
what her mother said to her three sisters. But having learned the
hard way with the infection she caught, she gave them some useful
advice.

' "Dear sisters," she said, "we shall do what our mother wants,
and bring wealth into the home, at no cost to our health or beauty.
We shall be *Houris*, artists, spiritual whores, and we shall get vile
unprincipled creatures to take care of the material side of the business. Watch me for a few days from this dark room, and after that
you can copy me. No one shall as much as lay a finger on my breast.
I intend to keep it pure, and the rest as well. My mouth shall never
suffer another's touch. As for common embraces, I'll have nothing
to do with them. We owe everything to our mother, now our father
has so cruelly abandoned us, but I don't intend her plans or our
condition to stop us finding a husband and bringing him the flower
of our virginity like any respectable girl. And don't imagine, sisters,
that what I'm suggesting will bring in less money! On the contrary,
men take immense pleasure in a virgin's caresses. All we need to do
is make sure we change places quickly. I mean to invent a new kind
of pleasure. They'll have all four of us. That will stop them growing
forgetful, fickle, or weary. The moment of satisfaction a fifth girl
will take care of, so they won't tire of us, but of her . . . So just be
guided by me."

'And that was what Sophie said. Her sisters kissed her, deeply
moved, and her mother was full of admiration. She was declared
their senior.

'That very same evening, while her mother still had only one
outsider working for her, she put the theory into practice. Madame
Ogret went out alone and "picked up" a man. When she came back,
she handed him over to Sophie, who had been rehearsing her three
sisters. Sophie took him in hand, and Angélique replaced her when

she slipped away. The young blonde was dazzlingly beautiful, and soon the mark was completely captivated. She slipped away in her turn, and the man fell into Adèle's arms! He was astounded . . . but no sooner had he satisfied the sense of sight, to which the four sisters were allowed to refuse nothing, Zéphire appeared and Adèle slipped away. The man tried to take his pleasure with the lovely child. Zéphire had a natural talent, and raised him to feverish heights . . . Then the journeywoman appeared and finished the job with the minimum of skill.

'Madame Ogret had seen everything. She wept with joy, kissed her daughters, and said these remarkable words to Sophie: "Sophie! Well named indeed, for you have true wisdom! Sophie! I am your mother, but I shall do as you say, even more so than your sisters! You're the mistress here, and everything shall be done as you command!"

'And indeed, Sophie runs things admirably. She has girls of every type; it was she who arranged the purchase of the black girl and the copper-coloured one, and put them with the Houris to make a group.

'Sophie has acquired a suitor out of the men who've seen her. This man, who's quite respectable, made careful enquiries into Sophie's conduct, and is now head-over-heels in love with her. But though she loves him she hasn't yet granted him her flower. She wants to get married and he's made his mind up to it. But he won't get anything until everything is signed and sealed.

'Tomorrow I'll tell you Angélique's story. I think you've had your money's worth today for your six francs.' Elise left and I came home to write down the extremely odd and amazing story! Paris! Paris! what a strange city! . . . But the Revolution will cut down on such abuses!

from L'Année des dames nationales *(1791–94)*

22 February: Maid of Thionville Defiled by Her Vile Husband

Thionville, seventy leagues North-East of Paris, is a fortified town in French Luxembourg, on the Meuse, which is crossed at that point by a fortified bridge.

In this Calendar, the characters shown are as varied as the regions. We see here reviewed all the fancies, whims and prejudices of men . . . and of women, and sometimes their most loathsome vices, as in the present tale.

Agnès Roussi, born in Thionville to an honest man distinguished by exceptional merit, was endowed with all possible charms, sound intelligence and an excellent heart. In her youth, she was doted on by her father and was his only comfort in the many sorrows and great suffering caused him by his wicked wife. When she grew up, Agnès was pained to see her mother's wrongdoings, of which she had clear evidence on more than one occasion. Her unnatural mother was jealous of her because of her beauty and spread slanders about her as soon as she was sixteen; Agnès, in her misery, decided to ask a childless aunt if she would take her into her home . . .

It was at her aunt's house that the girl had the misfortune to be seen by a villain from Paris, and the greater misfortune to take his fancy. The monster, black in body and soul, was called Guae. Pretending to be wealthy, he asked for Mademoiselle Roussi's hand in marriage and managed to deceive her aunt. The aunt impressed on her niece that her father, frustrated by his wicked wife, would never be able to set her up properly; that he was wretched, persecuted by such a Fury; that she had another sister, who was the apple of her mother's eye; and so since here was a suitor with an income of a thousand crowns, on top of his situation, and the only son of an honest couple, she ought to take him despite his ugliness and his repulsive face . . . Agnès recognised the force of her arguments and relying on her aunt's assessment of his character and morals tried to overcome her repugnance for Guae's face. Little did she know that the eyes and the face are the mirrors of the soul, and the monster was as vicious as he was deformed . . . Guae was introduced to Monsieur Roussi, a good judge of men, who declared from the first that he would have none of the man. The aunt, completely taken in, got Agnès' mother on her side. The girl herself was urged to plead with her father . . . There's no better way to bring an affair to a successful conclusion than to further it through the person who will lose by it. That individual, trying to persuade a third party, manages to persuade herself, and is amazed to find she now wants the thing she had shrunk from. That was Agnès' position. Rendered powerless by an aunt she trusted and a mother she feared, she repeated their arguments as though they were her own, went against the views of a father she worshipped, and married against his wishes.

She was very soon sorry. On the first night, this honest, decent girl found she had been handed over to a Parisian libertine with all

the vices of an office clerk, that most corrupt of all men, and was
forced to swallow all the foul inventions of his filthy lechery. She
was stripped naked, examined, praised and defiled . . . by the eyes,
the hands and the mouth of the villain. Agnès tried to stop him,
dying of shame . . . How would she have felt if she had known that
two of the scoundrel's friends, that he had hidden there himself,
could see all her charms and were sullying them with their wicked
eyes? . . . In bed, there were fresh infamies. The two witnesses
could see and hear them, because the despicable Guae had left two
candlesticks with four candles burning. 'Come on, do your duty!'
And her duty was an act of turpitude . . . 'Help me!' the innocent
girl cried. 'That's good! A virgin! I can tell! etc. . . . ' Tired by his
long excesses, all retailed by his ugly mouth, the monster finally fell
asleep. This was of no benefit to Agnès, who fell prey to fresh
horrors . . .

In view of the heat (it was June), Guae had thrown himself into a
single bed. His two abominable friends, excited by what they had
just seen and by the sight of the naked Agnès, who got up to wash as
soon as she heard the monster snoring, agreed to take her in turns.
Agnès unwittingly assisted them by putting out the four lights.
They tossed a coin and one of them went first to replace the husband
. . . Agnès, beginning to drowse off, thought it was Guae, and
resigned herself. The despicable creature was deep asleep. The
second friend succeeded the first, when the latter left off satisfied,
and she had to respond to the spurs of a fresh rider . . . The unhappy
young woman, completely inexperienced, thought miserably that
all her nights, in future, would be spent like this . . . They left her at
daybreak, without Guae ever once waking to her cries. Agnès,
exhausted, slept in her turn.

Guae was first to wake up, got out of bed, slipped on a dressing-
gown and went to find his worthy friends, who paid him ambigu-
ous compliments that the vile fellow, stupid as he was, only half
understood. He next offered to show them the perfect charms of his
sleeping wife. He put them in position and without too many
precautions uncovered all he wanted to show. Agnès was still
overwhelmed with exhaustion and gave no sign of life but the
voluptuous rise and fall of her bosom . . . The despicable Guae, her
shameless owner, profaned every sanctuary in front of his friends.
'Be grateful for just one thing!' they said to him. 'If it weren't for
that, we would tie you and gag you, and take your wife right in
front of you.' Guae laughed horribly at the threat. He let Agnès

sleep on, so she would be fresher, and ordered a cold bath. As soon as she was awake, he made her get in it in his presence (his friends saw everything) and held a strange conversation with her: 'Did your mother tell you what a husband would do to you?' 'No, certainly not!' 'Well, now you've got some idea.' 'Ah, marriage is a terrible thing!' 'Ha! You don't know everything yet! In your new condition, you have to stay clean as a whistle, and after the . . . ' (pointing to the chamber-pot) 'you must sponge yourself clean. For your husband, you have to be completely visible and completely accessible.' 'Heavens, what a way to talk!' . . . He said and did even worse than that, excited by the libertine ideas he must be stirring in his two friends . . .

During that day, Agnès was downcast. She had a talk with her aunt and her mother together. What she said amazed them! They asked for details, and the ones Agnès gave seemed to them frightening, inconceivable, and in fact unbelievable . . . They thought her imagination must be distorting and magnifying what had happened . . . They invited the husband to a private talk and remonstrated with him. The monster burst out laughing. 'What! Twenty-four times! How can you possibly keep it up?' Guae looked astounded at the triple count. He admitted what was true and denied the rest. He added with a snigger he thought his wife was a woman with a good appetite, and she'd tripled the dose in her dreams. He went to fetch Agnès. But she refused to say a word about such things in front of him. After he'd moved out of hearing, she went into even more particular detail of what had happened. Guae, suspecting as much, had crawled closer on hands and knees until his head was at Agnès' feet and he heard her stories. He was extremely surprised by the naïve detail he caught. He could see his wife was innocent, but he had his suspicions of his two friends.

He went to find them and stunned them by saying his wife had recognised them in the night and just confessed everything to her aunt and her mother. They blushed and were in some confusion. However, they denied it resolutely and even offered to fight Guae, which he refused. He had to admit that he hadn't recognised himself in certain details he had overheard his wife giving her aunt and mother, and had wanted to test them both. He was still no less convinced he had been dishonoured, and was quite sure of it the next night when he had his wife describe in detail the three different ways she'd been taken. He recognised the techniques of the two traitors, and when she told him the times things had happened –

which weren't his – it confirmed the fatal discovery.

Beside himself with rage, he said to his wife: 'You've been defiled. I'll forgive you if you help me get my revenge. Those jokers will be back in Paris before we are, and they mustn't be able to boast to my friends that they've had you.' 'What do you want me to do?' 'Smile at them, lead them on. Then I'll catch them.' 'I shall never, ever smile at them.' 'Yes you will, or . . . ' (he did despicable things to her) 'you will, or I'll torment you like that every day.' Agnès saw she was lost. But what could she do? . . . Her father had not been to the wedding; he was broken-hearted by it all . . . She said nothing, even to her aunt, and obeyed the monster's instructions as best she could.

Emboldened by this first success, next night Guae set out all his plans in detail. 'They've had you,' he said to his wife, using the crudest terms possible, 'and they shall have you again. I've changed my mind. You can be wife to all three of us and each one can pay for you for a week. You can go one week to Duval and the next to Lépinai. They've had you, so they can have you again; it's the only way I have to keep them quiet. If you refused, it would do you no good! . . . You belong to me. Your father doesn't want to see you again, and your mother told me to be hard on you . . . My friends agreed everything with me this morning. You'll belong to three men and a lot of women would like to be in your shoes. If I need a patron, you'll get me one. You're pretty; that's your dowry, and I intend to use it.' This brutal speech was an ordeal for Madame Guae. She said nothing in reply, simply repelling the monster's caresses. He knelt at her feet . . . She looked enchanting that day! She wore a short, well-cut dress, her feet were charmingly shod; her foot not the smallest, but the shapeliest in the world, instead of spoiling her shoe, increased its charm; her complexion, usually pink, was lily-white; there was a touching languor in the blue eyes under her ebony brows. Such was Agnès. The rutting monster bellowed with lust. But he concealed his feelings . . .

Eager for revenge, he left the next day. In Paris, the odious Guae realised his evil plans. His two accomplices assisted him. The monster had no delicacy of feeling. Once satisfied, Guae was happy to hand over his wife . . . When his desire for her returned, he was furiously jealous . . . What more needs be said? Nowadays there are no laws, no swift justice, no help to be got from magistrates. One evening Agnès was taken by the monster to one of his friends and left naked, locked in with him . . . She tried to struggle . . . Guae came back, tied her legs to the bedpost and held her arms . . . He unfastened her each time, and washed her, so that Lépinai could satisfy all his caprices (to harden himself, he had exhausted himself three hours before). He treated Agnès like this all night . . . The next day she tried to run away. She was caught and locked in . . . In the darkness, she was deceived . . . The two despicable friends got their way by these methods.

Agnès bore a son, who looked like Duval, and Guae tried to kill him. He was prevented. He was foully abusive and from then on would call his wife nothing but Madame Duval. From that time, he made her perform lewd movements for him, and if she refused he *spurred her on*, that is, suddenly twisted the flesh of her arm. He went further. As a result of his jealousy, he conceived the horrible notion of taking her to a brothel to make love to her there. In that way he got the Madam used to seeing the unsuspecting Agnès coming in quite freely. One Sunday evening, when everything was ready to carry out his foul plan, Guae took his wife there and told her to stay, saying he would come shortly to collect her. What he wanted was to degrade the woman Duval had made a mother. As he left, he told the Madam she could make use of the woman and make her earn something. The delighted woman, whose best customer had just arrived, told him she had a *new girl*, and introduced Agnès. The old libertine was charmed by her and paid over a louis. Left alone with the surprised Agnès, he addressed her decently, and she answered in the same way; they were soon laughing together. All of a sudden the man pulled off her fichu, saying; 'There's a fine bosom!' Agnès thought she must have been sold and betrayed; however, the only person in the world she was afraid of was Guae and he wasn't there, so she thrust the insolent creature away. He insisted; she stared at him scornfully. He hit her . . . The house was in uproar! The watch arrived. Agnès was handed over. The Madam said what she knew about her: that she had been in her house several times, that day in particular, with a man she'd picked up. The watch passed on what was said to the Commissioner, who, being at supper, refused to listen to Agnès, who was sent to Saint-Martin. The following Friday, she was sent straight to the Hospital; the Lieutenant of police never asked questions, just passed sentence. She was locked up for three months with prostitutes without anyone coming for her; Guae, the only one who knew, not having dared tell his two friends. Agnès was only able to speak to the Sisters the day she was due to leave. Certain that the dreadful Guae was waiting to get her in his clutches again, she begged them to keep her until she got an answer from her father, to whom she was about to write. They reluctantly agreed, but only after they saw her letter.

The answer came after a week, brought by Monsieur Roussi himself. He took charge of his daughter. He took her not to Thionville but to Morhange, where he entrusted her to the most respectable of his friends. She became like a daughter to them, and there she still lives, among decent, moral people. Incredibly, the despicable Guae, still unpunished, is spreading the rumour that she is her own father's mistress, kept by him in secret . . . We publish this dreadful tale at the request of Monsieur Roussi and Madame Guae.

from L'Anti-Justine *(1798)*

The Wicked Husband

The moment is coming when I shall get Conquette-Ingénue back again. My greatest desire, even when I lay in the arms of Victoire's friend Madame Moresquin, was to cuckold Vitnègre! Conquette met me one day on the bridge of Notre-Dame. She was unhappy and she came and threw herself into my arms. I was so moved that all my old anger evaporated. My delightful daughter was even lovelier in her sufferings. My first impulse was to take hold of her cunt. But we were in the street . . . I went straight to see her the following evening, at the time she had told me her husband, or rather the Monster, was never at home. And indeed, I found her alone and at this very first visit she admitted she had a lover. I was delighted to hear such a secret; it indicated to me that Vitnègre was due for cuckolding. I caressed and coaxed her, and urged her to let Timori (her suitor) put it to her. But I soon gathered that it was a completely platonic affair on both sides, and Conquette-Ingénue was consoling herself with a limp prick for her debauched husband's brutalities. She enjoyed talking about her lover. And since I was the only person she could talk to safely, and I promised besides to help them see each other, she was very affectionate with me.

On my second visit, Conquette told me some of the vile things Vitnègre had recently been up to. One day, as she was bending down to pick something up, he got one of his friends to take hold of her cunt. She screamed. 'Feeling a cunt is nothing,' said Vitnègre, coldly . . . And to his friend: 'Didn't I tell you her cunt hair was smoother than silk? . . . And inside is even smoother . . .' Conquette made to leave the room. He pulled her brutally back, put her across his knees, pulled her skirts up over her thighs and held her cunt, trying to show it off, or caress her, and all the time saying how much pleasure she gave when she was fondled, if she wanted to. 'She's like a whore, though,' he added, 'you have to thrash her to make her do her duty.' Then he tried to uncover her breasts. She got away. But he caught her with a kick . . .

A few days later the same friend came to dinner. After coffee, noticing his wife had pissed and washed herself, Vitnègre said to the friend, Culant: 'Her cunt's pretty clean! Why don't we both suck her off? We could do it by trick, or use force – though if it's got to be force, don't be surprised at the noise she makes! . . . If you want to try the first way, here's a key; it opens the door of the little room that gives onto the corridor. You come in when I get tired, and I say very loud: "Come on, Madame, show me your fine cunt, and let's do it again." And give it to her! I'd like to see the whole world fuck the bitch, she's not wide enough . . .' They called Conquette back in. The husband made her sit between them in front of the fire, took out his mulatto's prick and balls and told his friend to do the same. Seeing him hesitate: 'Get his breeches off at once, bitch, or I'll tear out your cunt hair in handfuls!' He reached out to her cunt; she cried out. Culant exposed his prick and balls straight away, asking Vitnègre to let her off. 'Right then, bitch, jerk us both off, one in each hand . . . I'm her master,' the villain said, 'she's completely in my power.' Conquette was crying. The friend asked Vitnègre again to let her off . . . 'All right, shall I make her suck my prick, down here in front of me, on her knees, and I'll come in her mouth? I used to come in my first wife's mouth, she died of it, but I used to love it.' Culant pointed out it would ruin a very pretty little mouth. 'All right, I'll suck her off.' 'I'd get too hard if I saw that!' said Culant. 'Go into that other room.' Vitnègre pushed Conquette into the room, and sent in Culant in his place. Then he went out gaming. Culant sucked off Conquette, but didn't dare fuck her; his prick was so small that she couldn't have mistaken him for Vitnègre. He still came six times, and Conquette twice as many. Then he left, giving her a thump to convince her it was Vitnègre. But when he got back that evening, the monster said to his wife: 'Well then, you bitch, did you get well sucked off? It wasn't me, I wouldn't do you the honour of coming six times; it was that friend of mine. But you knew it was him, you whore, you came twelve times and you never come for me. Good clout he gave you, hey? Did you feel it?' The villain burst out laughing. 'Right, you bitch of a lawyer's bastard, now you're a whore, and I mean to make something out of that cunt of yours.' Terrified, Conquette swore to herself she would leave him. It was the day after that that she met me, and from then on she started to resist the monster.

I found my daughter's story revolting, though she told it more discreetly than I have done here. I promised her immediate help . . . . At the same time, like all tales of licentious brutality, it made me stiff as a Carmelite. I asked might I have certain favours? She blushed; but she let me kiss a pretty green shoe she had on for the first time. I was satisfied with that. However, on the next day's visit I laughingly slipped my hand up her back, and without her realising got round to her breasts; she struggled then, but I won. Then I got a lock of her hair; and then, to see how far I could get without frightening her off, I pestered her for a little tuft of hair from her silky cunt. She gave it me, but she was terrified her husband might notice! To calm her down again, I got her talking about her lover and during this conversation one liberty followed another and I got to her cunt. She was so engrossed in her subject that I think in fact she thought it was Timori with his hand on her mound! . . . I told her while I was fondling her that I'd found her somewhere to stay when she left Vitnègre. She blushed with pleasure and kissed me . . . I put my tongue in her mouth and she touched it with hers . . .

Delighted, I was about to ask her to tell me how she lost her virginity when we heard Vitnègre. I dashed into the dark ante-chamber, intending to escape by the door into the corridor. To my extreme surprise I saw a monk being let in by that door! He didn't see me; I hid behind a large couch. Vitnègre came in immediately by the door of the room I had just left. 'Reverend Father, do you want to fuck her before dinner?' The monk, his eyes devouring pretty Conquette through the glass, seemed lost in thought . . . A moment later he answered: 'No; go into the room where the light is, as we agreed, play with her, and show me her breasts, her arse and her cunt. I want to keep myself for tonight.' 'Oho! That'll cost you extra.' 'No; I like fucking in bed, sucking tongues, breasts, fucking cunt, arse, breasts, all the rest, biting, tearing off nipples . . . Go on . . . Get your prick out and get her warmed up . . . Be rough with her!' Vitnègre took off his breeches and went into his wife, who was still frightened of him. 'Come on, bitch, I want to fuck, don't I?

You see how hard I've gone, just looking at that pretty green shoe?
. . . I heard a silly bastard behind you yesterday saying he'd like to
come in it . . . Get your kerchief off, so I can see your breasts . . .
Hey, they're pretty, white and plump! Hey, you bitch, I'd pull this
pretty bud off if I weren't frightened of spoiling them! . . . Walk
. . . What a rump for fucking! . . . Get your skirts up, you whore,
over your backside and your navel, so I can see what you've got . . .
Forward, show me your cunt . . . Turn round and show me your
arse . . . That's a pretty movement! . . . Go on, bitch-arse, bitch-
cunt, until I say stop . . . ' (She walked round a hundred times,
showing arse, cunt in turns) . . . Meanwhile, the monk was saying
to himself: 'That bastard's prick's not as big as mine, and he couldn't
take her! Ho, she'll shout tonight! . . . I wouldn't want that; I'd kill
her! She'd yell loud enough to bring the neighbours . . . I'm off.'
He slipped out, muttering: 'She's got to be killed; I shall kill
her! . . . '

At the same moment, Vitnègre said: 'Stop, you double-bitch.'
Then he came into the antechamber. 'What do you say?' he said.
'Do you want to try her?' I was as stiff as could be; I answered softly,
in the monk's place: 'Yes.' Vitnègre went back for his wife and
pushed her roughly in: 'Come on, by God, you bitch of a whore,
let's fuck you! . . . Ha, you're going to shout! But think on, bloody
doll's cunt, don't fetch the neighbours! Or I'll let them all in here
without getting off your bloody belly! . . . ' With these words, he
threw her onto her back with her skirts up, over the couch put in
there just for that, and left the room.

I leapt onto my daughter, who felt it slip painlessly in her and let
out . . . not a sound. 'Scream, will you!' I said softly. And she
shrieked her head off, realising she was being screwed by a stranger.
As soon as I came, with a delightful spasm that made her whole cunt
shiver, I slipped away before the neighbours turned up. She was still
screaming, so I sent them in to help her. When they went in, she was
standing up. 'I was just screwing my wife,' said Vitnègre. 'Take a
look; her thing's still covered with it. She's like a cat; she bites and
screams when she's enjoying it.' The neighbours laughed, and went
out again. Vitnègre had his supper and was fairly well behaved. He
was afraid his wife might find out she'd been fucked by a monk and
tell people. I dined in a bar opposite the house. I saw him go out and
went straight back in to my daughter, who told me the whole story.
To begin with, I said nothing.

I got her to tell me how she had, or so I thought, lost her

virginity. It was a story I really wanted to hear, and I knew it would
arouse me enough to fuck her again. She complied as soon as I had
got her in the right frame of mind by making her think about her
lover.

'Our first night and the next three each earned Vitnègre five
hundred louis, according to what he told me afterwards. As soon as
we got to his house, he lit four candles and stood them round the
bed and threw me back on it with my skirts up round my waist. He
turned me over and back again, examining me, kissing me everywhere. He made me lift my legs up in the air and then stand up on
the bed. "Wriggle your arse," he said, "like this, look" (showing me
how), "as if I were fucking you." I told him that wasn't decent.
"That's enough! A wife is her husband's whore." He sucked me off.
He yelled at the top of his voice: "She's coming!" He made me get
hold of his huge member, big and black as a horse's. "Come on then,
let me fuck you, now this minute." He threw himself on top of me.
But he couldn't do anything. "Bugger me! They're lying bitches
who say your father took your virginity; you're virgin enough for
four. I wish everybody were here, to see with their own eyes . . ."
He rubbed me with cream back and front. He put out the candles
(my virginity was already sold) and pretended to get into bed. But it
was someone else; I was plagued all night by a huge prick that
couldn't do anything . . . ' At the bit in her story: 'She's coming!
she's coming!' I'd slipped a hand between my daughter's thighs,
meeting no objections on her part. At this point, I grabbed her cunt.
'Oh, father, are you going to be as hard on me as everyone else, and
on the day when . . . I've lost my virginity!' 'Lost your virginity!
Oh, my heavenly child! Is that really true?' 'No one has ever been
inside . . . what you're holding . . . until today.' 'Oh, my beloved
child, I'm not a man, I'm a god . . . You've made me too hard: will
you give me your precious favours? . . . or . . . I shall be in an
agony of cramp!' I swept her up in my arms and carried her into the
dark little room.

'You're all the same!' she said. 'Even my own father only wants
me for that hole!' 'And for your arse, your breasts, your mouth,
your eyes, your voluptuous waist, your provocative figure, your
legs, your fuckable foot, and your soul still so innocent and virginal,
despite all they've done to make you a whore.' As I spoke, I had her
bent over the bed and was pulling her skirts up at the back and
getting ready to take her from behind. I had to put cream on her.
She went on: 'It's my own fault! These stories set all the men on fire.

Timori only once came near to taking me and it was after that very same story, with a few less details.' In the meantime, she was pulling away from me so I couldn't get in. I complained tenderly: 'Do you want to make me ill, dear child?' She softened, and her lovely wide beautiful blue eyes turned moist. She bent over to put it in herself, helping me along, despite some pain, alleviated by the ointment, and said: 'When my sister and I saw you putting it to mother, all those times, over the foot of the bed, you used to shout out with pleasure! . . . Don't do that this time! Vitnègre might come back, might he not?' I promised to keep quiet, whatever ecstasy I felt . . . I pushed my way in. The lovely lady's pussy made little contractions. Satin was never so smooth as the inside of that heavenly cunt! And if it had been hairless it couldn't have been tighter. 'Ah, if your villain of a husband had known how priceless your divine pussy was he would have split you open even if it killed you.' 'No, he was afraid of spoiling me because his prick is too big. He frigs himself, or makes me frig him, with his fingers in my cunt hair, or his hand on one of my buttocks and comes . . . cursing . . . ' She contracted and came. I set off then, in sheer delight, yelling and shouting in spite of my promise: 'Wriggle your rump,' I called, over and over again, 'wriggle your cunt my angel, will you? . . . Good . . . Good! . . . And again? . . . Again? . . . ' She was contracting and coming again, and the bottom of her cunt was nipping and sucking the tip of my prick . . . I came three times without coming out of her and she came perhaps ten times. I could feel it by her convulsions. Finally, she swooned away . . . I came out as soon as her juices stopped flowing. She went and washed straight away, for fear that when Vitnègre came in he would take hold of her cunt and sniff it, as he usually did, even in front of people he brought in with him.

We went to talk in the light, to relax a little. I told her of the whole episode with the monk, for whose benefit Vitnègre had made her give the lengthy display of her arse, breasts and cunt. I described how big the monk's prick was, twice the size of the Monster's, and what barbaric delight the dreadful creature had shown at the prospect of splitting her open and killing her the next night, with his prick as big as a coach shaft . . . . She threw herself into my arms: 'Oh, father dear, save me, and I'm yours for ever!' 'Of course I shall save you . . . ' I explained how and why the fat monk had left, assuring her I would have stabbed him if he'd tried to rape her then and there. I told her in detail how her loathsome husband had given her to me in the belief that he was giving her to the monk, who had paid for her. 'You recall, my charming child, how I put it to you? It was I, against all hope and all likelihood, who robbed our enemies of your heavenly virginity.'

Conquette placed a pretty kiss on my mouth. 'But how are you going to save me?' 'I'll come for you in an hour, take you away from here, and you can spend the night in your new room. As soon as you're safe, I shall use your key to let the pretty whore from Port-au-blé through the dark antechamber and into your bed. I've already told her she's to come and spend the night with me. I shall keep watch. As soon as Vitnègre and the monk get here, I'll slip out. I'll listen to what happens, and we'll see tomorrow.' My daughter was delighted . . .

I shall indeed save her; but I would have done better to take her away at once. Instead, I diverted myself by hearing her story of what happened on the second and third nights of her marriage.

XV
Donatien-Alphonse-François, marquis de Sade (1740–1814)

from *Aline et Valcour* (1795)

Though he provided throughout the nineteenth century the (often suppressed) point of reference for most explorations or exploitations of the erotic, Sade's proper recognition as one of the most significant of French writers came only with Apollinaire and the surrealists in the early twentieth century. Scholarly editions of his novels, short stories, plays, political writings and voluminous correspondence are now plentiful, thanks largely to the efforts of Maurice Heine and Gilbert Lély; Bataille, Paulhan, Blanchot and Barthes have provided illuminating studies; Justine, Juliette *and even the* 120 Journées de Sodome *appear in respectable paperback in French and English.*

Aline et Valcour *is a novel that displays Sade's eroticism in its two modes, exotic fantasy and sentimental realism, and in its inseparable connection with the political responses into which he was drawn by social and personal circumstances. Eroticisation turns to commodity the suffering – moral and physical – imposed by an authority misusing excessive and undeserved power. The Président de Blamont, Aline's father, intent on exploiting the women of his household for his own pleasure, incarnates Sade's double resentment of his wife's family, who abused parental power to keep him in prison under* lettres de cachet *for a substantial part of his life, and of the* noblesse de robe, *the Parliamentary magistrates who displaced the old feudal nobility.*

In the episode that follows, 'Delcour' is Blamont, 'Mirville' the financier Dolbourg, to whom Blamont intends to marry Aline (on whom Blamont himself also has incestuous designs). These identities are disclosed later; at this stage, the reader has only just begun to suspect that the mysterious Sophie, discovered giving birth in the woods, could be the daughter of Madame de Blamont, whom her father had kidnapped and passed off for dead.

Incest, power abused, humiliation, threats, physical pain, tearful victim – there are here all the ingredients of the more familiar fantastic rituals of Justine *and* Juliette, *but more discreetly presented. In Sade's writing, extremes of outrage or transgression are linked to explicit fictionality; Sophie, by the current conventions of realism a 'rounded' character, is less subject to abuse than the cardboard figure of Justine.*

Sophie's Story

'My name is Sophie, Madame,' she said, addressing Madame de Blamont, 'but I would find it very hard to tell you anything of my family; I know only my father and I am quite ignorant of the circumstances in which I came into this world. I was brought up in the village of Berseuil by a vineyard worker's wife called Isabeau and was on my way to find her when you came upon me. She was my nurse, and she told me as soon as I was old enough to under-stand that she wasn't my real mother and I was only boarded out with her. Until I was thirteen, I had no visits from anyone except a gentleman from Paris, who, according to Isabeau, was the one who had brought me to her house and whom she told me in confidence was my father. Nothing could be simpler or more monotonous than the tale of my early years, up to the fatal moment when I was snatched from the refuge of innocence and cast against my wishes into the depths of vice and debauch.

'I was about to enter my thirteenth year when the man I speak of came to see me for the last time with one of his friends, the same age as he was, that is, about fifty. They sent Isabeau out and both looked me over carefully. The friend of the man I had been given to believe was my father was lavish with his praise . . . I was charming, pretty as a picture . . . Alas! It was the first time I had been told so, and it never crossed my mind that nature's gifts were to be the source of my ruin . . . and the cause of all my misfortunes! The two friends combined their scrutiny with a few light caresses; occasionally they even indulged in one or two which were entirely lacking in decency. . . . Then they spoke quietly together . . . I even saw them laugh . . . Why, then! Can criminal thoughts be a source of laughter? Can a heart be joyful hatching plots against innocence? Oh, the effects of corruption! And how little I guessed where they would lead! And for me the outcome was a bitter one. Isabeau was called back in . . .

' "We are going to take your young pupil from you," said Monsieur Delcour (that was the name of the man I had been told to look on as my father); "Monsieur de Mirville likes her," he went on, indicating his friend, "he'll take her to his wife and she will look after her like her own daughter . . ." Isabeau began to cry. I threw myself into her arms, as griefstricken as she was, and we mingled our tears and sorrow . . .

' "Oh, sir," said Isabeau to Monsieur de Mirville, "the child is purity and innocence itself, I know of no fault in her . . . Take care of her, sir, I would be in despair if anything bad happened to her . . . "

' "Bad?" interrupted Mirville, "I'm taking her from you to make her fortune."

ISABEAU: May Heaven preserve her from making her fortune at the price of her honour.

MIRVILLE: A wise virtuous woman, our good nurse! As they say: virtue's flown to the villages.

ISABEAU to Monsieur Delcour: I seem to recall, sir, you said on your last visit you would leave her at least until she had performed her first religious duties.

DELCOUR: Religious duties?

ISABEAU: Yes, sir.

DELCOUR: Well, hasn't it been dealt with?

ISABEAU: No, sir, she hasn't yet learned enough of her catechism; the priest put it off till next year.

MIRVILLE: Oh, my Lord! We're not going to wait till then, I promised my wife she would have her tomorrow . . . and I want . . . But really! Can't those wretched things be dealt with anywhere?

DELCOUR: Absolutely anywhere, and just as well at home as here. Don't you think, Isabeau, that there are as good guides for young ladies' souls in the capital as in Berseuil? . . .

'Then, turning to me: "Sophie, do you want to see your fortunes threatened when now's the time to settle them? . . . and the slightest delay . . . "

' "Alas, sir, " I broke in innocently, "if you're talking of fortunes, I would rather you settled Isabeau's, and let me stay with her for

ever." I fell back as I spoke into the arms of my loving mother . . .
drenching her with my tears . . .

'"There, there my dear," she said, pressing me to her bosom. "I
am glad you mean so well, but you don't belong to me . . . Obey
those who are responsible for you, and may you never lose your
innocence. If you fall into disgrace, Sophie, remember kind mother
Isabeau, you'll always find a bite of bread in her home. It may take
some effort to earn, but at least you'll eat it pure . . . it won't be
bought with shame, or watered with tears of sorrow and
despair . . . "

'"I think that's enough, good woman," said Delcour, tearing me
from my nurse's arms. "This tearful scene's very touching, but it's
holding us up . . . let's be off . . . " I was snatched up, we leapt into
a coach that swept along at lightning speed and got us to Paris that
same evening.

'If I had had a little more experience, what I saw, heard, and felt in
that coach would have told me long before the journey ended that
the duties waiting for me were quite different from those I had
performed at Berseuil, that my future destination involved something quite other than attendance on a lady, and that in a word the
innocence my good nurse had urged me to take such care of was
very near to being violated. Monsieur de Mirville, who I was sitting
next to in the carriage, soon made it impossible for me to doubt his
dreadful intentions. The darkness favoured his liberties, and my
naïvety encouraged them, Monsieur Delcour found it great fun,
and we reached the height of indecency . . . My tears flowed
profusely . . .

'"Blast the child," said Mirville . . . "it was going perfectly . . .
and I was thinking, before we get there . . . But I don't like hearing
them howl . . . "

'"Oh, come, come," said Delcour, "and when was a warrior
ever frightened by the noise of victory? . . . When we went for your
daughter the other day, round by Chartres, did you see me take
such fright? There was just the same tearful scene . . . but before
we'd got to Paris I had the honour of being your son-in-law . . . "

'"Ah, but you lawyers are excited by tears and laments," said
Monsieur de Mirville. "You're like hunting dogs, you never savour
the kill so well as when you've had the creature at bay. I've never
seen such hard hearts as Bartolo's henchmen. It's not for nothing
people say you swallow the game raw so you can have the pleasure
of feeling it quiver between your teeth . . . "

'"It's true," said Delcour, "that financiers are rumoured to be much softer-hearted . . ."

'"Faith," said Mirville, "we don't kill people; we know how to pluck the pigeon, but at least we don't slit its throat. Our reputation is better than yours, and everyone basically calls us decent people . . ."

'It was with platitudes of this kind, and more remarks I didn't understand, because I'd never heard them before, but which seemed the more horrible for the words that went with them and the shameless actions with which Mirville punctuated them; it was with such horrors, as I say, that we travelled to Paris, where we finally stopped.

'The house where we got out wasn't quite in Paris, and I didn't know where it was situated; now I know more I can tell you that it was close to the Gobelins gate. It was about ten in the evening when we stopped in the courtyard. We got out. The carriage was dismissed and we went into a room where supper seemed about to be served. An old woman and a young girl of my own age were the only people waiting for us. We sat down to eat with them. I quickly realised during supper that the young girl, Rose, was to Monsieur Delcour what I thought Monsieur de Mirville wanted me to be to him. As for the old woman, she was meant to be our housekeeper. Her role was explained to me at once, and I learned at the same time that this was the house where I was to live with my young friend, who was none other than Monsieur de Mirville's daughter, whom Monsieur Delcour and he had been talking about fetching from round by Chartres. Which proves, Madame, that the two gentlemen had given each other their two daughters for mistresses, without either of the two unhappy creatures knowing any better than the other the second part of the bonds that attached them to their two fathers.

'You will allow me to suppress, Madame, the indecent details of the supper and the dreadful night that followed them. There was another room, smaller and more artistically furnished, set aside for these shameful episodes. Rose and Monsieur Delcour went in with us. Rose, who already knew what was to happen, made no objections. Her example was urged on me, to persuade me to temper the harshness of my own refusals; and to make me conscious of their futility, I was threatened with violence if I decided to persist . . . What can I say, Madame? I trembled . . . I cried . . . nothing stopped the monsters, and my innocence was defiled.

'The two friends separated about three in the morning. Each
went to his own apartment for the rest of the night, and we
followed those whom Fate had destined for us.

'There Monsieur de Mirville lifted the last veil from my destiny.

'"You can have no further doubt," he said harshly, "that I have
taken you on as my mistress; your condition has just been made
clear in a way that can leave you no uncertainty. You need not
expect a brilliant fortune or a wild existence; the rank Monsieur
Delcour and I hold in the world compels us to take precautions
which necessitate your isolation. The old woman you have seen
with Rose, who will also take care of you, will answer to us for the
conduct of you both. Any misdemeanour or attempt to escape
would be severely punished, I warn you; for the rest, be decent,
good, sweet and charming. The difference in our ages will prevent
your developing a feeling for me which in any case I don't
particularly want, but I do at least wish to see in you, in return for
what I give you, the obedience I would be entitled to expect if you
were my legitimate wife. You will be fed, clothed, and so on, and
have a hundred francs a month to spend as you like; it's not a great
deal, I know, but what use would you have for more in the solitude
in which I must keep you? Beside, I have other arrangements which
are quite ruinous. You're not my only dependant . . . for which
reason I won't be able to see you more than three times a week, and
the rest of the time you'll be left alone. You can amuse yourself here
with Rose and old Dubois; each in her own way has qualities which
will help you lead a pleasant life, and without realising it, my love,
you'll end up thinking yourself quite well off."

'His fine speech over, Monsieur de Mirville got into bed and
ordered me to take my place beside him. I shall draw a veil over the
rest, Madame, there's enough there to show you the dreadful fate in
store for me. I was all the unhappier because it was impossible to
avoid it; the only creature with authority over me . . . my father
himself, had forced me to yield and given me a vicious example to
follow.

'The two friends left at midday and I became better acquainted
with my warden and my companion. The circumstances of Rose's
life were exactly the same as mine; she was six months older than
me. Like me, she had spent her life in a village, brought up by her
nurse, and only been in Paris for three days; but the great dis-
similarity between her character and mine always prevented me
from making friends with her; she was silly, heartless, lacking in

delicacy and in any kind of principles. The innocence and modesty that nature had given me were a poor match for so much vivacious indecency. I was forced to live with her and we were united by the bonds of misfortune, but never by those of friendship.

'As for Dubois, she had the vices of her age and condition. She was imperious, spiteful, interfering, much fonder of my companion than of me; as you see, there was nothing there to make me form any strong attachment to her and I spent my time in that house almost entirely in my own room, immersed in reading, of which I'm very fond, and which I easily made into my main occupation, thanks to an order from Monsieur de Mirville never to let me run out of books.

'Nothing could have been more ordered than our lives. We walked as much as we liked in a very beautiful garden, but never went outside its bounds. Three times a week the two friends, who only appeared then, arrived together, had supper with us, enjoyed their pleasures in front of one another for two or three hours afterwards, and then went to spend the rest of the night each with his own mistress, in his own apartment, which was ours the rest of the time . . . '

'But how shameful!' interrupted Madame de Blamont . . . 'Really! Fathers in front of their daughters!'

'My dear friend,' said Madame de Senneval, 'don't let us look further into these dreadful depths; the unhappy creature might tell us of atrocities of quite another kind.'

'How do you know that we don't need to know them?' said Madame de Blamont. . . . 'Young lady,' continued this eminently decent and respectable woman, with a blush, 'I don't know how to put the question . . . but did nothing worse ever happen to you?' Seeing that Sophie didn't understand her, she asked me to explain quietly what she meant.

'Madame,' Sophie answered, 'I think perhaps the only thing that did restrain them on that point was a sort of jealousy, which dominated both of them. This is, at least, the only emotion to which I can attribute a restraint . . . which in those hearts would surely not have been motivated by virtue. It is wicked, I know, to judge one's neighbour without proof, but a multitude of other divagations . . . other vile and degrading acts made me so convinced of the moral depravity of the two friends that I can certainly only attribute their propriety on the point you raise to a feeling more dominant than their debauchery; and I never saw any stronger than their jealousy.'

'It is difficult to reconcile it with the communal pleasures you have described,' said Madame de Senneval.

'And particularly with the other dependants Monsieur de Mirville acknowledged,' added Madame de Blamont.

'I see that,' said Sophie. 'This is perhaps one of those instances when two passions clash violently and only the most powerful survives; but what is quite certain is that each one's desire to preserve his own property, a desire born of jealousy too obvious to doubt, was always uppermost in their hearts, and stopped them from perpetrating . . . horrors . . . which my companion, I know, would only have laughed at, and which would have seemed to me more terrible than death itself.'

'Carry on,' said Madame de Blamont, 'and please do not be offended that my concern for you made me tremble on your account.'

Sophie continued, still addressing Madame de Blamont: 'Up to the episode that secured me your protection, Madame, there is little left to tell you. After I joined the household, my salary was paid with scrupulous exactness, and with no reason to spend anything, I saved it all with the intention of perhaps one day finding an opportunity to send it to my good Isabeau, who was constantly in my thoughts. I had the temerity to inform Monsieur de Mirville of my intention, certain that he would himself furnish me with the means of executing my project . . . What an innocent I was! How could I expect compassion from such a man! Did pity ever dwell in the breast of vice and debauchery?

'"You must forget these provincial impulses," Monsieur de Mirville told me brutally; "the woman has been much too well paid for the little care she took of you; you owe her nothing more."

' "And what of my gratitude, sir, such a pleasant feeling to harbour, and so delightful when it finds expression?"

' "Never mind all that; all this stuff about gratitude is illusion. I've never seen any advantage in it; I only like to harbour feelings that pay. Let's hear no more of it, or else, since you seem to have money to spare, I won't give you any more."

'Rejected by the one I decided to have recourse to the other, and spoke of my plan to Monsieur Delcour. He was even more harsh in his disapproval and said if he were in Monsieur de Mirville's place he wouldn't give me another penny, since all I thought of was throwing my money out of the window. I had to give up my benevolent design, for lack of the means to perform it.

'Before I come to the incident that precipitated the unhappy catastrophe of my story, I should tell you, Madame, that the two fathers had more than once, in front of us, ceded to each other authority over their daughters, each asking the other not to spare them when they were at fault; their aim being to inspire in us the restraint, submission and fear by which they sought to chain us. Whether they took advantage of their authority I leave you to imagine for yourselves. Monsieur de Mirville, who was extraordinarily brutal, treated me in particular with unbelievable harshness on the slightest impulse; and although he did this in front of Monsieur Delcour, the latter never came to my defence, any more than Mirville defended his own daughter when Delcour mistreated her similarly, which happened just as often. And now, Madame, I must make a confession. Completely culpable, and a full accomplice in the wretched relationship I had been swept into, I found both my duty and my feelings betrayed by nature. To complete my punishment, she decided to plant in my bosom a pledge of my dishonour. It was about this time that my companion, tiring of the life she led, told me she was planning to escape.

' "I don't want to attempt it alone," she said to me one day, "I've managed to win over the gardener's son . . . He's my lover . . . He's said he will set me free. It's for you to decide if you want to share our fate. It might be better for you to wait until you've had the baby . . . I'll still make every effort to save you. I'll find you a lover and he can come and get you out of here, and if you like we can be together again."

'I was not very happy with the last part of the plan for a future connection; I wanted my freedom, but in order to live a very different kind of life from the one my companion planned to follow. Nevertheless, I accepted her offer, agreeing with her it was better for me not to escape until after I had had the baby. I begged her not to forget me, and to make all the arrangements for that moment.

'Although she herself was anxious to leave quickly, it took some time to make the necessary preparations, and the arrangements were not complete until about two months before the end of my term. The moment came; she was about to escape. And then one day, the eve of the day she had chosen for her departure, and also of the day on which I had the good fortune to meet you, she slipped up to her room for money for the gardener, who was to find her a lodging, and in the meantime asked me to stay with the young man, who was in a hurry to go and apparently unwilling to linger. I was to urge him to wait a moment . . . Then, fatal moment that sealed my misfortune! or rather my good fortune, since this was also the chance that raised me from the abyss. As luck had it, something happened then that hadn't happened for three years: Monsieur de Mirville came in alone and was in my room before I had time to get the young man out of sight. He slipped out quickly, but not without being seen.

'I can't describe the raging anger that immediately seized Mirville. The first weapon to hand was his stick, and with no respect for my condition, without stopping to find out whether I was guilty or not, he overwhelmed me with insults, dragged me across the room by the hair, threatened to trample underfoot the fruit I carried in my bosom, which he now saw as proof of his humiliation. I would have died under his blows – you can still see the bruises – had not Dubois come running up to tear me from his hands. He fell into a colder rage . . .

'"I shall still punish her cruelly," he said . . . "Close the doors . . . let no one in, and send the prostitute straight up to her room . . ."

'Rose, who had heard everything and was very glad to have escaped through this error a punishment she alone deserved, took care to say nothing and the thunder broke on my head alone . . . My tyrant soon followed me up. His eyes glittered with a hundred different passions, among which I saw ones more dreadful than anger, whose effects, distorting the muscles of his hateful countenance, made him seem even more terrible . . . Oh, Madame, how can I convey to you the fresh indignities of which I was the victim! They insult nature and decency, I can never describe them . . . He ordered me to take off my clothes . . . I threw myself at his feet with repeated protestations of innocence, and tried to soften his heart by pointing to the sad fruit of his vile love; poor child, kicking and squirming in my bosom, he already cowered at his father's knees . . . as if begging mercy for me . . . My condition did not move Mirville, who only saw in it, he said, a further proof of the infidelity he suspected; everything I pleaded was mere deception, he was sure what had been going on, he had seen for himself, nothing could pull the wool over his eyes . . . I put myself in the state he required; as soon as it was done, savagely painful bonds assured him of my compliance.

'I was treated to that shameful humiliation that schoolmasters like to inflict on children . . . But so cruelly . . . and so harshly . . . At last I turned pale, and swayed under my bonds . . . My eyes closed, and what the savage went on to do to me, I don't know . . . I came back to consciousness in Dubois' arms . . . My tormentor was striding up and down the room, urging more speed in the attentions bestowed on me . . . not out of pity, the monster . . . but to be rid of me the sooner . . .

' "Right," he exclaimed, "is she ready?" Seeing me still in the state of nakedness he'd imposed: "Dress her, Madame, for God's sake, and get her out of here . . . "

'He asked for my keys, took back everything he had given me and gave me two crowns, with the words: "Here you are, it's more than you need to get you to one of the whores this town is full of; no doubt she'll be delighted to take in a creature who behaves in the way you have done in my house . . . "

' "Oh, sir," I wept, unable to stay silent in the face of this last insult, "I have only ever committed one crime, and you alone made me do it. Judge of my repentance by my suffering, and don't insult me in my misery."

'At these words, which must have touched his heart, if a tyrant's heart were ever open to compassion, if corruption and crime did not always close it to the cries of the innocent, he seized my arm, dragged me to the doors of the house and threw me into a little street that led to one of the garden gates . . . Let your sensitive heart, Madame, figure my situation, alone at nightfall on the out-skirts of a completely unknown town, in my delicate condition, with scarcely enough money to get me away, my whole body torn and bleeding, without even the consolation of tears: alas! I could shed no more.

'Not knowing where to go, I threw myself down on the threshold of the gate that had just been closed on me . . . onto the smears of my own blood, and resolved to spend the night there. "Cruel as he is," I thought, "he won't forbid me the air I still have the misfortune to breathe . . . He won't deny me shelter like the animals, and heaven will have pity on my unhappiness and perhaps let me die here in peace." There was a moment when I thought myself lost: I heard steps close by . . . had he sent people to find me? Did he mean to finish off his crime, take the last remnants of a life I hated? Or was it perhaps remorse inspiring a moment's pity in that heart of clay? Whatever their purpose, the steps went quickly by;

day came, and I got to my feet and decided at once to return to dear
Isabeau's dwelling, certain she would not refuse me the refuge she
had always promised . . .

'I set out on my journey . . . It was my fourth day on foot,
dragging myself along as best I could, battered and bruised, shaking
with fear, exhausted by the burden I carried in my bosom, hardly
daring to eat, in case my small supply of money would not take me
to Berseuil. I thought I was almost there and then I got lost and my
pains forced me to stop. That was when I had the good fortune to
meet this gentleman,' said Sophie, indicating me, 'and however
dreadful my situation may be,' she continued, looking at Madame
de Blamont, 'I look on it as a favour from Heaven, since it has
secured me the protection of a lady whose compassion has aided
me, and whose kindness will help me find the woman I think of as
my mother. I am young, I dare to say also that I am virtuous, and if I
have stumbled, I call God to witness that it was not my wish . . . I
shall atone for my faults, weep for them for the rest of my life . . . I
shall help my good Isabeau in her house, and though I may not have
the wealth that crime brought me, I shall at least find peace and no
longer be gnawed by remorse.'

The whole assembly burst into tears; Sophie, too moved to
control her own, asked us to leave her alone for a moment. We
withdrew to pursue our conjectures, and since the mail is about to
leave I must leave you, dear Valcour, with your own, with the
assurance that I shall send you as soon as possible any further detail
we are able to establish concerning this unhappy episode.

XVI
Honoré de Balzac (1799–1850)

from *Contes drolatiques* (1832–37)

*Balzac's pastiche of the ribald mediaeval tale, part of the Romantics'
nostalgic reinvention of the robust innocence of the Middle Ages, is a sharp
contrast to the darker modern passions depicted in the novels of* La Comédie
humaine.

Ribald Tales of Three Pilgrims

When the Pope left his good city of Avignon to dwell again in
Rome, many pilgrims were caught out who had set off for the
Comtat and now had to cross the high Alps to reach the Eternal
City, where they hoped for the remission of some singular sins. All
the roads and inns were filled with men wearing the chain of the
order of the Brotherhood of Cain, prime penitents all, all wicked
lads burdened with leprous souls, thirsting to bathe in the Papal
piscina and carrying gold and precious jewels to redeem their sins,
pay for the Papal Bulls and reward the saints. They may have drunk
water on the way there, but if the innkeepers offered it on the way
back you can be sure they asked instead for holy water from the
cellars.

At that time, three pilgrims came to Avignon only to be disappointed, for it was already bereft of the Pope. When they turned
down the Rhone valley for the Mediterranean coast, one of the
three, who was bear-leading his son, ten years old at the most, left
the party. Around Milan he turned up again unexpectedly without
the boy. So at supper that evening they held a banquet to celebrate

the return of the pilgrim they thought had abandoned the idea of penitence when he found no Pope at Avignon.

Of the three Rome-seekers, one was from Paris, the second from Germany, and the third, who had doubtless hoped to improve his son's education by the journey, came from the duchy of Burgundy, where he held a number of fiefs and was a younger son of the Villiers-la-Faye family (Villa in Fago), called La Vaugrenand. The German Baron had met up with the citizen from Paris this side of Lyons and both of them had fallen in with La Vaugrenand in sight of Avignon.

In this inn, then, the pilgrims' tongues were considerably loosened, and they agreed to travel to Rome together for mutual protection against the robbers, nighthawks and cut-throats whose vocation it was to relieve pilgrims of the weight on their bodies before the Pope relieved them of the weight on their conscience. Having drunk deep, the three companions fell into conversation, wine being the key to eloquence, and every one of them admitted he had left home on account of a woman. The serving-girl watching them drink told them that out of a hundred pilgrims who stopped at the hostelry ninety-nine had taken to the road for just that reason. The three sages then turned to consider how pernicious is woman's influence on man.

The Baron showed them the heavy gold chain he was carrying in his hauberk as an offering to good Saint Peter, and said his case was such that ten chains like that wouldn't get him off. The Parisian unfastened his glove and revealed a ring with a white diamond, saying he was taking a hundred times that much to the Pope. The Burgundian untied his cap and disclosed two wondrous pearls destined for fine earrings for Our Lady of Loretto, admitting he would sooner have left them round his wife's neck.

The serving-girl broke in to say their sins must have been as great as the Viscontis'.

They were so great, said the pilgrims, that every one of them had made a solemn vow never to fornicate again for the rest of his days, however beautiful the woman might be – and that on top of whatever penance the Pope gave them. The serving-girl was amazed they had all taken the same vow. The Burgundian added that this vow had been the reason for his slowness on the road after they got to Avignon. He had been very much afraid that his son might take to fornication, despite his tender years, and he had sworn to stop all men and beasts in his household and on his estates from fornicating. The Baron asked what had happened, and the nobleman told them the following tale.

'As you know, the good Countess Jeanne of Avignon in her day made a decree compelling all whores to live in a special quarter, in brothels with closed red shutters. As we passed in your company through that damned quarter, my son noticed the houses with the closed red shutters and his curiosity was aroused. You know what these ten-year-old devils are like, they see everything. He pulled at my sleeve, and went on pulling to get out of me just what those houses were. To put an end to it, I told him young lads had no business in those places and should stay out if they valued their lives, because that was where men and women were made, and it was so dangerous for anyone who didn't know how to do it properly that if an ignoramus went in, flying cankers and all kinds of other wild things would go for his face. The lad was terrified and followed me to the inn shaking with fright and not daring even to look at the brothels. But while I was in the stable seeing the horses were looked after, the lad slipped away like a thief and the maid had no idea where he was. I was very much afraid it was something to do with the whores, but I knew I could trust the regulations that stop them letting in children of that age. At suppertime, the young rogue came back, no more embarrassed than our divine Saviour with the doctors in the temple. "Where have you been?" I asked. "The houses with red shutters," was his answer. "You little villain," I said, "I'll see you whipped for that." He started weeping and whining. So I told him if he told me what had happened, there'd be no whipping.

' "Well," he said, "I made sure not to go in because of the flying cankers and the wild things, so I just hung on to the bars on the windows to watch how men are made." "And what did you see?" I asked. "Well," he said, "I saw a beautiful woman being finished off, all she needed was just one peg that a young workman was hammering in with all his might. As soon as it was done, she turned round, said something, and kissed her maker." "Go and get your supper," I said. That night I went back to Burgundy and left him with his mother, terrified in case the next town we went into he took it into his head to hammer his own peg into some girl.'

'You often get things like that from children,' said the Parisian. 'My neighbour's boy let out his father was being cuckolded by something he said. I wanted to know if they were teaching him religion properly at school, so I asked him one evening: "What's

Hope?" "He's one of the King's fine halberdiers who comes to our house when my father's out," said he. And in fact, Hope was the name that the sergeant of the King's halberdiers went by in his company. My neighbour went red with shame, though he looked in the mirror to put a good face on it and said he couldn't see any horns.'

The Baron commented that what the boy said was rather good: Hope is a bitch who comes and sleeps with us when the real things in life have gone.

'Is a cuckold made in God's image?' asked the Burgundian.

'No,' said the Parisian, 'God in His wisdom never took a wife, that's why He's happy for eternity.'

'But,' said the servant, 'cuckolds are made in God's image before they get their horns.'

Then the three pilgrims set to cursing womankind and blaming them for all the evil in the world.

'Their cunts are wide as helmets,' said the Burgundian.

'Their hearts are as straight as bill-hooks,' said the Parisian.

'Why do you see so many men on pilgrimage and so few women?' asked the German Baron.

'Their damned cunts can't sin,' answered the Parisian. 'Cunts acknowledge neither father nor mother, commandments of God or Church, nor divine nor human laws. Cunts know nothing of doctrine, don't understand heresies, can't be got for anything, arc innocent of everything, always laughing it off. They don't understand anything at all, and that's why I hate and detest them.'

'So do I,' said the Burgundian, 'and I'm beginning to understand the alternative version one scholar wrote of the Biblical verses about Creation. In his account (we call it a *Noël* where I come from) he explains why women's cunts are so imperfect. They're not like female cunts of other species, no man can quench their thirst, because there's so much diabolical passion in them. This *Noël* says that while the Lord God was making Eve, God turned his head to look at a donkey braying in his Paradise for the first time, and the devil seized his chance and stuck his finger into her, because she was too perfect. He made a burning wound, the Lord carefully put a stitch in, and that's how we got virgins. The stitch was meant to keep women closed up, and children were meant to be made like God made the angels, with pleasure as much above our carnal experience as heaven is above earth. When he saw the new seal, the devil was wild at being outwitted, so he pulled on Lord Adam's skin while he was asleep and stretched it out like his own devil's tail, but because the father of mankind was lying on his back, the appendage came to be at the front. And by the law of similarities that God made to rule his worlds, the two devil's inventions conceived a passionate desire to be joined together. This was the source of the first sins and the sufferings of the whole human race, because God, seeing what the devil had done, decided he'd see what became of it.'

The serving-girl said there was a lot of sense in what they said. Women were wicked creatures, and she knew some she would rather see under the grass than on top of it. The pilgrims noticed then that the girl was rather beautiful, feared they might be tempted to break their vows, and went to bed. The girl went and told her mistress that she had some scoundrels for guests and recounted what they had had to say about women.

'Hey,' said the landlady, 'I don't care what notions customers have in their heads, as long as their purses are fat.'

But when the girl told her about the jewels: 'That,' she said, visibly moved, 'is an issue that concerns all women. Let's go and have a word with them, I'll take the nobles and you can have the good citizen.'

The landlady, the biggest whore living in the duchy of Milan, went off to the room where my Lord de la Vaugrenand and the Baron were in bed, and congratulated them on their vows, saying women wouldn't lose much by them. She thought though that to fulfil those vows properly, they needed to know if they could stand just a little temptation. Thereupon she offered to get in bed beside them, being curious to see whether they'd mount her, which had never happened before in any bed where she'd lain with a man.

At breakfast next day, the servant had the ring on her finger and the mistress had the gold chain round her neck and the pearls in her ears. The three pilgrims stayed in the town for about a month, spending all the money in their wallets, and all agreed that they had only heaped those curses on womankind because they'd never sampled the women of Milan.

Back in Germany, the Baron remarked he only had one error to be sorry for in his whole life, and that was being in his own castle. The citizen of Paris came back all covered in scallops, and found his wife was with Hope. Milord from Burgundy found Milady de la Vaugrenand so dejected that he nearly killed himself consoling her, despite all he had said.

This proves an inn is no place to shoot off your mouth.

XVII
Alfred de Musset (1810–57)

from *Gamiani* (1833)

The black irony and outrageously violent passion of Gamiani *may surprise readers who know only the Musset of the light comedies and exquisite lyric poetry ('Les Nuits', 1835–37) but they pervade – in more discreet form – the drama* Lorenzaccio *(1834) and, to a lesser extent, are present too in the novel* Confession d'un enfant du siècle *(1836).*

Alcide, intrigued by Gamiani, the mysterious Italian Countess, has spied on her seduction of Fanny and later joined the pair, uninvited. The two experienced lovers listen to Fanny's account of how she first lost her innocence. Later, Alcide eavesdrops as Gamiani tells Fanny the story of her own initiation.

Fanny Initiated

FANNY: At the age of fifteen I was still innocent, I assure you; I had never even stopped to think about anything to do with the difference between the sexes.

I lived a carefree and no doubt happy life; and then one burning hot day, alone in the house, I felt a sort of need to relax, to make myself comfortable.

I got undressed and lay down almost naked on a divan . . . Oh, I'm so ashamed! . . . I stretched out, parted my thighs, tossed and turned in all directions. Without realising it, I fell into the most indecent attitudes.

The stuff the divan was made of was icy-cold. Its coolness gave me a pleasant feeling of delightfully sensual friction over my whole body. Oh, I breathed so freely, bathed in the pervasive warmth and sweetness of the air! Such ravishingly sweet voluptuous pleasure! I was in ecstasies of delight. My whole being seemed flooded with new life, I felt taller and stronger, as though I were drawing in a divine breath, blossoming in the beautiful rays of the sun!

ALCIDE: Why, Fanny, you're a poet!

FANNY: Oh! I'm describing exactly what I felt. My eyes wandered complacently over my body, my hands fluttered over my neck and my breasts. Lower down, they stopped; and despite myself, I fell into a deep reverie.

The inexplicable words *love* and *lover* came over and over again into my thoughts.

Then I felt so alone. My relatives and my friends were forgotten. I felt a dreadful sense of emptiness.

I stood up and looked sadly round.

For a few moments, I was pensive and still, with drooping, melancholy head, hands clasped together, arms hanging down.

Then, touching and examining myself once again, I wondered whether all that might have some end or purpose.

I knew instinctively that there was something missing that I couldn't define but that I wanted and desired with all my soul.

I must have looked distraught; from time to time I burst out into frenzied laughter, opening my arms as though to seize the Object of my desires! I even embraced myself. I clasped and caressed myself with my own arms; I had to have something real, a body to press and squeeze: in my strange delusion, I took hold of myself, thinking it was someone else.

Through the windows, I could see the distant lawns and trees and I was tempted to go out there and roll on the ground or lose myself high up among the leaves. As I gazed on the sky, I longed to fly through the air, vanish into the mists of heaven with the angels.

I thought I was going mad; the hot blood was rushing to my head.

Frantic, beside myself, I suddenly hurled myself headlong onto the cushions. I held one clenched between my thighs and another pressed in my arms; I covered it with mad kisses, embraced it with passion, I think I even smiled at it, I was so intoxicated, so wholly at the mercy of my senses. Suddenly I stopped, quivered, I seemed to dissolve, to sink and to swoon. 'Oh, my God!' I cried out, 'Oh, my God!' And all at once I leapt up in terror.

I was soaked right through.

I couldn't understand anything of what had happened to me; I thought I had hurt myself and I was very frightened. I fell onto my knees, begging God to forgive me if I had done wrong.

ALCIDE: Delightful innocent! Did you not tell anyone what had frightened you so much?

FANNY: No! Never! I wouldn't have dared, and an hour ago I still didn't know; you've given me the answer to the puzzle.

Gamiani at the Convent

GAMIANI: . . . and straight after I discovered that in the Convent of the Redemption all the sisters indulged in private in frenzies of sensuality, and had a secret meeting-place for their orgies where they frolicked undisturbed. This loathsome Sabbat began with compline and ended at matins [. . .]

My own disposition being well suited to a life of sensual pleasure, I agreed to be initiated into their Saturnalian mysteries. The chapter approved my admission and I was presented two days later. I arrived naked, according to the rule. I gave the required oath and then to complete the ceremony bravely prostituted myself on a giant wooden phallus set there for the purpose. I had scarcely completed my painful libation when the whole band of nuns threw themselves at me like a crowd of cannibals. I submitted to all their whims, adopted the maddest, lewdest positions and finally finished up with an obscene dance, after which they declared me victorious. I was exhausted. A vivacious, lively little nun, more refined than the Superior, took me off to her bed; she was the most outrageous lesbian Hell ever created. I fell passionately in love with her and we were nearly always together for the great nocturnal orgies.

FANNY: Where did you hold your Lupercalia?

GAMIANI: In a vast room adorned with everything that art and the genius of debauchery could invent. Entry was by two great doors closed in Oriental fashion by rich gold-fringed tapestries, embroidered with a thousand fantastic patterns. The walls were hung with dark blue velvet in a broad frame of cunningly carved lemonwood. Tall mirrors reaching from floor to ceiling were set round the room at equal intervals. During the orgies, the groups of naked, frenzied nuns were repeated in a thousand different reflections, or stood out sharp and brilliant against the tapestried panels. To sit on there were divans and cushions, better suited to games of pleasure and lascivious poses. The floor was covered with a double carpet of a delicate material delightful to touch. On it were depicted in startling, magic colour a score of groups of lovers in different lewd attitudes, guaranteed to revive flagging desires. Everywhere, on the ceiling, in paintings, the artist's palette presented the eye with speaking images of frenzied debauch. I remember one particular fiery Thyad tormented by a Corybant. I could never look at that picture without being aroused immediately.

FANNY: It must have been a delightful sight!

GAMIANI: And as well as the luxurious decorations, there were the intoxicating scents and flowers. An even, temperate warmth and a tender, mysterious light falling from six marble lamps, a soft, opaline glow. The whole atmosphere worked in you a mysterious kind of spell, blended with sensual reverie and uneasy desire. It was the Orient with all its luxury, poetry and careless sensuality. It was the mystery of the harem, with its hidden delights and above all, its inexpressible languor.

FANNY: How sweet a place to while away ecstatic nights with one's beloved!

GAMIANI: Why, certainly, Love would gladly have set up his temple there; but every night, the foul din of orgies turned it into a squalid den.

FANNY: How did that happen?

GAMIANI: On the stroke of midnight the nuns came in, dressed in simple black tunics that brought out the whiteness of their skin. They were all barefoot and their hair hung loose. A magnificent banquet appeared as if by magic. The Superior gave the signal and each leapt promptly to answer. Some were seated, others lay back on the cushions. Exquisite dishes and hot spicy wines vanished before their devouring appetites. Faces worn out by debauchery, cold and pale in daylight, gradually turned warm and bright. Bacchic vapours and aphrodisiac spices set bodies on fire, made heads swim. Conversation became lively, grew to a confused din, and ended unfailingly in obscene talk and manic challenges, tossed to and fro among the songs, laughter and shouts and the noise of glasses and bottles. All at once, a hot-blooded, impetuous nun would fall on her neighbour and seize her in a violent embrace, electrifying the whole crowd of them. Couples formed, twisting and twining in hot embraces. Lips smacked noisily against flesh, or met and mingled in frenzy. Then, smothered sighs, faint words, cries of passion or exhaustion. Soon their unbridled kisses looked for something more than cheeks, breasts or shoulders. Dresses were pulled up or thrown aside. It was a unique sight, this chain of supple, graceful, naked female bodies, twisting and pressing against one another with all the sophistications and all the impetuosity of consummate lechery. A couple finding the climax of their pleasure too long in coming for their impetuous desire would leave the group for a moment to draw breath. Each would survey the other with eyes of flame; each would vie with the other to find the lewdest and most seductive pose. The one who triumphed in debauchery would find herself suddenly attacked by her distraught rival, thrown on her back, covered with kisses, devoured and consumed with caresses right into the hidden centre of pleasure. The attacker took a position where she was open to the same onslaught, two heads disappeared between two sets of thighs to leave a single body, twisting and convulsing, uttering a single muffled groan of lust and pleasure, and then a twin shout of joy!

'They're coming! They're coming!' the damned nuns would immediately echo. Crazed, distraught, they would hurl themselves on each other like maddened beasts loosed into the arena.

In the urgent search for their own climax, their ardent efforts intensified. The leaping, bounding groups clashed together and fell in tangled heaps to the ground, tense, panting, worn out by their orgies of lust; a grotesque confusion of naked, swooning, fainting women piled up in ignoble disorder. So it was that dawn often found them.

FANNY: What wild folly!

GAMIANI: They went further than that; they tried all kinds of things. Because we had no men, our inventions were all the more excessive. We knew all the priapic legends and obscene stories of ancient and modern times. We outdid them all. Our imaginations outstripped Elephantis and Aretino. It would take too long to tell you of all the tricks, artifices and wonderful philtres we had to revive our strength and to arouse and satisfy our desires. You'll have an idea if I describe the unusual treatment we gave one nun to arouse her passions. First we plunged her into a bath of warm blood to bring back her vigour. Then she drank an erotic potion, lay down on a bed and we massaged her whole body. We used magnetic powers to put her to sleep. As soon as she was slumbering soundly, we exposed her to best advantage, whipped her till the blood came, and stuck sharp pins in her. The victim would wake up in the middle of the torture. She would sit up distraught, stare at us with crazed eyes and fall straight into violent fits. Six people could scarcely hold her down. The only thing that could calm her was being licked by a dog. Her madness would come flooding out. But if relief didn't come, the wretch would go to even more dreadful extremes and clamour for a donkey.

FANNY: A donkey! Heaven have mercy!

GAMIANI: Yes, my dear, a donkey. We had two well-trained docile beasts. We weren't to be outdone in anything by the women of Rome, who used them in their Saturnalia [. . .]

FANNY: Gamiani, you fill me with such transports! I can't bear it much longer . . . How did you finally come to leave this diabolical convent?

GAMIANI: In this way: after one tremendous orgy, we had the idea of turning ourselves into men by strapping on dildoes, spearing each other with them in turn and then running round the room like madwomen; I was the last link in the chain, the only one riding but not ridden. Imagine my surprise when I was vigorously attacked by a naked man who had somehow slipped in among us. At my involuntary cry of terror, the nuns broke apart and fell immediately on the unhappy intruder. Each was determined to enjoy a real conclusion to desires aroused by a tiring imitation. The creature was soon worn out by excess of attention. You should have seen him, so weak and exhausted, his sheath hanging limp, all the signs of his virility as negative as could be. I had considerable trouble bringing a spark of life into this rag of humanity when it came to my turn to taste the prolific elixir. However, I managed it. Lying on top of the half-dead fellow, my head between his thighs, I sucked master Priapus so skilfully that he woke from his slumbers red and rosy, lively and at your service. Meanwhile, another nimble tongue was caressing me; and before long I began to feel the onset of unbelievable pleasure, which I crowned by sitting in delightful glory on the sceptre I had just conquered: I gave and received a flood of ecstasy.

This final excess finished the man off. Nothing would revive him. And can you believe it? As soon as the nuns realised the wretch was no longer any use, they unhesitatingly decided to kill him and bury him in one of the cellars, in case some indiscretion should compromise the convent. I opposed this wicked plan, but with no success: in less than a second, one of the lamps was taken down and the victim hauled up in its place with a slip-knot . . . I averted my gaze from the dreadful sight . . . But to the mad creatures' great surprise, hanging him produced the usual effect. Marvelling at this wonderful demonstration, the Superior climbed up onto a step and to the frenzied applause of her worthy accomplices mated with the dead man in mid-air, pegged herself onto a corpse!

That isn't the end of the story. Either too thin or too old for the double weight, the rope stretched and snapped. The dead man and the living woman fell to the ground so heavily that all the nun's bones were broken and the hanged man, only half-strangled, came back to life and in his dying spasms threatened to kill the Superior.

A thunderbolt falling on a crowd would cause less consternation than this scene spread among the nuns. They all fled in terror, thinking the devil had come. The Superior was left to fight the dead man alone.

The whole adventure seemed likely to have terrible consequences. Eager to avoid them, I escaped the same night from that den of crime and debauchery.

XVIII
Émile Zola (1840–1902)

from *La Faute de l'abbé Mouret* (1875)

Against the abuses, corruptions and degradations imposed on humanity by the capitalist society of the Second Empire, depicted in the Rougon-Macquart cycle (1871–93), Zola draws a Utopia of peaceful, fecund Nature. Serge, Father Mouret, a village priest in his twenties, betrays his vows of chastity for the sixteen-year-old Albine, seduced by the beauty of le Paradou, the park run wild. The moment of bliss is short-lived: the forces of guilt reclaim Serge as the couple leave the garden, and Albine dies of grief. However, the book is an act of faith in the indomitable redemptive power of Nature.

The allegory is heavy — Fantasia underwritten by D.H. Lawrence. The pessimism generated by Zola's well-documented observations of the real ills of the present, combined with his reluctance to condone revolutionary solutions antagonistic to his private interests, drives him to these extremes of erotic escapism.

Paradise Regained

They went downstairs and walked among the garden, Serge still smiling. He saw nothing of the greenery except its reflection in Albine's bright eyes. Seeing them come, the garden shook with a long burst of laughter, a murmur of satisfaction fluttering from leaf to leaf to the end of the deepest avenues. For days now it must have been waiting for them, just like this, arms round each other's waist, at one with the trees, looking over the grassy beds for their lost love. A solemn 'Hush!' raced under the branches. The two o'clock sky, blazing hot, urged drowsiness. Plants stood on tiptoe to watch them pass.

'Can you hear them?' asked Albine softly. 'They're quiet when we come close. But in the distance they're waiting for us, whispering together which way to send us . . . I told you we needn't worry about the paths. The trees are stretching out their arms to show me the way.'

The whole park in fact was pushing them gently on. Behind them, a fence of bushes reared its thorns to stop them going back. In front, the grassy carpets unrolled so smoothly there was no need even to look at their feet, they just followed the gentle slope of the land.

'The birds are coming with us too,' Albine went on. 'It's the tits this time. Can you see them? Running along the hedgerows, stopping at every turning to make sure we don't get lost. Oh, if we knew what their singing meant, they're surely calling us to be quick!'

Then she added: 'All the creatures in the park are here. Can't you feel them? There's a great rustling behind us: it's the birds in the trees, the insects in the grass, stags and deer in the coppices, even the fish, fins flicking through the silent water . . . Don't turn round, you'll frighten them, but it must be a magnificent procession.'

They were still walking on, with no feeling of tiredness. Albine spoke only to enchant Serge with the music of her voice. Serge was obedient to the least little pressure of her hand. Neither knew where they were, but they knew they were travelling straight to their goal. And the further they went, the more discreet the garden became, hushing the sighing shadows, the babbling waters, the ardent animal life. There was only a great quivering silence, an awed expectancy.

Instinctively Albine and Serge looked up. Before them stood a massive bank of foliage. As they hesitated, a doe, watching them with lovely soft eyes, leapt into the thicket.

'That's it,' said Albine.

She went first, her head turned away again, pulling Serge with her; both vanished into the rustling, parted leaves and all was quiet again. They stepped out into a world of tranquil delight.

In the middle stood a tree drenched in such thick shadow it was impossible to say what it was. It was gigantic. Its trunk breathed like a human breast, its branches stretched out like protecting arms. It looked good, vigorous, powerful and fertile; it was the oldest thing in the garden, father of the forest, the grasses' pride and the friend of the sun, who rose and set daily over its summit. From its green vault showered all the delight of creation: scent of blossoms and birdsong, drops of light, fresh waking dawns and the sleepy warmth of twilight. Its potent sap poured through its bark, bathing it in a mist of fertility, transforming it into the symbol of earth's virile power. The tree was enough to bring enchantment to the clearing. The others round about formed the impenetrable wall that left it standing alone in the heart of a tabernacle of half-light and silence; there was nothing but greenery, without a scrap of sky or a glimpse of horizon, just a rotunda, walls draped in the tender silk of the leaves, floor covered with the satiny velvet of moss. It was like entering the crystal heart of a spring, limpid green light, a sheet of silver drowsing in the reflection of the reeds. Colours, scents, sounds, shivers, all was vague, transparent, nameless, a blissful swoon where all things fainted and died. Through the still branches untouched by the breeze trailed a bedroom languor, the glow of a summer night on the bare shoulder of a woman in love, love's indistinct murmur, dissolving of a sudden into a great soundless spasm. A nuptial solitude peopled with creatures embracing, an empty room where somewhere, behind the drawn curtains, passionately entwined, Nature lay sated in the arms of the sun. From time to time, the tree's back cracked; its limbs stiffened like a woman in labour; the living sweat that poured from its bark rained heavier still on the surrounding grass, exuding languorous desire, flooding the air with abandon until the clearing paled in a spasm of pleasure. And the tree would collapse and sink, with its shadow, its grassy carpets, its belt of thick coppices: ecstasy personified.

Albine and Serge stood enchanted. The moment the tree spread its gentle branches over them they were free of the dreadful anguish that tormented them. Gone was the fear that made them flee one another, the hot, desperate struggles where they bruised and tore each other, not knowing what enemy they fought with such fury. They were filled instead with complete confidence, supreme serenity; they yielded to one another, slipped slowly into the pleasure of being together, far away in the depths of a miraculously secret hiding-place. Still unaware as yet what the garden wanted, they left it free to dispose of their love; they waited quietly for the tree to speak. The tree so blinded them with love that the mighty, regal clearing began to vanish, became no more than a cradle of scent.

They stopped and sighed, captivated by the musky coolness.

'The air tastes like fruit,' murmured Albine.

Serge in his turn said softly: 'The grass is so alive I seem to be treading on the hem of your dress.'

Their voices were lowered in holy awe. They felt no urge to look up, to see the tree. They were well aware of its majesty, weighing on their shoulders. Albine's glance asked if she had exaggerated the magic of the green woods. In answer, two brilliant tears ran down Serge's cheeks. Their joy in being there at last was more than words could express.

'Come,' she whispered in his ear, in a voice softer than the breeze.

She went first and lay down at the foot of the tree. She held out her hands to him, smiling; he smiled too as he stood there and held out his own. She took hold of them and pulled him slowly to her. He fell down beside her and held her close to his heart. The embrace filled them with delight.

'Oh, do you remember,' he said, 'that wall that stood between us? I can feel you now, there are no barriers left . . . Am I hurting you?'

'No, no,' she answered. 'It's good.'

They lay silent, still holding each other tight. A delicious feeling stole over them, smooth and gentle as a film of spilt milk. Then Serge ran his hands over Albine's body murmuring: 'Your face is mine, your eyes, your mouth, your cheeks . . . Your arms are mine, from your fingernails to your shoulders . . . your feet are mine, your knees are mine, all of you belongs to me.'

He kissed her face, eyes, mouth, cheeks. He kissed her arms, swift little kisses running from fingers to shoulders. He drenched her in a rain of kisses, great raindrops, warm as the drops of a summer shower, falling everywhere, beating her neck, breasts, hips, flanks. It was a peaceful, unending invasion, that took possession of the tiniest veins under the pink skin.

'I want to take you so I can surrender myself,' he said. 'I want to surrender myself to you wholly and for ever. I know now you are my mistress and my queen; I want to kneel down and worship you. I'm here to obey you, to lie at your feet attending on your wishes, hold out my arms to protect you, blow away the fluttering leaves that threaten your repose . . . Oh, deign to let me efface myself, become absorbed in you, become the water you drink and the bread you eat. You are my destiny. From the moment I woke up in this garden, I began to walk towards you, I grew to manhood for your sake. My goal and reward have always been the vision of your grace. You went by in the sunlight with your golden hair, a promise proclaiming that one day you would show me the meaning of creation, earth, trees, waters, heavens, whose key still escapes me . . . I am yours, your slave, ready to listen, my lips on your feet.'

All this he said, bowing to the earth, worshipping Woman. Albine, in the glow of her pride, let herself be worshipped. She offered her fingers, lips, breasts, to Serge's devout kisses. She felt like a queen as he lay so strong and humble before her. She had conquered him, he was at her mercy, a single word from her would seal his fate. And what made her all-powerful was the voice of the garden all round them rejoicing in her triumph, assisting her with its slowly swelling sound.

Serge's words became incoherent and his kisses began to stray. He murmured again: 'I want to know . . . I want to take you and keep you, I want to die, I want to fly away with you, I don't know . . .'

They were both lying back, unable to speak or breathe, heads spinning. With an effort, Albine lifted a finger to tell Serge to listen.

It was the garden that had willed their fall. For weeks it had connived at love's slow apprenticeship. Then at this last moment it had led them to the green bower. Now it was the tempter and all its voices taught them love. From the beds came scents of swooning flowers, long whispers of love-affairs among the roses and the voluptuous pleasures of the violets; never had the sunflowers beckoned with such ardent sensuality. The wind from the orchard carried scented gusts of ripe fruit, odours of rich fecundity, the vanilla scent of apricots, and the musk of oranges. From the plains rose a deeper note, the sighs of a thousand grasses kissed by the sun, plaints and lamentations from countless crowds, all in heat, melting at the rivers' cool caress, the nakedness of the running water, edged by the willows whispering dreams of desire. The forest murmured of the mighty passion of the oaks, the organ notes of the tall plantations, solemn music for the marriage of ash, birch, hornbeam and plane in the deep leafy sanctuaries; bushes and copses rang with roguish delight, the noisy din of lovers playing chase, tumbling down at the ditches' edge, snatching at pleasure, with a great rustling of branches. As the whole park locked and coupled, the harshest embraces came from far off among the rocks, where the heat cracked the stones that swelled with passion and the thorny plants pledged their tragic love, and no comfort came from the nearby springs, on fire from the sun slipping down into their beds.

'What are they saying?' murmured Serge, bewildered. 'What do they want, what are they asking for?'

Albine said nothing, but held him close.

The voices were clearer still. It was the turn of the creatures in the garden to call them to love one another. The grasshoppers sang a deadly sweet song of love. The butterflies' fluttering wings scattered kisses. Sparrows swept by sudden passions bestowed swift, ardent caresses, like sultans in a harem. In the clear water, fish swooned and deposited their eggs in the sunlight, frogs croaked their passionate, melancholy calls: mysterious passions everywhere, seeking grotesque satisfactions in the blue-green blandness of the reeds. In the heart of the woods, nightingales burst into laughing song, threaded with sensual delight, and stags bellowed, drunk senseless with lust, dying exhausted at the side of near-disembowelled mates. On flat rocks by scrawny bushes, adders, twined two by two, hissed softly, while huge lizards brooded over their eggs, spines vibrating, throbbing with ecstasy. From corners far from the pools of sunlight, from shadowy gulfs, came the hot animal odour of creatures all in rut. And all this swarming life quivered with new birth. On every leaf, a fertile insect; in every clump of grass, a growing family; flies on the wing, stuck together, were impregnated before they touched the ground. The invisible particles of life inhabiting matter, the very atoms of matter, made love, coupled, set the ground shaking with pleasure, turned the park into an immense shudder of fornication.

And then Albine and Serge understood. He said nothing, but he wrapped his arms around her tighter and tighter. They were surrounded by the fatal necessity of procreation. They gave in to the insistent garden. The tree whispered to Albine what mothers whisper to brides on their wedding night.

Albine yielded. Serge took her.

And the whole garden swooned with the lovers, in a last cry of passion. The trees bent as though in a mighty wind; the grass let slip an ecstatic sob; the fainting flowers with parted lips breathed out their souls; the very sky, flaming with the setting sun, filled with motionless, swooning clouds from which superhuman rapture rained. It was a victory for all the creatures, plants and things in the garden who had willed these two children to enter the eternity of life. The park burst into thunderous applause.

XIX
Guy de Maupassant (1850–93)

'Marroca' from *Mademoiselle Fifi* (1882)

*Disciple of Flaubert, and on the aesthetic wing of Naturalism, Maupassant first published his short stories in the popular press (*Le Gil Blas, Le Gaulois*) and then in separate collections. 'Marroca' appeared in* Mademoiselle Fifi *in 1882.*

The love/death association that for other writers invokes all the terrors of the imagination is here sanitised by the Naturalist and turned into game by the simple characterisation and the farcical slant. The craftsmanlike twist in the tail stimulates surprise, but no erotic shiver of horror. In his introduction to the 1974 Pléiade edition of the Contes, *Louis Forestier points to the intellectual nature of Maupassant's eroticism: his heroes love only their idea of love. 'Pleasure,' says Forestier, 'doesn't come from pure sensation, but from a whole environment, which the true adept of sexual pleasure savours in his intelligence.'*

'Marroca' (1882)

Friend, you asked me to send you my impressions, my adventures, and especially my love stories from the land of Africa that has called me so long. You were looking forward to laughing over what you called my black passions; you already pictured me coming home with a tall black woman in my train, her head swathed in a yellow scarf, swaying along in her brilliantly coloured dresses.

No doubt the turn of the blackamoors will come; I've already seen several women who've made me think I would enjoy dipping into that ink. But I happen to have begun with something better and quite out of the ordinary.

You wrote in your last letter: 'When I know what love is like in a country, I know that country so well I could describe it, even though I've never seen it.' Let me tell you, here they love with intensity. From the first few days you can feel a kind of quivering passion, desires welling up, sudden tension, a nervous prickling in your fingertips arousing to exasperation the powers of love and every capacity for physical sensation, from the mere touch of the hand to the need that shall be nameless that makes us do so many foolish things.

Let's be quite clear. I don't know whether what you call love of heart and soul, sentimental idealism, Platonic love, can exist in this atmosphere; I doubt it. But the other love, that of the senses, which has its good side – its very good side – is terrifyingly intense in this climate. The heat, the steady burning fever in the air, the suffocating blasts from the South, the waves of fire from the great desert close by, the heavy sirocco, more devastating, more parching than flame, a whole continent eternally afire, its very rocks burnt by a huge, devouring sun, all inflame the blood, madden the flesh, turn men into beasts.

Let me come to my story. I'll pass over my first days in Algeria. I visited Bône, Constantine, Biskra and Sétif, and finally came to Bougie through the Chabet gorges and by a matchless road in the middle of the Kabyle forests that run along the coast, two hundred yards above sea-level, winding in and out of the high scalloped mountain, down to the wonderful gulf of Bougie, as beautiful as the gulfs of Naples, Ajaccio and Douarnenez, the finest I know. (I leave out of the comparison the incredible bay of Porto, ringed with red granite, home of the fantastic, blood-red stone giants called the 'Calanches' at Piana, on the west coast of Corsica.)

From a long, long way off, before journeying round the great basin with its calm, sleeping waters, you can see Bougie. The town is built on the steep slopes of a towering mountain topped with woods: a splash of white on the green slope, like the foam on a waterfall cascading into the sea.

As soon as I set foot in the tiny, charming town, I knew I would stay there a long time. All around, the eye embraces a complete circle of fantastically shaped peaks, jagged, hooked and horned, so close-packed that the open sea is almost invisible and the gulf looks like a lake. The blue water, milky-blue, is wonderfully transparent, and overhead the azure sky, deep azure, as though covered with two coats of paint, spreads out its amazing beauty. Each seems to mirror the other, casting back the shared reflection.

Bougie is a city of ruins. Docking at the quay, you confront a magnificent pile straight out of the opera. This is the old Saracen gate, smothered in ivy. And in the mountainous woods round the city there are ruins everywhere, sections of Roman wall, bits of Saracen monuments, remains of Arab constructions.

I had rented a little Moorish house in the upper town. You know what these dwellings look like; writers have often described them. There are no windows on the outside; an inner courtyard gives light from top to bottom. There is a big cool room for daytime on the first floor and a terrace at the top for night.

I at once adopted the custom of hot countries: that is, taking a siesta after lunch. In Africa that's when the heat is suffocating, when you can no longer breathe, when streets, plains, long blinding roads are all empty and everyone sleeps, or tries to, with as few clothes as possible.

In my room with its Arabian pillars, I had had installed a wide, soft divan, covered with carpets from Djebel-Amour. I stretched out on it, wearing more or less the same costume as Hassan, but I couldn't rest, tormented by my continence.

Dear friend, there are two torments on this earth I hope you never experience: lack of water and lack of women. Which is worse? I don't know. In the desert, a man would commit the most hideous crimes for a glass of clear, cool water. What wouldn't a man do in certain towns on the coast for a lovely, fresh, healthy girl? There's no shortage of girls in Africa! On the contrary, there are swarms of them; but, to pursue the comparison, they're all as foul and noxious as the muddy liquid in the Saharan wells.

One day, even more edgy than usual, I tried to close my eyes, but to no avail. My legs were quivering, as though stung by something inside; I tossed and turned on my carpets in an agony of restlessness. Finally, I could stand it no longer; I got up and went out.

It was July, and a torrid afternoon. The paving-stones in the streets were baking hot; my shirt, soaked straight through, clung to my body; all along the horizon floated a thin white vapour, the burning mist of the sirocco, heat you could almost touch.

I went down by the sea, walked round the harbour and started out onto the bank along the pretty bay where the bathing is. The mountain cliff, covered with clumps of trees and tall scented plants

with heady perfumes, forms a ring round the creek and great dark
rocks run into the water all around its edges.

There was no one out; nothing moving; no animal crying or bird
flying, not a sound, not even a ripple, as the drowsy sea lay
motionless in the sun's heat. But in the baking atmosphere I seemed
to feel a kind of fiery throbbing.

Suddenly, behind one of the rocks half-covered by the silent
water, I caught a slight movement; I turned round, and I saw
bathing in the water, thinking herself quite alone with the sun at its
height, a tall naked girl, with the water up to her breasts. She was
looking towards the open sea, splashing softly, without seeing me.

An amazing tableau: the beautiful woman in the glassy, trans-
lucent water, under the blinding light. She was an incredibly
beautiful woman, tall and statuesque.

She looked round, screamed, and half-swimming, half-walking,
hid completely behind her rock.

She had to come out, so I sat on the bank and waited. She
carefully poked round her head, piled high with black hair fastened
up any old how. Her mouth was wide, with fleshy lips, her eyes
huge and brazen, and her skin, slightly tanned by the climate,
seemed carved out of old ivory, firm and smooth, good stock,
slightly coloured by the Negro sun.

She shouted: 'Go away.' Her rich voice, a little loud, like all the
rest of her, had a throaty accent. I didn't move. She added: 'You
shouldn't stay there, Monsieur.' The *r*s, in her mouth, rolled like
waggon wheels. I still didn't move. The head disappeared.

Ten minutes went by; then the hair and the brow and the eyes
reappeared, slowly and carefully, like children playing hide-and-
seek, peeping round to watch the seeker.

This time, she looked furious; she shouted: 'You're going to
make me catch cold. I won't leave as long as you're there.' I got up
then and moved off, but turned round several times. When she
thought I was far enough away, she got out of the water, bent over,
her back to me; and she vanished into a hollow in the rock, with a
skirt hung over the entrance.

I went back next day. She was bathing again, but this time
dressed in a full costume. She burst out laughing, showing me her
brilliant teeth.

A week later, we were friends. A week after that, we were even
more so.

She was called Marroca, doubtless a nickname, pronouncing it as though it had fifteen rs. The daughter of Spanish colonists, she had married a Frenchman called Pontabèze. Her husband was a civil servant. I never knew exactly what he did. I could see he was very busy, and that was all I asked.

So, changing her bathing-time, she came every day after I had had lunch to take her siesta at my house. What a siesta! Call that resting!

She was really a wonderful girl, rather an animal type, but superb. Her eyes were always glistening with passion; her part-open mouth, her pointed teeth, even her smile had a hint of savage sensuality; and her strange breasts, long, straight and pointed, like fleshy pears, firm and elastic as if there were steel springs inside, gave her whole body a certain animality, turned her into a kind of inferior but magnificent being, a creature meant for wild love, and woke in me thoughts of the obscene Gods of the Ancients who indulged their affections freely among the leaves and grasses.

And there was never a woman so full of insatiable desires. Her violent passions and howling embraces – grinding teeth, bites, jerking convulsions – gave way almost immediately to deep, death-like sleep. Then she would wake up suddenly in my arms, ready for new embraces, her bosom swelling with kisses.

Beside that, her mind was simple as two and two make four, and a ringing burst of laughter did away with the need for thought.

Instinctively proud of her beauty, she shunned the slightest veil and moved round my house, running and frolicking, with bold, unselfconscious shamelessness. Sated at last with love, her cries and writhings all exhausted, she would sleep her deep, peaceful sleep by my side on the divan; while the overpowering heat brought out tiny drops of sweat on her sunburnt skin and drew from her body, from the arms folded under her head, from all her hidden folds, the musky scent that attracts the male.

She would sometimes come back in the evening, when her husband was on duty somewhere or other. Then we would lie out on the terrace, flimsily covered in delicate, filmy Oriental cloth.

When the great luminous moon of the hot countries rose full in the sky, lighting up the town and the gulf and the encircling frame of the mountains, we could see lying on all the other terraces an army of silent ghosts, standing from time to time, changing places, and lying down again in the languorous warmth of the calm sky.

Despite the brilliance of these African nights, Marroca would insist on being naked, even under the bright rays of the moon; she scarcel · thought about all the people who could see us, and often, despite ny fearful entreaties, she would fill the darkness with long, vibrant ries, making the dogs howl in the distance.

As I vas dozing one evening under the wide firmament bespattei d with stars, she came and knelt on my rug and brought her full lips close to my mouth: 'You must,' she said, 'come home and sleep with me.'

I didn't understand. 'What do you mean, home?'

'Yes, when my husband's left, you must come and sleep in his place.'

I couldn't help laughing. 'What on earth for, when you come here?'

She replied, speaking into my mouth, blowing her warm breath into the back of my throat, wetting my moustache with her breath: 'To give me something to remember.' And the *r* of remember trailed on and on, like a torrent crashing over the rocks.

I still couldn't understand what she was thinking. She put her arms round my neck. 'When you're gone, I'll think of that. And when I kiss my husband, I shall pretend it's you.' And the *r*s rolled in her throat like the rumbling of well-known thunder.

I murmured, touched and very amused: 'You're just crazy. I'd rather stay at my house.'

I have in fact no liking at all for romantic trysts under the family roof; they're traps, and idiots are always caught in them. But she begged, pleaded and even wept, adding: 'You'll see how I can rrreally love you.' *Rrreally* echoed like a drumroll beating attack.

Her desire seemed to me so strange I could make no sense of it; then, as I pondered, I thought the answer must be some deep hatred of her husband, one of these secret revenges, the woman enjoying deceiving the man she loathes, and wanting to deceive him in his own house, his own bed, between his own sheets.

I asked her: 'Is your husband very cruel to you?'

She looked annoyed: 'No, very kind.'

'But you don't love him?'

She stared at me with her big, surprised eyes. 'Yes I do, I do, very much indeed, but not as much as you, dearr hearrrt.'

Now I was completely in the dark, and while I was trying to work it out, she planted on my mouth one of the caresses she knew were so potent and then murmured: 'You'll come, won't you?'

But I resisted. She got dressed at once and went away.

She didn't appear again for a week. When the week was up, she came again, stopped serious-faced in the doorway of my bedroom and asked: 'Will you come home to sleep with me tonight? If you won't, I'll go away again.'

A week, friend, is a long time, and in Africa that week was as bad as a month. I shouted: 'Yes' and opened my arms. She threw herself into them.

She waited in the darkness in a nearby street, and led me there.

They lived in a little low house by the harbour. First I went through a kitchen, where they ate, and then into the clean, white-washed bedroom, with photographs of relatives all along the walls and paper flowers under glass covers. Marroca seemed mad with delight; she jumped up and down, saying: 'You're at home, it's your house.'

And I acted, in fact, just as I did at home.

I was slightly embarrassed, I have to admit, and even anxious. As I hesitated, in this unknown place, to part company with a certain garment without which a man caught off his guard is clumsy and ridiculous, and incapable of doing anything, she tore from me by force the sheath of my virility and took it into the next room with the rest of my clothes.

I finally regained my confidence and demonstrated as much to her to the best of my ability. After two hours sleep was still a long way from our thoughts when a sudden, violent banging on the door made us both jump; and a loud male voice shouted: 'Marroca, it's me!'

She leapt up: 'My husband! Quick, hide under the bed.' I was groping around in panic for my trousers; but she pushed me, panting: 'Oh go on, go on.'

I lay down flat and slipped without a murmur under the bed where I'd been so comfortable on top.

She went into the kitchen. I heard her open a cupboard, close it, then come back with something I couldn't see, that she quickly put down somewhere; since her husband was growing impatient, she answered in a firm, calm voice: 'I can't find the matches,' then suddenly: 'There they are, I'm coming.' And she opened the door.

The man came in. All I could see were his feet, and they were huge. If the rest was in proportion, he was a colossus.

I heard kisses, a smack on bare flesh, a laugh; then he said in a Marseille accent: 'Forgot my wallet, had to come back. You must have been fast asleep.' He went to the dressing-table and rummaged

around for an eternity looking for what he wanted; then, Marroca
having lain down on the bed again, as if totally tired out, he came
back to her and obviously tried to fondle her, since she replied with
a barrage of furious *rs*.

His feet were so close that I had a mad, stupid, inexplicable desire
to touch them very softly. I refrained.

Not getting very far, he grew irritable. 'You're in a nasty mood
today,' he said. But he gave in. 'Goodnight kid.' The sound of
another kiss; then the huge feet turned away, I saw the nails in them
as he moved off, into the next room, and the street door slammed
shut.

I was saved!

I came slowly out of my hiding-place, a humble, wretched thing,
and while Marroca, still naked, danced a jig round me, shrieking
with laughter and clapping her hands, I dropped heavily into a
chair. I jumped up again quickly; there was something cold under
me, and since I was no better dressed than my partner in crime, I felt
the contact. I looked round. I had just sat on a little hatchet for
chopping wood, sharp as a knife. How had it got there! I hadn't seen
it when I came in.

Marroca, seeing me jump, was choking with laughter, shouting,
coughing, both hands clutching her belly.

I thought her amusement improper and out of place. We had been
gambling foolishly with our lives; I still felt the chills running down
my spine and her giggling hurt my feelings.

'What if your husband had seen me?' I asked.

She answered: 'No danger.'

'What! No danger! That's a stiff one! He only had to bend down
to find me.'

She had stopped laughing; she was just smiling, staring at me
with her huge wide eyes, filling up with fresh desire.

'He wouldn't have bent down.'

I insisted: 'Well, look! If he'd just dropped his hat, he'd have had
to pick it up, and then . . . I was all right, wasn't I, in this get-up.'

She put her round muscular arms on my shoulders, and in a
lowered voice, as though she were saying: 'I love you,' she
murmured: 'Well then, he wouldn't have got up again.'

I didn't understand: 'Why not?'

She gave a knowing wink, stretched her hand towards the chair
where I'd just sat down; and her pointing finger, the crease in her
cheek, her parted lips and her bright, fierce, savage, pointed teeth all

showed me the little hatchet for chopping the wood, with its sharp, glittering blade.

She made as if to pick it up; then, pulling me close to her with her left arm, pressing her leg against mine, with her right arm she sketched the movement for beheading a man on his knees . . .

And that, my friend, is what this country means by conjugal duty, love, and hospitality!

XX
Joris-Karl Huysmans (1848–1907)

from *À rebours* (1884)

Huysmans, art critic and novelist, began his writing career as a Naturalist (e.g. Marthe, histoire d'une fille, *1876) but was influenced by the mystical revival of the 1880s towards Symbolism (*À rebours, *1884) and occultism (*Là-bas, *1891) and eventually became a convert to Catholicism (*La Cathédrale, *1898). The following piece is made up of two extracts. The first characterises the aristocratic disdain for contemporary life that is the context of des Esseintes' escapist vision of love as destruction, intellectualised into the form of art. A superficial, convoluted, formal beauty hides an inner terror of the real. See also the Introduction.*

La Femme fatale

Edgy and ill-at-ease, irritated by the meaninglessness of the clichés in common currency, he was turning into one of those people described by the Jesuit Nicole, sensitive to everything, flaying his own skin, wincing at the patriotic and social nonsense trotted out in the papers every morning, exaggerating to himself the extent of the success an omnipotent public grants always, indiscriminately, to works with no content or style.

Already he dreamed of a sophisticated Thebaid, a comfortable desert, a warm, solid Ark where he could flee the endless flood of human stupidity.

Only one passion – women – could have moderated the scorn for all things with which he was afflicted, but even that had worn thin.

He brought to the delights of the flesh his crabbed, depraved appetite, and a blunted palate that soon grew bored. In the days when he had rich young playboy friends, he had been to lavish suppers where drunken women unfasten their blouses at dessert and bang the table with their heads; he had been backstage, tried his hand at actresses and singers, endured, on top of the innate stupidity of the female, the raving vanity of third-rate theatricals. He had kept notorious whores and contributed to the wealth of agencies who provide dubious pleasures for a price; and finally, sated, tired of the monotony of luxury, the same old caresses, he had thrown himself headlong in among the dregs of society, hoping to find fresh fuel for his desires in the contrast, thinking he might stimulate his jaded senses with the titillations of dirt and poverty.

Whatever he tried, he was overwhelmed by tremendous boredom. He made furious efforts, resorted to the dangerous caresses of experts, but then his health suffered and his nervous system got worse; the nape of his neck was already sensitive and his hand shook – gripping a heavy object, it stayed steady, but with something light, like a small glass, it was weak and wobbly.

The doctors he spoke to terrified him. It was time to stop this way of life, give up the practices that were sapping his strength. He was quiet for a time; but soon his imagination caught fire again and called him back to the battlefield. Like young girls in puberty craving spoiled or abject meats, he resorted to imagining and then indulging in special passions and deviant pleasures; and that was the end; apparently content with having drained all experience, worn out with their efforts, his senses fell into a lethargy, and impotence threatened.

He found himself back on the same old path, sobered, alone, abominably weary, begging for an end that the weakness of his flesh would never let him attain.

As his desire to withdraw from a loathsome world of revolting boorishness became more acute, so also did his need to see no more pictures of humanity toiling away in Paris between four walls or wandering the streets begging for money become more imperative.

Having washed his hands of modern life, he was determined to bring into his cell no germs of future disgust or regret; what he wanted was subtle, exquisite painting, steeped in old dreams and ancient corruption, far removed from our days and ways.

For the delectation of his intellect and the delight of his eyes, he wanted a few evocative pictures that would sweep him into the world of the unknown, open up trails of new conjecture, shatter his nervous system with erudite hysterias, complex nightmares, visions of cool atrocity.

There was one artist above all others whose work plunged him into deep ecstasy: Gustave Moreau.

He had bought Moreau's two masterpieces and for nights at a time would stand dreaming in front of one of them, the picture of Salome, figured as follows:

There was a throne, like the High Altar in a cathedral, and overhead countless vaults springing from squat columns like Romanesque pillars, enamelled with multicoloured brickwork, studded with mosaics, encrusted with sardonyx and lapis lazuli, in a palace like a basilica, of mixed Moslem and Byzantine design.

In the middle of the tabernacle above the altar with its sweep of half-circular steps sat Herod the Tetrarch, a tiara on his head, legs stiff and straight, hands on his knees.

His face was parchment yellow, furrowed with wrinkles, ravaged by old age; his long beard floated like a white cloud over the jewelled stars studding the orphrey robe that lay moulded over his chest.

Around the motionless statue, frozen like a Hindu god in hieratic pose, burned dishes of perfume, pouring forth billowing vapours pierced by the glinting jewels set in the sides of the throne, like the glowing eyes of animals; and the vapour rose and rolled under the arcades, where the blue smoke mingled with the golden dust of the broad rays of sunlight that fell from the domes.

In the perverse scent of the perfumes, the overheated atmosphere of the church, her left arm stretched out in a gesture of command, her right arm bent, holding up to her face a huge lotus flower, Salome steps slowly forward on the points of her toes, to the accompaniment of a guitar, its strings plucked by the fingers of a crouching woman.

Her face withdrawn, solemn, almost august, she moves into the lascivious dance that will waken the numbed senses of the old Tetrarch; her breasts quiver, and their tips stiffen, rubbed by her swirling necklaces; the diamonds fixed on her moist skin sparkle; her bracelets, belts and rings spit sparks; over her triumphal robe, sewn with pearls, patterned with silver, woven with gold, her tunic of gold and silver mail, every stitch a jewel, flashes and flames, intersecting serpents of flame, swarming over her matt flesh, her tea-rose skin, like magnificent insects with dazzling wings, streaked with crimson, spotted with dawn yellow, mottled with steel-blue, striped with peacock green.

Totally concentrated, her eyes vacant, like a sleepwalker, she cannot see the trembling Tetrarch, or her mother, fierce Herodias, watching over her, or the hermaphrodite or eunuch standing sword in hand at the foot of the throne, a terrifying figure, veiled to the cheeks, his castrate's breasts hanging like gourds under his tunic splashed with orange.

This figure of Salome, that haunts artists and poets, had obsessed des Esseintes for years. How often he had read in Pierre Variquet's old Bible, translated by the theologians of Louvain, the gospel of Saint Matthew, that narrates in short, simple lines the beheading of the Precursor; how often he had dreamed between the lines:

'On the day of the feast of Herod's nativity, the daughter of Herodias danced before the crowd and was pleasing in Herod's sight.

'So he swore an oath to give her whatever she should ask.

'And she, prompted by her mother, said: Give me the head of John the Baptist, on a plate.

'And the king was grieved, but because of his oath, and those sitting at table with him, he ordered it should be given her.

'And he sent a messenger to the prison, to behead him.

'And the head of John was brought on a plate and given to the girl; and she gave it to her mother.'

But neither Matthew, Mark, Luke or the other Evangelists enlarged on the maddening charms or the depraved movements of the dancer. She was obscured, lost, mysterious and ecstatic, in misty far-off ages, not for grasping by precise down-to-earth minds, only accessible to over-excited, shattered brains, neurotic visionaries; resisting painters of the flesh like Rubens, who decked her out like a Flemish butcher's wife; incomprehensible to writers, who have never caught the disturbing exaltation of the dancer, the refined grandeur of the murderess.

In the work of Gustave Moreau, where the concept far exceeded the Biblical facts, des Esseintes finally saw realised the strange, superhuman Salome of his dreams. She was no longer the entertainer forcing from an old man a cry of lust and desire, with a depraved twist of her haunches; breaking the strength and the will of a king with her quivering breasts, jerking belly and shivering thighs. She became, in a fashion, the symbolic deity of untamable Lust, the goddess of immortal Hysteria, accursed Beauty, and the sign of her election was the catalepsy that seized her rigid flesh and hardened muscles; she was the monstrous, indifferent, irresponsible, heartless beast, poisoning, like Helen of old, everything that came near, all who saw her, everything she touched.

This vision of her belonged to the theogonies of the Far East. She was no longer part of the Biblical traditions, could not even be assimilated to the living image of Babylon, the royal Whore of the Apocalypse, adorned like her with jewels and royal crimson, and painted as she was; for the Whore was not hurled by a fateful power, a supreme force, into the seductive abjection of debauch.

And the painter seemed intent on stressing his desire to stay outside time, to give her no exact origin, country or historical moment, setting his Salome in the heart of this extraordinary palace, with its confused, grandiose architecture, dressing her in fantastic, sumptuous garments, mitring her with a vague kind of diadem shaped like a Phoenician tower, like Salammbo wore, and finally placing in her hand the sceptre of Isis, the sacred flower of India and Egypt, the great lotus.

Des Esseintes tried to work out the meaning of the emblem. Did it have the phallic significance given it by the primordial religions of India; did it proclaim to old Herod an offering of virginity, an exchange of blood, an impure wound sought and offered on the express condition of a murder; or was it an allegory of fecundity, the Hindu myth of life, existence held in woman's fingers, torn and crushed by the trembling hands of man swept by madness, crazed by the tumults of the flesh?

Perhaps too, arming his enigmatic goddess with the holy lotus, the painter had thought of the dancing girl, the mortal woman, the defiled Vase, cause of all sin and crime; perhaps he had remembered the rites of ancient Egypt, the embalming ritual in the tomb, when the priests and the chemists stretch out the dead woman's body on a table of jasper, and with their curved needles draw out her brain through her nostrils, and her entrails through an incision in her left flank, and then, before they gild her nails and her teeth, before they anoint her with perfume and bitumen, insert in her sexual parts to purify them the chaste petals of the divine flower.

Whatever his intention had been, the canvas exuded an irresistible fascination; but the water-colour entitled *The Apparition* was perhaps even more disturbing.

There, Herod's palace sprang up like an Alhambra on slender columns iridescent with Moorish tiles, fixed with silver mortar, golden cement; swirling arabesques ran from lozenges of lapis lazuli all along the cupolas, where rainbow gleams, flashes of prismatic light, slithered over inlaid mother-of-pearl.

The murder was done; the executioner stood impassive, his hands on the pommel of his long sword stained with blood.

The head of the saint had risen up from the plate set on the flagged floor and stared, pale, its colourless mouth hanging open, its neck crimson, dripping with tears. There was a mosaic around the face, with a shining aureole, radiating shafts of light under the porticoes, illuminating the dreadful ascent of the head, lighting up the round glazed eyeballs, fixed in a kind of spasm on the dancer.

Salome, with a gesture of terror, is pushing away the frightening vision that nails her motionless on the tips of her toes; her eyes are dilated, her hand clutches her throat convulsively.

She is almost naked; in the heat of the dance, the veils are come undone, the brocades have fallen to the floor; she is dressed only in jewelled cloths and shining minerals; a gorgerin clasps her waist like a corselet, and a marvellous jewel, like a magnificent clasp, glitters in the cleft between her breasts; lower down, a belt runs round her haunches, hiding the top of her thighs where a huge pendant hangs, dripping with a river of emeralds and carbuncles; finally, from the rest of her body, naked between the gorgerin and the belt, her belly swells, indented by a navel with a hole like an engraved onyx seal, milky-coloured, tinged with finger-nail pink.

In the burning rays emanating from the Precursor's head, all the facets of the jewels catch fire; the stones come to life, outlining the woman's body in glowing streaks; points of fire pricking at her neck, legs, and arms, red as coals, purple as jets of gas, blue as burning alcohol, white as starlight.

Flames leap from the dreadful head, still dripping blood, dark purple clots hanging from the trailing beard and hair. Only Salome can see it, its sombre gaze never falls on Herodias, dreaming of hatred finally realised, or the Tetrarch, leaning slightly forward, his hands on his knees, still panting, maddened by the nakedness of the woman drenched in musky scents, smothered in balms, in the smoke of incense and myrrh.

Like the old king, des Esseintes would stand overwhelmed,

exhausted, dizzy, in front of this dancer, less majestic and less haughty, but more disturbing than the Salome of the oil-painting.

In the unfeeling, pitiless statue, the innocent and dangerous idol, the eroticism and the terror of human existence had finally dawned; the great lotus had disappeared, and the goddess had vanished; now the actress, whirled into ecstasy by the dance, was in the grip of a terrifying nightmare, and the courtesan stood hypnotised, petrified by fear.

Here, she was truly a whore; obedient to her hot, cruel female nature; she was alive, more sophisticated and yet more primitive, more hateful, and more exquisite; she stirred more vigorously a man's lethargic senses, bewitched and enslaved his will more surely, this tall, entrancing flower of Venus, grown in a sacrilegious bed, raised in a hothouse of impiety.

As des Esseintes said, no water-colour had ever before attained such brilliance; never before had poor chemical colours showered onto the paper such flashing brilliance of jewels, or such equally brilliant gleams from stained-glass windows struck by the sun's rays, such fabulous, blinding splendour of cloth and flesh.

Lost in contemplation, he pondered the origins of the great artist, the mystical pagan, the visionary who stood apart from the world and saw shining in the heart of Paris the cruel visions and fairytale transformations of another age.

Des Esseintes found it hard to say what school he belonged to; occasional vague echoes of Mantegna and Jacopo de Barbarj; occasional confused memories of da Vinci and Delacroix' feverish colours; but overall, the influence of such masters was hardly noticeable: the truth was that Gustave Moreau was like no one else. With no real predecessor, and no possible descendants, he remained unique in modern art. Going back to ethnographic sources, to the origins of mythologies and comparing, disentangling, their bloody mysteries; bringing together and fusing into a single piece the legends come out of the Far East and transformed by the beliefs of other nations, he found there the justification for his blending of architectures, his luxurious, unexpected mixtures of fabrics, his hieratic, sinister allegories sharpened by the anxious insight of an entirely modern neurosis; and he remained for ever in eternal anguish, obsessed by symbols of love and perversity beyond the human, divine debauch, consummated without abandonment and with no hope.

There was a strange magic in his erudite, hopeless works, an incantation that stirred the very depths of being, as in some of Baudelaire's poems, and the spectator stood dumbfounded, thoughtful, disconcerted by an art that went beyond the limits of painting, borrowing from the writer's art its most subtle powers of evocation, from the art of Limoges its most wonderful brilliance, and from the lapidary and the engraver their most exquisite delicacy. The two figures of Salome, for which des Esseintes' admiration knew no bounds, lived constantly in front of him, hanging on the walls of his study on special panels between the rows of books.

XXI
Rémy de Gourmont (1858–1915)

from *Histoires magiques* (1894)

Essayist, critic and novelist, de Gourmont was one of the founders of the Symbolist review, the Mercure de France. *His works include* Sixtine, roman de la vie cérébrale *(1890),* Le Latin mystique *(1892),* Histoires magiques *(1894),* La Physique de l'amour: Essai sur l'instinct sexuel *(1903; tr. by Ezra Pound, 1926).*

'Péhor', published in the Histoires magiques, *written in a clear and sensuous prose, is a study in the psychology and the physiology of ignorance and repression. Church and family pervert Douceline's healthy sensuality and lively imagination. In his essay 'La Jeune Fille d'aujourd'hui' (1901), de Gourmont inveighs against the myth of the 'sweet young thing' which he sees as an invention by men to secure male interests: 'As long as men need to be sure they're the fathers of their own children, they will approve every means experience can offer to preserve the virginity of young girls.' The fate of Douceline is an ironic morality tale.*

'Péhor' (1894)

Spirited and poor, imaginative and half-starved, Douceline learned early to kiss and caress, found pleasure in stroking her hand down little boys' cheeks or the nape of little girls' necks, who yielded like cats. For no reason at all, she would set to kissing her mother's hands while the knitting needles clicked, and banished to a chair to do penitence would play at smacking her lips on the palms of her hands, her arms, her knees, pulling them up naked one after another; and then she would look at herself. Like any curious female, she had no sense of shame. Scolded for it in crude, sarcastic terms, she conceived a perverse affection for the despised, forbidden spot; her hands followed her eyes. She kept the vice all her life, never spoke of it in the confessional, kept it hidden with frightening cleverness, even in her most reckless moods.

She was passionately excited by the preparatory exercises for her first communion. She would beg holy pictures, or pennies to buy them, steal her friends' pictures out of their prayer books. She was not very fond of the Holy Virgins; she preferred the Jesus ones, the gentle Jesuses with their pink-washed cheeks, fiery beards and blue eyes inscribed in the diffuse light of a halo. There was one with a Visitandine nun at his feet, showing her his heart, streaming with light, while the nun was saying: 'My beloved is all mine and I am his.' Under another Jesus with loving, slightly leery eyes, it said: 'A glance from his eyes has wounded my heart.' From a Sacred Heart stuck by a dagger dripped blood the colour of red ink, with the rubric, debasing one of the loveliest metaphors of mystic theology: 'What better can the Lord give his children than this wine that makes virgins bring forth fruit?' The Jesus spurting this crimson jet had an encouraging, affectionate face, a robe historiated with little golden flowers, and exceptionally delicate, transparent hands starred with two little squashed redcurrants: Douceline worshipped him at once, made him a vow and wrote on the back of the picture: 'I give myself to Our Lord Jesus Christ, because he has given himself to me.'

Often, peeping into her missal, she would gaze on the encouraging, affectionate face and murmur, lifting it to her mouth: 'Yours! Yours!'

Of the mystery of the Eucharist she understood not a word, receiving the Host without emotion, remorse for her sacrilegious confessions, or any attempt at love: all her heart was given to the affectionate, encouraging face.

Then in place of the catechism of perseverance they gave her the 'Shield of Mary' to read. A passage noting Jesus' preference for beautiful souls and his contempt for beautiful faces caught her interest. She gazed at herself in the mirror for hours at a time, decided she was definitely pretty, was sorry for it, wished she could be ugly, prayed fervently, gave herself a fever and woke one morning with her face covered in spots. In her ensuing delirium, she babbled words of love. Once cured, she thanked Jesus for the white marks scarring her forehead and gave herself up to long ejaculatory prayers, kneeling behind a wall on sharp stones. Her knees bled: she kissed the wounds, sucked the blood and said to herself: 'It's the blood of Jesus, for I have his heart.'

Weakened and anaemic after her fever, for some weeks she forgot her vice; the familiar movements started up again in her sleep. She would wake up half polluted and fall asleep again. One morning, her fingers were covered in blood; she was frightened and got straight out of bed, but the blood was everywhere. Her mother was asleep. She tore the image with her dedication out of the prayer book where she had sewn it and went out shivering in her nightdress to bury it in a deep hole. She came back in tears and fainted.

She was forced to believe her mother's explanations. But it wasn't natural. She blamed the Jesus she had instinctively smothered under the grassy earth, the silent haven of the dead. The bloody Jesus was dead. She quietened down, while her mother put her back to bed and gave her a book of saints' lives to read.

Douceline read the saints' lives, storing up strange names that echoed in her ears, as she drowsed, like the sound of bells: one name sounded louder than any of them, noisier than the three bells that rang on high Sundays, echoing and re-echoing in her brain: Pé-hor-Pé-hor-Pé-hor-Pé-hor.

Demons are obedient, like dogs. Péhor is fond of young girls, and remembers the days when he used to inflame the genitals of Cozbi, the royal Madianite, daughter of Sur: he came, and loved Douceline for the sake of her fresh puberty, already tarnished; he took up residence in the dwelling-place of vice, sure of favours and caresses, sure of the obscene embrace of feverish hands, with no need to fear the sword of Phineas, who in former days cut short with a single blow the joys of Cozbi and the joys of Zambri, son of Salu, who had penetrated the daughter of Sur.

The bedroom would light up in the middle of the night, and all the things in it be ringed by a halo, as though become luminous, radiating light. Then, a lull; and in a shadowy redness, closing all the portals of sight, he would come. She would feel his approach, and straight away shivers would start to run up and down her skin, slight at first, then in one precise place. The harbinger light would penetrate through the red shadow, worming into all the fibres of her being, and then there was nothing but the red shadow and without warning, swift jets of soft light, in a faster rhythm; finally, an explosion like fireworks, an exquisite rending, stretching, elongating her brain, spine, marrow, membranes, nipples and all her most sensitive flesh; the little hairs on her skin stood on end like grass rippled by a low wind. And after the last convulsion, little tremors inside: through half-open valves, pleasure filtering, running through her veins to every cell and nerve-ending. Then Péhor would leave his hiding-place and grow to the stature of a handsome young male and Douceline, unamazed, gaze on him in admiration and love. She would draw him down beside her, his head on her shoulder, and fall asleep knowing nothing except Péhor in her arms.

In the daytime, she found pleasure in remembering the nights, delighting in the shamelessness of each stage, the intense caresses, the devastating embrace of Péhor, invisible and intangible while her pleasure lasted, rising up as if by magic when her joy flowered, scattering scent. Who was Péhor? She never knew, heedless of everything but fleshly satisfaction, stupefied by spasm after spasm, living in a carnal dream; a Psyche with no knowledge of man, originator of her own debauch, she would give herself to the dark angel in the red shadows or a dazzling cerebral brilliance, with no will of her own and holding nothing back.

She was getting on for fifteen when a pedlar took advantage of her as she slept the exhausted sleep of adolescence in the pasture where she was minding the family cow. Feeling no pain, completely deflowered by Péhor's audacious inventions, she let him do it. The faces the fellow pulled seemed to her ridiculous, and when he finally sat up and looked at her tenderly, she got up, burst out laughing and walked away, shrugging her shoulders.

She was punished for letting him do it. Péhor never came back.

Now while she minded the cow in the pasture she dreamed to her shame of the pedlar. After some weeks, she had a fright and having seen pregnant women lighting candles to the good Virgin for a safe birth she stuck an enormous one on the candle spikes, so as not to be pregnant.

When her request was granted she was duly grateful, gave herself up to prayer, left her cow and her pasture and went telling long strings of beads, kneeling on the flagstones in front of the beneficent image: she thought its face affectionate and encouraging, as she had once thought Jesus' face.

But even without Péhor, her vice gnawed away at her. Her cheeks grew hollow, she started to cough, her spine was painful, her head would suddenly start spinning and she would find herself lying under the cow's hooves, while it snuffled and lowed over her. She shivered so hard one morning that she couldn't get her stockings on. Back in bed, her belly started to hurt: her inflamed ovaries were throbbing under the pricks of a whole packet of needles.

In the distress and wretchedness of her bed, she was visited by unexpectedly ingenuous fantasies, reminders of her earlier innocence. In spurious ecstasies, she saw God the Father, all in white, like the friar who once preached the sermon for Lent; little images of Saint John, all in silver, playing with curly, beribboned baby lambs on the moss of the heavenly groves, and a Holy Virgin in cloudy blue.

In her last days, the comforting apparitions left her, as if Heaven refused to connive with her any longer. The devil's hypocrisy was exposed and the impenitent sinner returned to him who by force of unspeakable terrors had become her master for eternity. Péhor came back to reside in the secret dwelling-place of the impurities to which she had given her consent. Douceline felt herself ravaged by painful caresses, thistles slowly brushing her skin, lines of live ants running over her bloated, near-putrid genitals, ripe and ready to burst like a fig. For hours of unending agony she heard Péhor's laugh ring in her belly, like the deathbell on the eve of Good Friday, that seems to rise from the tombs. Péhor would revel in his laugh of demonic satisfaction, and then, for a joke, swell up to bursting with stinking winds and release them in a sudden explosion. Then he would begin to take her in a tender embrace, with an ironic bite in place of a spasm. Douceline would scream, but Péhor, it seemed, could scream louder, strident shrieks filling her stomach, which trembled with the vibrations . . . There was a tremendous tumult in his foul den, and then a terrible feeling of crowding, suffocating at the top of her stomach: Péhor was rising. He dug his claws in passing into Douceline's heart, clung and tore at the spongy holes in her lungs, and then her neck swelled like a serpent disgorging its slimy prey, and thick gobs of blood spurted out in a shameful, drunken hiccough. She drew a breath, almost fainting, her eyes closed, sculling with her hands in the gentle waves of the shipwreck carrying the damned girl into the abyss . . . A kiss stinking of excrement fastened itself precisely on her lips, and the soul of Douceline left this world, sucked into the entrails of the demon Péhor.

XXII
Pierre Louÿs (1870–1925)

from *Aphrodite* (1896)

Louÿs was closely connected with the Symbolist movement and a disciple of Hérédia, the Parnassian poet. His fascination with pagan antiquity produced the brilliant hoax translations Chansons de Bilitis *in 1894 and* Aphrodite: moeurs antiques *(1896). Other works include* La Femme et le pantin *(1898);* Les Aventures du roi Pausole *(1900).*

The following extract presents a version of eros in which the destructive powers of love are invoked to bring the individual to the highest self-fulfilment. In Aphrodite, *the beautiful courtesan Chrysis promises herself to the sculptor Demetrios on the fulfilment of three tasks, including the theft of the jewels on the statue of Aphrodite. Chrysis is punished by execution and on the pattern of her dead body Demetrios models his loveliest statue. The carefully constructed gardens that surround the temple of the goddess, evoked in the chapter below, are the formal symbol of this equivalence between self-fulfilment and self-abandonment. Prostitution is the highest form of religion, and death the finest form of prostitution.*

Aphrodite *should be read alongside Louÿs' later* Trois Filles de leur mère *(1926; published posthumously). The two are complementary, despite the discrepancy in tone between the classical discretion of the first and the explicit coarseness of the second. Thérèse and her daughters, the modern prostitutes who invade the narrator's bedroom, have as strong a sense of vocation as Chrysis, and the sense of shame and violation in the text derives not from them but from the narrator, whose responses are conventional. As the Preface to* Aphrodite *argues, the nature of sexuality is entirely dependent on the nature of culture.*

The Gardens of the Goddess
Reproduced by kind permission of Editions Albin Michel, 22 rue
Huyghens, Paris.

The temple of Aphrodite-Astarte stood outside the city gates, in
huge gardens full of flowers and shade which the waters of the Nile,
carried in by seven aqueducts, kept miraculously green whatever
the season.

This forest of blossoms on the edge of the sea, the deep running
streams, the lakes, the dark meadows, had been carved out of the
desert by the first Ptolemy, more than two centuries ago. Since
then, the sycamores planted at his command had turned into giants;
under the influence of the fertile waters, the lawns had grown into
prairies; the ponds widened to lakes; nature had turned a park into a
whole country.

The gardens were more than a valley, more than a region, more
than a country: they were a whole world, closed by stone bounds
and ruled by a goddess, the soul and centre of this universe. The
circumference was ringed by a terrace, eighty stadia long and
thirty-two feet high. It was less a wall than a colossal city, of
fourteen hundred houses. An equal number of prostitutes dwelt in
this holy city, representing, in this single place, seventy different
nations.

The sacred houses were built on a uniform plan: the door of red
copper (a metal sacred to the goddess) had a phallus for knocker,
which struck against an embossed buffer representing the female
genitals; the courtesan's name was carved above, and the initials of
the customary phrase:

Ω.Ξ.Ε

ΚΟΧΛΙΣ

Π.Π.Π

On each side of the door, two rooms opened off, built like shops,
with no wall on the garden side. The right-hand one, the 'display
room', was where the courtesan sat in all her finery on a tall chair at
the hour when the men came. The one on the left was for lovers
who wanted to spend the night in the open air without lying on the
grass.

When the door was open, a corridor led into a wide court with
marble flags with an oval-shaped pond in the middle. A peristyle

cast a ring of shade round this great splash of light, a belt of coolness protecting the entrance to the seven rooms in the house. At the far end stood the altar, of pink granite.

All the women had brought with them from their own land a little image of the goddess, which they set up on the domestic altar and worshipped in their own tongue, without understanding one another. Lakhmi, Ashtaroth, Venus, Ishtar, Freya, Mylitta, Cypris were the religious names of the divine form of their Desire. Some worshipped her in symbolic form: a red pebble, a conical stone, a huge spiny shell. Most of them set on a pedestal of soft wood a crude statuette with skinny arms, heavy breasts and over-developed hips, her hand pointing to the curly triangle on her belly. They would lay a branch of myrtle at her feet, strew rose petals over the altar, and burn a tiny grain of incense for every prayer answered. She was the confidante of all their sorrows, witness of all their labours, and supposed source of all their pleasures. At their death she was placed in their tiny fragile coffins to guard their tombs.

The loveliest of the girls came from the kingdoms of Asia. Every year, the ships carrying to Alexandria the gifts of tributaries and allies unloaded with the bundles and the wineskins a hundred virgins chosen by the priests to serve in the sacred garden. There were Mysians and Jews, Phrygians and Cretans, girls from Ecbatana and Babylon, the shores of the Gulf of Pearls and the holy banks of the Ganges. Some were white-skinned, with faces like cameos and unyielding breasts; others, dark as the rain-soaked earth, golden rings threaded through their nostrils, their short, dark hair scattered over their shoulders.

Some came from further away still; tiny, slow-moving little creatures, whose language no one knew, who looked like yellow monkeys. Their eyes were elongated at the temples; their straight black hair was strangely dressed. These girls remained as shy as lost animals for the whole of their lives. They knew all the movements of love, but refused kisses on the mouth. Between brief encounters, they could be seen playing together, sitting on their tiny feet, engaged in childish games.

In one lonely stretch of grassland lived a band of the fair, pink daughters of the Nordic peoples, sleeping out on the grass. There were Sarmatians with their triple braids, sturdy legs, square shoulders, who wove themselves garlands from tree branches, and wrestled hand-to-hand for amusement; snub-nosed, big-breasted hairy Scythians, who would only copulate like animals; gigantic

Teutons who terrified the Egyptians with their hair light as an old
man's, and their flesh softer than a child's; Gauls red as cattle who
would laugh for no reason; young Celts with sea-green eyes, who
never went out naked.

In another place, the brown-breasted Iberians gathered together
by day. They had thick heads of hair, elaborately dressed, and
muscular bellies, which they never plucked smooth. Their
Alexandrians liked their firm skins and big rumps. They were hired
as dancers as much as mistresses.

The daughters of Africa lived under the broad shade of the
palm-trees: Numidians with white veils, Carthaginians clothed in
black gauze, Negresses wrapped in multicoloured costumes.

There were fourteen hundred of them.

Once a woman had entered there, she never left again till the first
day of her old age. She gave the temple half of what she earned, and
had to make do with the rest for her meals and her perfumes.

They were not slaves, and each was the proper owner of one of
the houses on the Terrace; but not all had as many lovers, and often
the more fortunate managed to buy neighbouring houses sold by
the occupants so as not to die of hunger. The vendors would take
their obscene statuettes into the park and look for a flat stone, for an
altar, in some corner where they then stayed. Poor tradesmen knew
that, and preferred to go to the women who slept on the moss, by
their open-air sanctuaries; but sometimes even they never came,
and then, two by two, the poor girls would unite their wretchedness in passionate friendships, turning almost into conjugal love,
households where everything was shared, down to the last woollen
tatter, and other indulgences consoled them for their long periods
of chastity.

Those who had no close friend offered themselves as willing
slaves to their more sought-after colleagues. The latter were forbidden to have more than a dozen of these poor girls in their service;
but there were twenty-two courtesans reputed to have reached the
maximum, who had selected a multicoloured band of servants
from every race.

If, in the course of taking their lovers, they conceived a son, he
was brought up within the temple to contemplate the perfect form
and serve its divinity. If they gave birth to a daughter, the child
belonged to the goddess. On the first day of her life, there was a
celebration of her symbolic marriage with the son of Dionysius, and
the High Priest himself deflowered her with a little gold knife, for

virginity displeases Aphrodite. Later, she would enter the Didascalion, a monumental school situated behind the temple, where the little girls learned in seven classes the method and theory of the erotic arts: the look, the embrace, the movements of the body, the variations of the caress, the secret techniques of lips, teeth and throat. The pupil could choose freely the day of her first experience, because desire is a command of the goddess, who must not be thwarted; on that day, she was given one of the houses on the Terrace. Some of these children, not even nubile, were among the most tireless courtesans, and the most often called-for.

The inside of the Didascalion, the seven classrooms, the little theatre and the peristyle in the courtyard were decorated with ninety-two frescoes summarising the teaching of love. It was the work of one man's entire life: Cleochares of Alexandria, the illegitimate son and disciple of Apelles, had finished them just before he died. Recently, Queen Berenice, who took a great interest in the famous School and sent her young sisters there, had commissioned from Demetrius a series of marble compositions to complete the decoration; so far, only one had been set up in the children's class.

At the end of every year, in front of all the assembled courtesans, there was a great competition that stirred the crowd of women to tremendous rivalry, because the twelve prizes that were awarded granted the highest privilege they could possibly imagine: entry to the Cotytteion.

This monument was so wreathed in mystery that no one nowadays can give any detailed description of it. We know only that it stood within the peribolus and was shaped like a triangle, the base of which was a temple to the goddess Cotytto in whose name unknown, terrifying debaucheries took place. The two other sides of the monument consisted of eighteen houses; thirty-six courtesans lived there, so sought after by rich lovers that they never gave themselves for less than two minae: they were the Baptes of Alexandria. Once a month, at full moon, they came together in the compound by the temple, crazed with aphrodisiac draughts and wearing ritual phalluses. The oldest of the thirty-six had to take a deadly dose of a fearsome love philtre. The certainty of a speedy death enabled her to experiment fearlessly with all the dangerous pleasures living women would shy from. Her foam-covered body became the centre and the pattern of the whirling orgy; amid wailing shrieks, cries, tears and dances the other naked women

would embrace her, trail their hair in her sweat, rub themselves
against her burning skin and draw fresh ardour from the uninterrupted spasms of her raging agony. For three years these women
lived in this way and after the thirty-sixth month this was their
ecstatic end.

Other less venerable shrines had been set up by the women in
honour of the other names of many-sided Aphrodite. There was
even an altar dedicated to Ouranian Aphrodite, to receive the chaste
vows of sentimental courtesans; another to Apostrophian
Aphrodite, who took away the memory of unhappy loves; another
to Chryseian Aphrodite, who could bring rich lovers; another
Aphrodite of Genetyllis, who protected girls in pregnancy; and
another to Aphrodite of Colias who sanctioned base desires,
because everything to do with love was worthy of reverence in the
goddess's eyes. But the virtue and efficacy of the private altars were
limited to minor requests. They were waited on without formality,
their favours were everyday ones and they were treated with
familiarity. Those whose prayers were answered set on them simple
flowers; those who were not satisfied defiled them with their
excrement. They were neither consecrated nor served by the
priests, and so to profane them was no sin.

The discipline of the temple was very different.

The Temple, the Great Temple of the Good Goddess, the holiest
place in all Egypt, the inviolable Astarteion, was a colossal building
three hundred and thirty-six feet long, raised up on seventeen steps
at the top of the gardens. Its golden doors were guarded by twelve
hermaphrodite slaves, symbolising the two objects of love and the
twelve hours of the night.

The entrance looked not to the East but to Paphos, that is, the
North-West; the sun's rays never shone directly into the sanctuary
of the great Divinity of the night. The architrave was supported by
eighty-six columns, dyed in crimson for half their height, swathes
of red from which the top half rose dazzling white, like a tall female
torso.

Between the epistyle and the coronis wound the long belt of the
Zophorus, decorated with fabulous erotic beasts: there were female
centaurs mounted by stallions, skinny satyrs climbing onto goats,
monstrous bulls leaping onto virgins, naiads covered by stags,
tigers making love to Bacchantes, lionesses seized by griffons. The
whole mass of creatures was in rut, swept by the holy and irresist-

ible passion. The male strained, the female opened, and the first tremor of life awoke in the fusion of the two creative sources. At irregular intervals the press of obscure couples gave way to a tableau of immortals: Europa bent under the weight of the magnificent creature from Olympus, Leda guiding the vigorous swan between her yielding young thighs. Further on, the insatiable Siren exhausted the dying Glaucus; the god Pan, standing upright, took possession of a dishevelled hamadryad; the Sphinx lifted her rump to the horse Pegasus – and at the very end of the frieze, the sculptor had represented himself, in front of the goddess Aphrodite, modelling after her in soft wax the folds of a perfect cteis, as if his whole ideal of beauty, joy and virtue had long ago fled into that precious, fragile flower.

XXIII
Octave Mirbeau (1848–1917)

from *Le Jardin des supplices* (1899)
Journal d'une femme de chambre (1900)

Originally a Right-wing journalist, Mirbeau shifted from 1885 onwards to an anarchist position. He was a collaborator on Le Journal *1894–98, and in 1899 wrote a number of pro-Dreyfus articles. Besides his novels, he also wrote short stories (*Lettres de ma chaumière, *1886).*

Both of the following novels, written in different modes, are attacks on the moral and political corruption of la Belle Époque. Le Jardin des supplices *(discussed also in the Introduction) uses the morbid eroticism of the Decadents to challenge the institutions within which they evolved. Clara, the English girl met on the boat who introduces the narrator to the garden and to the philosophy and the tortures of the East, attacks the greater evils of Western colonial exploitation and the religious hypocrisy that sanctions them: the massacre of young Indian princes at Candy, Arabs buried to the neck in the desert and left by French soldiers to die, missionary 'vultures' prowling through desecrated temples, sanctioning wholesale murder, bringing 'civilisation at the end of a torch, at the tip of sabre and bayonets'. The text, however, is ambivalent. What it offers is a literary anarchism which sees Clara's beauty as enhanced by her thirst for cruelty, writing her into that contemporary emblem, the* femme fatale; *and its political effectiveness is undercut by its portrayal of the erotic seduction of death, a vortex in which sense and reason vanish. Sated and sickened, the narrator finally rejects Clara, but not the 'truth' she represents. Corruption is presented as an eternal and inevitable part of life:*

Woman contains an elemental cosmic force, an invincible force of destruction, like nature . . . Being the matrix of life she is also, by the same token, the matrix of death . . . since it is from death that life is eternally reborn . . . and to destroy death would be to kill the only, fertile source of life . . .

The garden with its exotic carnivorous flowers, all the colours of decomposition, flesh-eating peacocks, luxuriant abundance nourished by human suffering and blood, is the natural symbol of the identity of love and eros. The alternative is the barren desert: no life without death.

The same impression is left by the satire of the Journal d'une femme de chambre, *a servant's-eye view of the depths of corruption beneath the rich trappings of provincial respectability. In her opening pages, Célestine tells of one of her first confrontations with an employer. The story has a certain grotesque comedy, created by her determinedly caustic and deflationary tone; but neither sarcasm nor platitudes can successfully distance the perverse and terrifying depths she would prefer not to contemplate, the master's violent fits, teeth clenched into the leather boot. She remains however in service, and her diary is an account of how she learns to survive by living like her masters.*

Mirbeau's eroticism attacks a decadence and a perversity which paradoxically it also embraces and celebrates. Within the limits of nineteenth-century language, such paradox is one of the few roads available into the darker areas of eros. The next steps, to a clearer and better understanding, will be taken by the surrealists, armed with a new aesthetics, a new psychology, and a new politics.

from Le Jardin des supplices *(1899)*

The Penal Colony: Impressions of Clara

The penal colony is built on the bank of the river. Its quadrangular walls enclose more than a hundred thousand square yards of ground. No windows: the only opening is the great gate, crowned with red dragons and reinforced with heavy iron bars. Watchtowers, square towers topped with stacks of curved roofs, mark the four corners of the sinister wall. Other smaller towers are spread along at regular intervals. At night, all the towers are lit up like lighthouses, casting over the colony, the plain and the river an accusatory light. The massive foundations of one of the walls, covered in slimy weed, plunge down into the deep, black, stinking water. A low gate leads across a drawbridge to the jetty, which reaches right into the middle of the river, crowds of ditty-boats and sampans moored to its wooden frame. Two halbadiers, spears in hand, guard the gate. On the right of the jetty a little gunboat, something like our own protection launches, lies motionless at anchor with the mouths of its three guns trained on the colony. On the left, as far downriver as the eye can see, twenty-five or thirty rows of boats mask the other bank with a confusion of rainbow-coloured boards, gaudy masts, rigging and grey sails. And from time to time the mighty paddleboats pass by, painfully propelled by the dry sinewy arms of the poor wretches in their cage.

Behind the colony, far, far into the distance, up to the dark line of mountains girdling the horizon, stretches the rocky earth with its brief undulations, blackish-brown in places or the colour of dried blood, bearing nothing but scrawny maples, faded blue thistles and stunted cherries that never flower. Endless desolation! Overpowering bleakness! . . . For eight months of the year the sky is blue, a blue washed with red, kindled by the reflections of an eternal blaze, a relentless blue no passing cloud dares cross. The sun bakes the earth, roasts the rocks, vitrifies the pebbles, which shatter underfoot like glass splintering or crackling flames. No bird ventures into the furnace-like atmosphere. Nothing lives there but invisible organisms, swarms of bacillae that at evening-time, when the dank vapours rise with the sailors' chants from the weary river, take on the clear forms of fever, plague and death.

What a contrast with the other bank, where the rich, fertile soil, covered with orchards and gardens, bears giant trees and wondrous flowers!

As we left the bridge, we had the luck to find a palanquin to carry us across the burning plain almost to the foot of the colony, whose gates were still closed. A band of police carrying spears with yellow streamers and huge shields that nearly hid them from sight kept in bounds the impatient, swollen crowd. The crowd grew bigger by the moment. There were tents for drinking tea, or for nibbling pretty sweetmeats, rose-petals and acacia blossoms rolled in delicate scented pastry and sprinkled with sugar. There were other tents where musicians played the flute and poets recited verses, while the punkah, waving in the fiery air, spread a slight coolness, a fresh breath on our faces. Wandering merchants were selling pictures, ancient tales of crime, figures of tortures and torments, engravings and ivories, bizarre and obscene. Clara bought a few of the ivories, saying to me:

'Look at these so-called barbaric Chinese – so much more civilised than we are, so much more in tune with the logic of life and the harmony of nature! . . . They don't think the act of love is something shameful that ought to be hidden . . . They glorify it, praise every movement and every caress . . . like the Ancients, who didn't treat the phallus as an object of infamy, or an image of impurity, but as a God! . . . And look how much Western art has lost from being forbidden to express the magnificence of love. Eroticism with us is a poor, stupid, chilling thing . . . it always comes in a tortured mask of sin, while here it still has all the vital fullness, the whinnying poetry, the quivering grandeur of nature . . . You're just a European lover . . . a poor, timid, shivering little soul indoctrinated by Catholicism with a foolish fear of nature and hatred of love . . . Catholicism has twisted and perverted the real meaning of life for you . . . '

'My dear Clara,' I objected . . . 'is it natural to seek delight in decay and nourish one's desires on the dreadful sight of pain and death? . . . Is that not in fact a perversion of the nature you say you worship, to justify, perhaps, the criminal and monstrous nature of your sensuality?'

'No!' retorted Clara, 'because Love and Death are the same thing! . . . and because decay is Life eternally resurrected . . . Look . . . ' She broke off suddenly and asked me: 'Why do you say that? . . . How funny you are! . . . ' And with a delightful pout, added: 'It's so tiresome how little you understand! . . . Why don't you see? . . . Why do you still not see, it's not love, even, but lust, love at its most perfect, that reveals and refines all a man's mind and faculties . . . lust, and nothing else, that makes your personality complete? . . . Look . . . when you make love, for instance, have you never thought you could commit a magnificent crime . . . transcend, in your own self, all the social taboos, law, everything? . . . And if you never have, then why make love?'

'I can't argue with you,' I stammered . . . 'It feels like being in a nightmare . . . The sun . . . the crowd . . . the smells . . . and your eyes, your voluptuous, tormenting eyes . . . your voice . . . your wickedness . . . it all frightens me . . . drives me mad!'

Clara gave a short, mocking laugh. 'Poor sweetie!' she sighed comically. 'You won't say that tonight when you're in my arms . . . and I make love to you.'

The crowd was becoming increasingly animated. Crouching under sunshades, their long red robes spread round them like pools of blood, frenzied bonzes, banging gongs, poured crude invective on the passers-by, who appeased their curses with large flat coins, piously dropped into metal bowls.

Clara took me into a tent embroidered with peach blossom, sat me beside her on a heap of cushions, and stroked my brow with her electrifying hand, the hand that dealt oblivion or ecstasy, saying: 'Heavens, dear, it's taking so long! . . . Every week it's the same . . . It takes them for ever to open the gate . . . Why don't you say something? . . . Do I frighten you? . . . Are you glad you came? . . . Do you like it when I caress you, you dear, beloved wretch! . . . Oh, what beautiful, tired eyes! . . . It's fever . . . and me, too, isn't it? . . . Say it's me? . . . Do you want some tea? . . . Or another pastille?'

'I want to go! . . . I want to sleep!'

'Sleep! . . . How strange you are! . . . Oh, you'll see, shortly, how beautiful . . . how terrible it is! . . . And what extraordinary . . . unknown . . . wonderful desires it stirs in the flesh! . . . We'll go back by the river, in my sampan . . . And spend the night in a flower-boat . . . You'd like that, wouldn't you?' She tapped my hands lightly with her fan. 'You're not listening. Why don't you listen to me? . . . You're so pale and sad . . . And you're not really listening at all . . . ' She nestled close to me, her whole body against mine, sinuous, wheedling: 'You're not listening, wretch,' she went on, 'and not even touching me . . . Stroke me, darling . . . Feel how cold and hard my breasts are . . . '

And in a lower voice, cruel, voluptuous green flames leaping from her eyes, she told me: 'Listen! . . . A week ago . . . I saw something extraordinary . . . My dear love, I saw a man whipped for stealing a fish . . . All the judge said was: "When a man's standing there with a fish in his hand, there's no need to assume every time he's a fisherman!" Then he condemned the man to be beaten to death with iron rods . . . For a fish, darling! . . . They did it in the garden of tortures . . . Imagine, there the man was, kneeling on the ground, his head resting on a kind of wooden block . . . the wood black with dried blood . . . His back and loins were naked . . . the colour of old gold! . . . I arrived just as a soldier grabbed his long pigtail and tied it to a ring fastened in a stone flag, set in the ground . . . Near the victim, another soldier was heating a tiny, tiny iron switch in a forge . . . And then . . . Listen! . . . Are you listening? . . . When the switch was red hot, the soldier would whip the man, with all his might, on his loins . . . The switch whistled through the air . . . sank deep into the muscles, and they sizzled, and a reddish vapour came off. . . Do you see? . . . Then the soldier left the switch to go cold in the flesh, and the flesh swelled and closed over it . . . Then when it was cold he pulled it out, hard, with a single movement . . . with little bleeding shreds of flesh . . . And the man screamed with dreadful pain . . . Then the soldier did it again . . . He did it fifteen times! . . . And dear heart, every time, I felt as if the switch were sinking into my loins . . . It was ghastly, and very sweet!'

Seeing I said nothing: 'Ghastly, and very sweet,' she echoed . . . 'And if you knew how handsome and strong the man was! . . . Muscles like a statue . . . Kiss me, dear love, kiss me then!'

Clara's eyes were rolled back. Between her half-closed lids I could see only the whites of her eyes . . . She said again: 'He didn't move . . . It made little waves over his back . . . Give me your lips!' [. . .]

A few minutes later, a murmur ran through the tents and the crowd. From behind my heavy lids which, despite myself, had almost closed listening to the horrors of Clara's story, I saw robes, robes, sunshades, fans, happy faces, evil faces, dancing, swirling, rushing . . . It was like huge flowers springing up, enchanted birds wheeling . . .

'The gates, dear heart,' cried Clara . . . 'they're opening the gates! . . . Come on, quick . . . And stop being so gloomy, please! . . . Think of all the lovely things I've told you about, that you're going to see! . . . '

I got to my feet . . . Taking me by the arm, she pulled me away with her, where to, I don't know . . .

[. . .] Leaning over me like the very embodiment of sin, Clara, with her mouth red as the cydonia blossom, Clara with her green eyes, the greyish green of the young fruit of the almond tree, brought me back to reality, pointing to the garden with a broad sweep of her arm, and saying: 'Look, my love, what marvellous artists the Chinese are, and how skilfully they make nature an accomplice of their refined cruelties! . . . In that dreadful Europe of ours, where the true nature of beauty is long forgotten, we torture in secret in the depths of prisons, or else in public squares, with vile, drunken crowds . . . Here the instruments of torture and death, stakes, gibbets, crosses, are surrounded by flowers, the miraculous silent enchantment of every flower that grows . . . You'll see them presently, mingled so closely with this splendid orgy of flowers, the harmony of this unique, magical nature, that they somehow become one with her, blossoming by a miracle from this earth, this light . . . '

I couldn't conceal a gesture of impatience.

'You're stupid!' snapped Clara . . . 'A stupid little beast, and you don't understand anything! . . . '

A harsh, dark line crossed her brow and she went on: 'Look! . . . Have you ever been at a celebration feeling ill, or unhappy? Then you know how your sadness was irritated, exacerbated, almost insulted by the happiness on people's faces, the beauty of everything around . . . It's an unbearable feeling . . . Think how it must feel for the victim about to die in torment . . . Think how much the anguish in his body and his soul is multiplied by all the splendour around him . . . and how much more atrocious is his death agony, more desperately atrocious, dear little heart! . . . '

'I was thinking of love,' I answered reproachfully . . . 'And here you are talking again about torture, always talking about torture! . . . '

'Well, of course! . . . it's the same thing . . . '

She was still standing beside me, her hands on my shoulder. The red shade of the ash seemed to wrap her round in a glimmer of fire . . . She sat down on the bench, and went on:

'And wherever there are men, there's torture . . . I can't do anything about it, dear baby, so I just try to accept it and enjoy it, because blood's a precious stimulant to pleasure . . . It's the wine of love . . . '

[. . .] The avenue twisted and turned, into sunlight and shadow, changing with every moment, and the lovelier its flowers became the more inexorably horrific were the sights mingled with them.

'Look closely, darling,' said Clara . . . 'Look all round you . . . Now we're in the loveliest and most interesting part of the garden . . . Oh, those flowers! Look at those flowers!'

She pointed to some strange vegetation growing in a part of the ground where water oozed in all directions . . . I went closer . . . On tall stalks, scaly and spotted with black like snakeskins, were great flat blades like flaring trumpets, dark decaying purple on the inside, and on the outside a greeny decomposing yellow, like the gaping throats of dead animals . . . From the bottom of the cones stretched long, bloody spikes, mimicking the form of monstrous phalluses . . . Attracted by the scent of corpses rising from these horrible plants, flies buzzed round in dense swarms, fell into the depths of the blade, covered from top to bottom with contractile silk threads which wrapped them round and held them captive, tighter than spiders' webs . . . And all along the stalks the fingery leaves clenched and twisted, like tormented hands.

'You see, dear heart,' explained Clara . . . 'these flowers aren't inventions of a sick brain, a genius in delirium . . . they're nature . . . Didn't I tell you nature loves death! . . . '

'And nature creates monsters!'

'Monsters! . . . Monsters! . . . There are no monsters! . . . What you call monsters are higher forms, or, simply, forms beyond the reach of your imagination . . . Aren't the gods monsters? . . . Isn't the man of genius a monster, like the tiger, or the spider, like every individual, living above the lies of society, in the divine, shining immortality of things? . . . Then I'm a monster too! . . . '

We had turned into a path fenced with bamboo, overrun with honeysuckle, scented jasmine, bignonias, branching mallow, climbing hibiscus, not yet in bloom. A moonseed wound its web of lianas round a column of stone. On top of the column grinned the face of a hideous god, his ears spread out like bats' wings, his hair rising in fiery horns. The base was hidden in incarvilleas, daylilies, moreas, bare-stemmed delphiniums, buried in their pink bells, scarlet thyrses, golden chalices and crimson stars. Covered with ulcers and devoured by vermin, a mendicant priest, apparently the guardian of the building, who was training mongooses to make backbreaking somersaults, heaped insults on us as we came into sight . . . 'Dogs! . . . Dogs! . . . Dogs! . . . '

We had to throw a few coins to the fanatic, whose invective surpassed the most insulting obscenities the foulest imagination could invent.

'I know him!' said Clara. 'He's like any priest of any religion . . . He's trying to frighten us to get our money . . . but he's not a bad devil!'

At intervals, in the recesses of the fencing, like summerhouses and flowerbeds, wooden benches, armed with chains and bronze neckbands, iron tables shaped like crosses, blocks, grills, gibbets, racks, beds covered with sharp blades, bristling with iron points, shackles driven into the ground, trestles and wheels, pans and cauldrons hanging over dead fires, all the tools of torture and sacrifice, displayed their bloodstains, dried and blackish, red and sticky. Pools of blood filled all the hollows; long trails of congealed blood hung from the dismantled machinery . . . Round all the instruments, the earth was draining away the last drops of blood . . . More blood starred the white jasmine with red, streaked the coral pink of the honeysuckle and the mauve of the passion-flowers, and scraps of human flesh, torn away by the lashing whips and leather thongs, hung here and there on the tips of leaves and petals . . . Seeing me waver and jib at the pools, whose spreading stains reached out to the middle of the avenue, Clara urged me on in a soft voice: 'This is nothing, darling . . . Come on!'

It was hard to go on. The plants, the trees, air and earth were full of flies, drunken insects, vicious fighting beetles, swollen mosquitoes. All the animal life of corpses burgeoned around us in myriads, in the heat of the sun . . . Foul maggots teemed in the red pools, fell in soft bunches from the branches . . . The sand seemed to be breathing, moving, lifted by the seething swell of maggot life. Deafened and blinded, our way was blocked every moment by the buzzing swarms, growing and multiplying, and for Clara's sake I feared their deadly stings . . . And from time to time we had the horrible feeling that our feet were sinking into the ground, sodden with the rain of blood!

'This is nothing, darling,' Clara said again . . . 'Come on!'

And then to complete the drama, human faces appeared . . . teams of workers, coming with casual steps to clean and mend the instruments of torture, the time for executions in the garden being over . . . They looked at us, surprised no doubt to meet at that time and in that place two creatures still on their feet, still alive, with heads, legs and arms . . . Further on, crouching on the ground like a painted ape, we saw a kindly, fat-bellied potter, glazing freshly-baked flower pots; next to him, a basket-maker, with precise, unhurried fingers, was weaving ricestraw and supple reeds, cunning shelters to protect the plants . . . a gardener sharpened his grafting-knife on a grindstone, humming a popular song, while an old woman, chewing betel leaves, nodding her head, was calmly clean-ing a kind of iron maw, with foul shreds of human flesh still clinging to the sharp points of its teeth. We saw children, too, beating rats to death and stuffing them into baskets. And along the fences, starving, ferocious, trailing the imperial splendour of their cloaks in the blood and mud, peacocks, flocks of peacocks pecked at the blood spurted into the hearts of the flowers, and clucked and snapped at the shreds of flesh sticking to the leaves, greedy for meat.

A sickly slaughter-house smell, hanging over and dominating all the other scents, turned our stomachs and choked us with an overwhelming desire to be sick. Even Clara, the spirit of the charnel-house, angel of rot and decay, her nervous excitement, perhaps, slightly lessened, had turned a little pale . . . The sweat stood out on her forehead . . . I saw her eyes turn up and her legs give way.

'I'm cold!' she said.

She gave me a look of real distress. Her nostrils, which always flared wide at the scent of death, had narrowed . . . I thought she was going to faint . . .

[. . .] Clara said nothing, gave no more explanations . . . She was listening to the heavy wings of the vultures passing over the trellissed branches, and above them, the cawing of countless flocks of crows, sweeping through the sky . . .

The gloomy avenue of tamarisks ended in a broad terrace set with peonies, which led us down to the pool . . .

The irises stood out of the water, their tall stalks displaying extraordinary flowers, with petals the colour of old stone vases; precious enamels streaked with the colours of blood; threatening crimsons, blues flamed with orangey ochre, velvety blacks with sulphurous throats . . . Some, huge and contorted, were like cabalistic signs . . . White waterlilies and Egyptian lotus spread their huge open flowers over the golden water, for all the world like severed heads afloat . . . We leaned for a few moments over the rail, watching the water in silence. An enormous carp, only its golden snout visible, was asleep under a leaf, and the goldfish swam to and fro between the cattails and the reeds, like red thoughts in a woman's brain.

from Journal d'une femme de chambre *(1900)*

A Pair of Boots

It was not the first time I had had a job in the provinces. Four years
ago I got a place . . . Oh, it didn't last long! . . . and the circumstances were really unusual . . . I remember that particular
adventure as if it were yesterday . . . The details are a bit risqué,
nasty even, but I mean to tell the story . . . Besides, I give fair
warning to my readers that my intention in writing this diary is to
hold nothing back, about myself as well as other people. I mean, in
fact, to put in it every ounce of sincerity I have, when it's needed,
and all the brutality of life. It's no fault of mine if souls stripped of
their veils and shown naked have such a rotten stench.

Here's how it was:
    I had been picked out in an employment bureau by a kind of fat
housekeeper to be a chambermaid for a certain Monsieur Rabour
from Touraine. I accepted the terms, and it was agreed I would take
the train on such a day, at such a time, to such a station. It all went
according to programme.
    Having handed my ticket over to the inspector, I found at the exit
a sort of coachman, with a surly red face, who hailed me:
    'You Monsieur Rabour's new chambermaid?'
    'Yes, that's me.'
    'Got a trunk?'
    'Yes, I have a trunk.'
    'Give me your luggage ticket and wait for me there . . .'
    He went through onto the platform. The officials hurried up.
They called him 'Monsieur Louis' in a friendly, respectful tone.
Louis looked out my trunk from the heap of parcels and had it
carried to a dogcart, standing by the barrier.
    'Right then . . . are you getting in?'
    I took my place beside him on the bench seat, and we set off.
    The coachman kept looking at me out of the corner of his eye. I
looked him over likewise. I saw straight away that this was a lout, a
rough peasant, a badly trained servant with no experience of service
in a big house. That put me out. I'm one who likes a fine livery.
Nothing gets me so worked up as white skin trousers, clinging
round sinewy thighs. And God, this Louis had no style, no gloves
for driving in, a blue-grey drugget suit too big for him, and a flat

shiny leather cap, trimmed with two rows of gold braid. No, really! They were way behind in that hole. On top of that, a brutal, sour face, but not a bad devil at bottom. I know the type. The first few days with new girls they act nasty and then it sorts itself out. Sometimes it sorts itself out better than you wanted.

We were a long time without saying anything. He was playing the big coachman, holding the reins high, making great sweeps with his whip . . . God, he was a laugh! I put on a respectable face and looked at the countryside, which was nothing special: fields, trees, houses, same as everywhere. He slowed the horse to a walk to go up a slope and suddenly, with a mocking smile, asked: 'Hope you've got a good stock of boots with you, then?'

'Of course!' I said, surprised by the question, which had nothing to do with anything, and even more surprised by the peculiar tone he asked it in. 'Why do you ask? . . . It's a bit of a stupid question, old fellow, eh?'

He gave me a bit of a nudge with his elbow, ran his eyes over me with a strange look I couldn't make sense of, both sharp irony and, I swear, delighted obscenity, and then sniggered: 'Would you believe it! . . . Go, on, act the innocent if you want . . . A joker, eh . . . a bloody joker!'

Then he clicked his tongue and the horse picked up speed again.

I was intrigued. What could that mean, then? Nothing at all, perhaps . . . I decided the fellow was a bit of a simpleton with no idea how to talk to women, and that was all he could think of to start a conversation which, in any case, I thought it best not to pursue.

Monsieur Rabour's estate was big and rather fine. A pretty house, painted light green, surrounded with wide flower-covered lawns and a pinewood smelling of turpentine . . . I love the country . . . but it's funny, it makes me sad and sleepy. I was completely stupefied when I got into the hall where the housekeeper was waiting, the same one who had taken me on in the agency in Paris, with God knows how many impertinent questions about my private tastes and habits. That ought to have put me on my guard . . . But you go on, seeing and putting up with worse and worse things every time, and you never learn . . . I hadn't liked the housekeeper back at the agency; here, she sickened me right off and I thought she looked like a repulsive old pimp. She was a fat woman, fat and short, short and blown out with yellowish fat, her hair in flat grey coils, voluminous great breasts and hands that were soft, wet, transparent and jelly-like. Her grey eyes were full of spite,

cold, calculated, vicious spite. The steady way she looked at you
raked you through, body and soul, almost made you blush.

She took me to a little room and left me at once, saying she would
go and find the master, because the master wanted to meet me
before I started my duties.

'You see, he hasn't seen you,' she added. 'I took you on, of
course, but still, you've got to suit the master . . .'

I looked over the room. It was kept spotlessly clean and neat. The
copper and brass, the furniture, the floor and the doors, thoroughly
polished, waxed and varnished, shone like mirrors. Nothing flashy,
heavy drapes or embroidered stuff like you see in some Paris houses;
an atmosphere of decent wealth, well-to-do, quiet, orderly provincial life. What a deadly boring place to live! . . . My goodness!

The master came in. What a funny little fellow, he did make me
laugh! Imagine a little old man, neat as ninepence, all pink and
fresh-shaven, just like a doll. Very upright, lively and very
unappetising, I swear! – he came hopping along like a little grass-
hopper in the fields. He bowed, and ever so politely: 'What's your
name, my dear?'

'Célestine, sir.'

'Célestine . . .' he said . . . 'Célestine? . . . Dammit! . . . Pretty
name, I don't say it isn't, but too long, child, much too long . . . I'll
call you Marie, if you don't mind . . . That's nice too, and it's
short . . . Besides, I've called all my chambermaids Marie. It's a
habit I wouldn't like to give up . . . I'd sooner give up the
person . . .'

They've all got this strange craze for never calling you your
proper name . . . I wasn't too surprised, I've already had all the
saints' names in the calendar . . . He kept on: 'You don't mind then
if I call you Marie? . . . Is it agreed?'

'Of course, sir . . .'

'Pretty girl . . . nice-natured . . . Good, good!'

He said all that playfully, very respectfully, and without staring at
me or peering at my bodice and skirts as though he could see
through them, like men usually do. He'd hardly looked at me.
From the first moment he'd come into the room, his eyes had been
stubbornly fixed on my boots.

'Have you got any others?' . . . he asked, after a short silence, in
which his eyes seemed to take on a strange shine.

'Names, sir?'

'No, no, child, boots . . .'

His pointed tongue licked quickly in and out over his lips, like a cat's.

I didn't answer right away. The word boots, reminding me of the coachman's randy cheekiness, had taken me by surprise. Did it mean something, then? . . . Asked again, more urgently, I finally answered, but in a voice that was slightly hoarse and disturbed, as if confessing a sexual peccadillo: 'Yes, sir, I do have others . . .'

'Shiny ones?'

'Yes, sir.'

'Very . . . very shiny?'

'Oh yes, sir.'

'Good . . . good. Yellow leather?'

'I haven't got any of those, sir.'

'You'll have to get some . . . I'll give you some.'

'Thank you, sir!'

'All right . . . all right . . . Be quiet!'

I was frightened; dark gleams had just come in his eyes . . . red cloudy spasms . . . Drops of sweat were pouring down his forehead . . . Thinking he was going to faint, I was about to call out, shout for help . . . but the attack passed, and after a few minutes he went on in a calmer voice, though there was still a froth of saliva at the corner of his mouth: 'It's nothing . . . It's over . . . Understand, child . . . I'm a little bit crazy . . . You're allowed to be at my age, aren't you? . . . So look, one thing is I don't think it's right for a woman to polish her own boots, let alone mine . . . I have great respect for women, Marie, and I can't allow that . . . I'm the one who'll polish your boots, your little boots, your dear little boots . . . I'll look after them . . . Listen carefully . . . Every night, before you go to bed, you'll bring your boots into my room . . . you'll put them by the bed, on a little table, and every morning when you come to open my windows . . . you'll get them back.'

And since I looked absolutely flabbergasted, he went on: 'Come on! . . . What I'm asking isn't much . . . it's very natural, after all . . . And if you're very nice . . .' Brusquely, he pulled two louis out of his pocket and gave them to me. 'If you're very nice and do as I say, I'll give you lots of little presents. The housekeeper will pay your wages every month . . . But I'll give you lots of little presents, Marie, just between the two of us. And what am I asking for? . . . Come on, it's nothing extraordinary, is it . . . Heavens, is it really so extraordinary?'

The master was getting carried away again. His eyelids flickered as he spoke, flickered and fluttered like leaves in a storm.

'Why don't you say something Marie? . . . Say something . . . Why don't you walk around a bit? Take a few steps, just so I can see them moving . . . see them come to life . . . your little boots . . .'

He knelt down, kissed my boots, kneaded them with feverish, caressing fingers, unfastened them . . . And while he kissed them, kneaded them, stroked and caressed them, he said in a begging voice, the voice of a crying child: 'Oh, Marie . . . Marie . . . your little boots . . . give them me, now . . . now . . . now . . . I want them now . . . give them me . . .'

I was powerless . . . paralysed with amazement . . . I no longer knew if I was really there or dreaming . . . As for the master's eyes, all I could see were two little white globes, shot with red. And his mouth was all smeared over with a kind of soapy froth . . .

In the end, he took away my boots and shut himself away with them in his room for two whole hours . . .

'The master likes you very much,' said the housekeeper, showing me round the house. 'Try and keep it up . . . It's a good place . . .'

Four days later, when I went to open the windows in the morning, at the usual time, in his bedroom, I almost fainted with horror . . . The master was dead! . . . Stretched out on his back, in the middle of the bed, his body almost completely naked, you could already feel in and around him the stiffness of a corpse. He hadn't struggled. No disarray in the bedclothes; on the sheets, not the slightest trace of struggle, convulsion, agony or hands clenched in the effort to strangle Death . . . I would have thought he was asleep, if his face hadn't been purple, a dreadful purple, a sinister purple, like an aubergine. And something else really horrific, that made me shake with terror, even more than that face . . . the master's teeth were clenched on one of my boots, clenched so tightly that after vain, dreadful struggles I had to cut the leather with a razor to wrench it away . . .

I'm no saint . . . I've known a lot of men and I know for myself all the lunatic, dirty things they're capable of . . . But a man like the master? . . . I don't know . . . You have to laugh, though, don't you, to think there are people like that . . . And where do they get their funny ideas from, when it's so easy and so nice to make love properly . . . like ordinary people . . .

Select Bibliography

Section A gives the most complete bibliographical information available for the first edition of texts translated, which by the nature of the subject is often very partial. Where possible, I have translated from these; otherwise, I have collated various later editions. Works cited in Section B have been restricted as far as possible to those referred to in the Introduction and Notes.

A. Works translated

Andréa de Nerciat, A. R., *Félicia ou Mes Fredaines*, London, 1775.

Anon., *Les Cent Nouvelles Nouvelles*, A. Vérard, Paris, 1486.

Argens, J. B. de B. d', *Thérèse philosophe, ou Mémoires pour servir à l'histoire de P. Dirrag et de mademoiselle Eradice*, The Hague, 1748.

Balzac, H. de., *Contes drolatiques*, Gosselin, Werdet, Paris, 1832–37.

Béroalde de Verville, F., *Le Moyen de parvenir*, 1610.

Bourdeille, P. de, *Vies des dames galantes*, Sambix le jeune, Leyden, 1666.

Crébillon, C.-P. J. de, *Tableaux des moeurs du temps dans les différents âges de la vie*, ?1750–60.

Diderot, Denis, *Les Bijoux indiscrets*, Au Monomotapa, 1748; first complete edition ed. Naigeon, Desray, Paris, 1798.

Gourmont, R. de, 'Péhor', in *Histoires magiques*, Mercure de France, Paris, 1894.

Huysmans, J.-K., *À rebours*, Charpentier, Paris, 1884.

Laclos, P. C. de, *Les Liaisons dangereuses*, Durand neveu, Paris, 1782.

Louÿs, P., *Aphrodite: moeurs antiques*, Mercure de France, Paris, 1896.

Maréchal, P. S., *Contes saugrenus*, Bassora, 1789.

Maupassant, G. de, 'Marocca' in *Mademoiselle Fifi*, Kistemaeckers, Brussels, 1882.

Millot, Michel, *L'École des filles*, Paris, 1665.

Mirabeau, H.-G.R., comte de, *Le Libertin de qualité*, first pub. as *Ma Conversion*, London [Malassis, Alençon], 1783.

Mirbeau, O., *Le Jardin des supplices*, Fasquelle, Paris, 1899.
Journal d'une femme de chambre, Fasquelle, Paris, 1900.

Musset, A. de, *Gamiani*, Brussels, 1833.

Rabelais, F., *Pantagruel*, Nourry, Lyons, 1532; 2nd ed. Juste, Lyons, 1542.

Restif de la Bretonne, N. E., *Le Palais-Royal*, Guillot, Paris, 1790.
L'Année des dames nationales, Geneva, 1791–94.
L'Anti-Justine, ou Les Délices de l'amour, Girouard, Paris, 1798.

Sade, D.-A.-F., marquis de, *Aline et Valcour*, Girouard, Paris, 1795.

Sentilly, le marquis de, *Le Rideau levé, ou l'Éducation de Laure*, Cythère [Malassis, Alençon], 1786.

Zola, E., *La Faute de l'abbé Mouret*, Charpentier, Paris, 1875.

B. Works consulted

Apollinaire, G., Fleuret, F., and Perceau, L., *L'Enfer de la Bibliothèque Nationale*, Mercure de France, Paris, 1913.

Bakhtin, M., *Rabelais and His World*, M.I.T. Press, London, 1968.

Bataille, G., *Eroticism*, tr. M. Dalwood, John Calder, 1962.
Oeuvres complètes, 8 vols., Gallimard, Paris, 1970–76.

Bayle, P., 'Éclaircissement sur les obscénités in *Dictionnaire historique et critique*, 2nd ed., R. Leers, Rotterdam, 1702.

Carter, A., *The Sadeian Woman*, Virago, London, 1979.

Cellard, J., and Rey, A., *Dictionnaire du français non conventionnel*, Hachette, Paris, 1980.

Charney, M., *Sexual Fiction*, Methuen, London, 1981.

[Choux, J.], *Le Petit Citateur. Notes érotiques et pornographiques. Recueil . . . pour servir de complément au Dictionnaire érotique du professeur de langue verte*, Paphos [Brussels], 1881.

Delvau, A., *Dictionnaire érotique moderne, par un professeur de langue verte*, nouv. éd. revue . . ., Basle [?Brussels, 187–].

Desnos, R., *La Liberté ou l'amour*, Gallimard, Paris, 1962.

Diderot, D., *Oeuvres*, Gallimard, Paris, 1951.

Faust, B., *Women, Sex and Pornography*, Penguin, London, 1982.

Foucault, M., *The History of Sexuality*, tr. R. Hurley, Vol. I, Penguin, London, 1981 (first French ed. Gallimard, 1976).
Language, Counter-Memory, Practice, Blackwell, Oxford, 1977.

Foxon, D., *Libertine Literature in England, 1660–1745*, rpt. from *The Book Collector*, London, 1964.

Fusil, C.-A., *Sylvain Maréchal, ou l'Homme sans Dieu*, Plon, Paris, 1936.

Gautier, Th., *Les Jeunes France*, Charpentier, Paris, 1883.

Gay, J., *Bibliographie des ouvrages relatifs à l'amour, aux femmes, au mariage*, 2nd ed. revue . . ., J. Gay, Paris, 1864.

Griffin, S., *Pornography and Silence*, The Women's Press, London, 1981.

Guirand, P., *Dictionnaire érotique*, Payot, Paris, 1978.

Huizinga, J., *The Waning of the Middle Ages*, Penguin, London, 1965.

Kearney, P. J., *The Private Case*, Jay Landesman, London, 1981.

Kristeva, J., *Desire in Language*, Basil Blackwell, Oxford, 1980.

Kronhausen, E. and P., *Pornography and the Law*, revised ed., Ballantine Books, New York, 1964.

Marcus, M., *A Taste for Pain*, Souvenir Press, London, 1981.

Marcus, S., *The Other Victorians: A Study of Sexuality and Pornography in Mid-Nineteenth-Century England*, Weidenfeld & Nicolson, London, 1966.

Maupassant, G. de, *Contes et Nouvelles*, Gallimard, Paris, 1974.

Mirabeau, H.-G. R., comte de, *Le Degré des âges du plaisir*, de l'imprimerie de la Mère des amours, Paphos, 1793.

Praz, M., *The Romantic Agony*, tr. A. Davidson, Oxford University Press, Oxford, 1933.

Rougemont, Denis de, *L'Amour et l'occident*, Paris, Plon, 1972 (tr. M. Belgion, *Passion and Society*, Faber and Faber, London, 1962, 2nd rev. and aug. ed.).

Sontag, S., 'The Pornographic Imagination', in *Styles of Radical Will*, Secker & Warburg, London, 1969.

Vocabula amatoria, London, 1896.

Voltaire, F. M. A. de, *Dictionnaire philosophique portatif*, London [Cramer, Geneva], 1764.